MW01101626

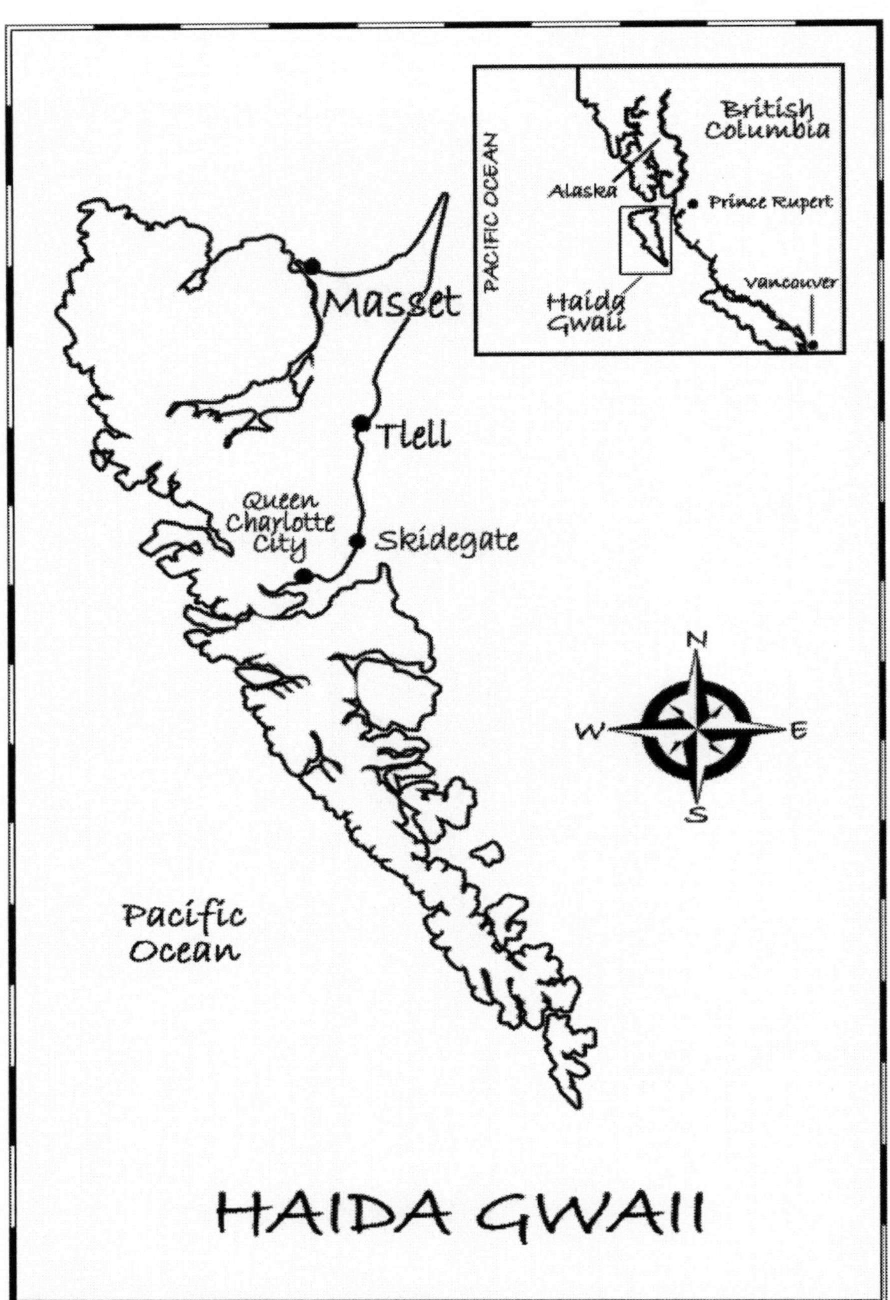
British Columbia
PACIFIC OCEAN
Alaska
Prince Rupert
Haida Gwaii
Vancouver
Masset
Tlell
Queen Charlotte City
Skidegate
N
W
E
S
Pacific Ocean
HAIDA GWAII

House of Northern Lights

For Wendy

11.10

House of Northern Lights

A novel

Valen Watson

RED SQUARE Books
A *Division* of Red Square Press

Los Angeles * Moscow

A RED SQUARE Press Book/ May, 2010

Moscow * Los Angeles

Cover Design by: Agnes Galecka

Cover Photo: Halldór Örn Óskarsson

Library of Congress Cataloging-in-Publication Data

Watson, Valen

House of Northern Lights: a novel / Valen Watson. – 1st ed.

p. cm.

ISBN: 978-0-9760398-9-1

1.Title

Published in the United States

Red Square Books are published by Red Square Press, a division of Knigy Krasny Kvadrat. Its trademark, consisting of the words "Red Square" and the portrayal of the square, is registered with the U.S. patent and Trademark Office and in other countries. Marca Registrada. Red Square Press, 7661 Curson Terrace, Los Angeles CA 90046

www.redsquarepress.biz

PRINTED IN THE UNITED STATES OF AMERICA

10 9 8 7 6 5 4 3 2 1

room. Even the stairs in the most ordinary of sugar maple have matching grain, as if it were sawn from one giant tree.

Everything here has been well cared for and in many ways belongs to the housekeeper, Ana Celia, who scrubbed, polished, greased, blessed and boxed everything regularly with creases and button loops neatly facing the same way. The house has been swept until brooms have turned to nubs, flannel cloths rotted around polish tins or burned in the rubbish heap.

The house with such history bears the mark of many. Broken pieces of a Lionel train in the attic are testament to the presence of children at one time. None since our occupation, only a certain stillness that comes from waiting, the smoothing of a never-ending current of chaos worn down to a patina by a thousand applications of beeswax and intense, concentrated effort.

♐♒♐♒♐♒

My friend Andrew comes to pick me up at the end of the week. His red Bronco pulls up the driveway alongside the back porch so I can load my boxes. He gets out warily and leans on the car door.

"Hey, Elle."

"Andrew."

He gives a nod to Mitch, who is positioned by the screen door with the dog at his heels. I load up the car while the men stay put. Along with the usual sundries, I've packed an impulsive assortment of goods: canned corn, tuna fish in foil packets, a large black umbrella rescued from the basement.

There are no goodbye hugs. I'm in the passenger seat when Mitch suddenly calls out, "Liselle!"

I turn, alarmed.

"Take the side streets, they are faster this time of day." Then he pulls Bobo into the house, neither man nor beast giving me so much as a backward glance. The door bangs shut, and all is quiet.

"So long." This is to the house.

The neighborhood slides into focus, as it always does once I've left the security of the front yard with all its peculiarities. Our street is

Following Simon Fraser

♐♒♐♒♐♒

My mother was right about me. If she was dead wrong when I was six, certainly her sunny observations of me have finally come true. I feel nothing. Absolutely nothing. I am riding around on my tricycle getting hit in the head with something thrown from either an older sibling or some well-meaning older sibling's friend, and the smile never wavers. Squeaking around corners, feet pumping rhythmically, I flash a good one at Mum-o of the brittle golden halo and nervous, fertile womb. *Oh, honey would you get me a cigarette? That's a good girl.* I think she referred to my patent shine as the *super-ego*, her little Protestant pridey.

But certain things did not factor into this assessment: potty trained only weeks before I hit kindergarten, I was an unfathomable wild-child with a foreign name and the exterior cultivation of a weed patch. Endearing only, it seemed, to kind adults and lost dogs. Avoided by children for reasons that were not clear, I became adept at searching for signs of entry before opening up the latch. I was, as my mother put it, "doing my best."

Ah, well. It has been a great relief to feel nothing these past few weeks. A much-deserved vacation. Nothing, nothing, nothing. With my hands on the wheel the nothing gives over to an overriding, gut-churning fear of having to drive over a thousand miles on a twisting, cliff-hanging two-lane highway that goes somewhat north if you don't count the three hundred dangerous curves marked with appropriate yellow warning signs. Even so, I remember why I learned to drive in the first place.

This is it: If you want to be the failure of young whitey, try riding the bus in Los Angeles. The bus is for the old, the sick, the feeble, or those so down and out they cannot afford to save up in a pitiless lifetime three hundred bucks for a balding '85 Datsun held together with chicken wire and electrical tape. The price of a ticket shaves off the truly destitute, so you don't see too many street people, mostly working stiffs who feed off thin slices of democratic trickle-down and live out whole generations inside peeling clapboard houses that flash by the sides of freeways. The bus is also home to crazies going from nowhere on Wilshire Boulevard to nowhere on Santa Monica Boulevard, punky smart asses, the angry, and the dead.

I couldn't afford a car, so for my first three years in Los Angeles I took the bus to my entry-level job, and every day I would get on and be smacked in the face with fear. Fear keeps you alive on the bus and in the metal shelters where you wait for the bus. Waiting in the shelter was the most dangerous. Too many dark hours spent assuming the position, head down, arms crossed, crotch hidden, and feet firmly planted. Every stop at the red light brought more of those predatory creatures who inhabit the dark recesses of automobiles expressly for *opportunity*, the ones who stare and sometimes smack their lips when you slide into view like a piece of meat in a shop window. "Look again, *fils de pute*, and you'll be sorry!" One of us is going to an early grave; I want it to be them, tires screeching at the green light, leaving an empty spot for some other schmuck to fill. It got so I just couldn't take it anymore, and once that happens you lose your nerve and they come looking for you.

So I found a guy with a car and learned to drive a stick shift in the parking lot of Love's Barbecue Restaurant. Later I practiced in the Veterans' Cemetery where the roads were as quiet as the voices from thousands of white crosses curving up in every direction. I passed the eternally resting at five o'clock every afternoon for two weeks, scraping gears and burning a lot of rubber.

My first car was a tiny blue Honda with a manual choke. Big rubber bumpers protected me from dings and the engine started to cough over sixty-five. Once the clutch cable snapped, twanging into uselessness like a broken guitar string and I was lucky to escape with my life, drifting unmolested to the curb. Haunted by a dark memory born sometime before an early birthday, I avoided freeways. My mother claimed I had been traumatized when I was little, though she couldn't isolate the specific incident. It could have been any number of near misses and minor accidents that peppered my childhood. Once she leaned over to retrieve a glove and drove straight into the neighbor's rose garden, ruining twenty years of meticulous grooming. Next to her as she sped along, heart thumping, foot pressing down on an imaginary brake, she taught me an early lesson in the transience of life. One moment you're an American Beauty rose and the next moment you're wheel slush.

The Honda came with the marriage, like a toaster oven or a good set of dishes. My husband did the freeway driving, except when I was forced to get about town on my own like a beetle skimming the soft shoulders in fear of being squashed.

Now there is no escape – I've reached that imaginary middle point where going backward is the same as going forward. The highway, blasted through bleak shale mountains, hugs the river named for explorer, Simon Fraser, who last century followed the caribou in a failed search for the mythical Northwest Passage. The two-lane, newly paved blacktop is a far cry from the hard slog it must have been long ago, but mountain terrain is still dangerous. There is no stretch free of roller-coaster curves, dips, and blind drops into steep valleys. My compact SUV, delivered from Los Angeles by rail, doesn't seem as hardy in this real wilderness.

I can't afford a motel so I pull off into a campground at two a.m. and sleep folded around my possessions. I'm supposed to be next to something called Little Bear Lake but the moonless light reveals nothing but a square of gravel in my headlights. The sky is clear and cold, a thousand stars drift across the windshield. Everything I own, everything I am, is inside this car. Sleep is quick and dreamless.

Early morning is a cup of coffee at the Busy Bee, the last café before the highway curves toward the west. Here, on the final stretch, the narrow blacktop stays inside the winding valley carved by the Skeena River, a sinewy rope of mountain water, opalescent turquoise, and fast moving. On the twisty road I keep sight of her but sometimes she surprises me, curving around and crossing my path. Together we push toward the sea.

For a second my eyes stray to static on the radio.

Out of the corner of my eye a white shape crosses the front of the windshield and I jam on the brakes *what the…?* It disappears into the sideways skid, to the shudder and wrench of steel like a tin can folding into itself, rubber burning, then silence. The car dies and all is quiet. I look out the front windshield, craning, then to the side. Nothing. Just the sound of my breath sucking in and out. I have to get out to look. The road is deserted. I crack open the door, cautiously rounding the front, hairs stiff, rising up everywhere. I see a dirty white paw first, leathery pads, as silent as the still, hot air just beyond the front tire. I creep closer, almost on hands and knees. The paw doesn't move so I circle around for a better look.

A wolf. The fur is thick and soft and cleaner than I expected. Maybe it is a stray Samoyed but no, the body is too lean, the snout too long. Nothing friendly about the face. It looks like an Artic wolf but this can't be their territory so far south. A finger of air ripples through the luxurious mane, and in this field of winter, soft gray tips quiver. I circle his head, sure now that it is a 'he,' and come around his flank. The sharp jaw is slack, black gums loose around the tips of powerful teeth stained to tea color. Dark weeping streaks beneath his eyes. For a long while I stand there. From somewhere metal ticks, crickets start up again and drone on. The sun is warm. I take a step closer. There is a small scratch on his face, the beginning of blood oozing. Otherwise he looks perfect, as if stretched out for a nap in a patch of sun, fur too soft and luxurious for something wild. I lean down, hand outstretched. To feel…

In that moment he explodes upward, knocking me back on my behind, a smack of pain. Before I can get my hands up over my face he's already lunged past me and has made it across the tarmac, the smell of fear and shit in his wake. I whimper like a baby and can't stop. From a safe distance he turns toward the sound, rewarding me with another jab of fear. We are both panting. *Shush, shush.* He and I remain in place, watching each other.

Despite the bloody gash, he seems unhurt. Without another glance he gallops off, disappearing behind a ridge of trees. After a moment, when I am certain he is really gone, I get up and limp back to the car, to the damp seat where the coffee spilled.

The road stays empty. A big gush of glacier runoff is arching down the side of one of the mountains to the west of the highway and twists like a string of pearls into an unseen pool below. No cars. Everyone who is going to has come and gone. It is a long time before I can unwrap my hands from the steering wheel and swing back onto the road. It seems only minutes before the last curve drifts into the beginnings of frontier sprawl that is Prince Rupert.

♐♒♐♒♐♒

Raw, smelling of cedar sap and new wood, this northern British Columbia port barely makes a dent in the mountain; it still feels as if it were only yesterday hacked out of the bush. Big statues of bear, colorful totem poles, and lots of bars everywhere. Not very pretty but a lot of energy and purpose. And as always, the deep red color of the old Hudson's Bay Trading Company remains in distinctive lumberjack plaid, wool caps, blankets and duffle coats. In the distance mill stacks belch oily, yellow steam. But right now I don't see the mills or the industrial pollution; everything smells fresh and eager, like the building-sized lots of sawn planks waiting to be shipped out all over the world. I suddenly feel good, better than I've felt in months.

By mid morning a light mist is falling. I set out along Broad Street looking for maps, last-minute supplies of tinned goods and some perishables that I'm sure I won't be able to get in Masset. Then, as I make my way down to the waterfront, the sun unexpectedly breaks from behind the clouds, quickly burning off the mist. I gaze up, traveling up and away into the open sky. Gulls pick among the beach sand, screeching and lifting off over the water.

The ocean has turned from gray to a deep greenish blue. Over to the south is the mouth of the Skeena. The delta ribbons out as strands of cream into the midnight blue water of the Hecate Strait. To the north is the Alaskan Panhandle, a forbidding panorama of glaciated mountains. Due west by a hundred miles or so lie the temperate Charlottes, surrounded by a warm Japanese current that keeps the mountainous archipelago wrapped in a steamy mist much of the time. Although the islands are rarely visible, I search for them. A ghostly smudge seems to float on the distant horizon, but perhaps it is just a trick of the eye.

After making inquiries at the Port Authority I find I've missed the daily ferry to the Charlottes so I have to stay the night. Sleeping in my car isn't an option here so I find a bed and breakfast and wait for morning. By six a.m. the town has come to life in a heavy, boiling fog, horns blaring up and down the waterway. My room, shapeless and dark but for the light from a small poodle lamp, reveals its age. Red plastic flowers sit on a Formica dresser next to the tiny metal washbasin with push levers for hot and cold. This is where I carefully clean my hands and face and wonder what I shall do if I don't like where I'm going. I haven't the money to come back. An enamel alarm clock ticks by the side of the bed, and from somewhere down below comes the aroma of bacon frying.

The retired Dunkirk veteran who runs the guesthouse sends me off with a promise we'll meet again. I crawl blind down foggy, empty streets, a bacon sandwich neatly wrapped in wax paper cradled in my lap. The terminal and the sea come into view together. Both are quiet.

Visibility is poor under a lingering fog bank that stretches clear across the strait but the ferry purser assures me they'll sail as scheduled.

Five hours to cross the Hecate Strait, so unpredictable it's been known to swallow ferries whole. I find a bench near the window and prop myself up to follow an endless supply of fog dripping off the railings and into the ocean. The mist is so heavy it swirls around us like a cloud, curling and trailing in our wake. Finally I stretch out and sleep, my knapsack under my head and my arms looped through the straps of my purse.

♐♒♐♒♐♒

In the rapidly falling night, the road to the Haida Village of Masset is deserted. Everyone is at a big party celebrating the completion of a town sculpture created to mark the birthday of their oldest *Naani,* who turned ninety-five today: **How the Raven Discovered The Sun,** the invitation reads in deep blue lettering, with the full story written inside. Harry had sent it down to me with a scrawled note. *"Just follow the road northwest until you see a big noisy place. That's where we'll be."*

At last, a sign marks the final yards of the Trans-Canada Highway. Both road and continent end here, unceremoniously severed at the shore of a vast, inky Pacific. A gust of cold wind blows by and the car shudders. With the engine off the dull roar of the ocean fills up the car with its presence and pushes everything else out except the sound of my blood thrumming.

The Village Hall sits along the highway, mere yards from the sea. Shaped like gymnasium, with a curved roof and large painting of a large-winged bird across the front wall. At short intervals, the main door opens, letting out a blast of light and noise. Young men drift in and out and look over toward my car curiously. Some of them cluster in small groups to talk and smoke.

Stalling for time, I open the invitation and by moonlight re-read the story inside. According to Haida legend, the Raven brought light into the world. He seized it by trickery from a box closely guarded by humans and in a heavenly battle with an Eagle, inadvertently brought the sun, moon and stars to a dark world. If the Raven were still up there watching this new world what would he think of his creation?

The night deepens, and with it the sense that the party may end soon. From within, the sound of a rhythmic drumbeat starts up and a group of costumed dancers come from around the corner and make their way inside. I have no choice but to get out, cross the parking lot and enter into the unknown.

Delkatla Street

♐♒♐♒♐♒

Let me tell you all about Matty, Phil, and others with lives formed around living and dead languages, gossip and strange spiritual references, all mixed together into one crazy mess when you are sitting there listening.

Phil, the Islands' only dentist, is up from Queen Charlotte City. He has a long, sharp-featured face framed by a wispy ponytail, a thinning fu Manchu moustache, and is wrapped from head to toe in a striped Hudson's Bay blanket. He's made himself comfortable sitting cross-legged on the floor of the tiny house I now share with Matty. Next to Phil, leaning back in an old rocking chair, expression frozen into a shy half smile is Kim, who does odd jobs around town and collects rare mushrooms for sale on the Mainland. Over in the corner, 40-something Quinnie reclines in a purple beanbag chair, a thin woman adorned with many beaded necklaces and other assorted jewels. Her languid form is like the ripened peach she is - still pungent but soon to turn. Introduced, she appraises me openly.

Matty, dark curly hair framing a bird-like face and sun-freckled skin, perches nearby, arms flung across the back of a folding chair, her eyes alive with pleasure as friends take in the newcomer. In the chattering chaos it appears they are more curious as to why she would let me into her domain, than who I am.

The living room, growing more crowded with arrivals, runs the length of the house. It flows into the kitchen area along the back where a small porch is stacked with rows of wood for the potbelly stove, our only source of heat. Two small bedrooms open directly into the living room; mine is jammed full with the boxed contents of my car. The place is all pre-fab, walls as thin as a fingernail, papered in fake veneer. Pale green linoleum floors, faded by many cleanings. A collection of small rugs to step on. Most of the walls are covered with artifacts: photographs, serigraphs, red and blue Chinese fans, a Pinocchio puppet, Indonesian masks and paper cuttings. A bookcase, filmy with dust, bows under the weight of tightly packed books, world maps and photo albums stuffed haphazardly upwards and downwards. Any leftover space has been plastered with a mortar of shells, pebbles and I-Ching coins; hardened collections of them flow down like lava to claim every available surface. Set back behind an oversized, rambling garden, the house rises up with a steeply pitched roof under a canopy of giant cedar branches. The ever-present wind brushes their feathery arms across the shingles like an animal scratching to get in.

With much fanfare, my benefactor, Harry, finally arrives to see if I've settled in. He stands for a moment in the doorway, massive frame wrapped in a heavy Oxford suit jacket, tucked wool scarf and tartan kilt. Boots and socks discarded by the door, he eases his bulk down next to me on the sofa and wraps a purple afghan around his lap. His feet, stretched out in front of him, are tipped with horny toenails, heels crusted with old calluses split along the fault lines of his enormous weight. At one point he hoists a meaty foot up over his knee, an amazing feat given the girth of his calves, and picks at a bulbous toe absentmindedly before seeing my look and quitting with a sheepish grin. At least he is nowhere near the popcorn being passed around. The sticky mixture has been liberally coated with garlic salt, yeast powder and a squirt of dark soy sauce. I can't seem to get enough of it.

Soon the fire roaring inside the big stove warms the house enough that we begin peeling off cardigans, neck scarves and other assorted woolens. The noise level has risen considerably as the group settles in to the warmth and the familiar. First order of business is to hash out the *doings* from the Naani's party, gossiping and speculating about arguments overheard, covert and overt handholding, butt cupping and other signs of passionate couplings which may or may not have been spied upon in the darkened corners of the gymnasium.

Everyone has an opinion. "Did you see who Norman was with?" "Big trouble there, and that's a fact!" Matty snorts and says something witty. She has kept me smiling from the moment we met, sitting side by side at the big long table where our neighborhood shared platters of sweet potatoes, vegetables, and bonfire-smoked salmon. I have yet to figure out how she pays the rent, but it has something to do with various grants she elicits from the Canadian Government relating to Haida issues. I do know it doesn't need to be much. Our total expenses here would barely pay the electric bill back home.

Most of the visitors spread about the room are neighbors; Harry is the closest. His small cedar-shake cottage where I'd found a measure of peace in the previous year is right across the street, overlooking the fishing harbor. I learned earlier that evening he'd leased his downtown Vancouver townhouse at the end of the summer to live in Masset full time. And there's Colleen, from two doors up. She lives in a converted church and has a face like a fox with an expression just as guarded.

Bottles of Moosehead and chunks of roasted black cod on rounds of dark rye that I sniff and decline before passing along have replaced the popcorn. It is a marvel how easily they have folded me into their midst. I experiment with the idea of my house, my harbor, my town.

Someone turned the snow globe upside down and the silvery bits float about as if they too were made of glass.

CBC Radio comes on in the dark. Disoriented I wonder if the time was somehow set wrong. Nine a.m. and the sun has yet to make an appearance. Then I remember the arctic timetable. Winter days grow shorter on both ends. I switch on the bedside lamp and lie perfectly still, swaddled by clean sheets and a down comforter wrapped in flannel. The cocoon smells pleasantly of borax and lemon-fresh Downy. My room is tidy. I have always been that way after a move. Everything out of the boxes and unpacked right away, clothes folded, rugs unrolled, bedspread shaken, pictures hung.

Matty has given me a monk's bed, small, high and narrow, just the right size for a tiny recess carved into one side of the room. It's three *tatami* mat size, just big enough for a laptop desk placed in front of the oblong aluminum sliding-glass window and a small wooden dresser now displaying a collection of family pictures.

The framed photos are always with me, I carry them from place to place carefully wrapped in tissue. Over there is my mother at twenty, brunette hair pulled back in the style of her youth, full lips and burnished skin. The photographer must have worshiped her - she looks so beautiful, so unspoiled, and so hopeful. Next to hers is a backyard portrait of the three of us kids, eyes squinting in the bright afternoon sun. Two years apart each, we all look like healthy Norfolk farm stocks, except for me, the reed-thin one in an Indian-print skirt made from thrift-store fabric. I've taken great pains to look at this photo, to study it. I see sameness in all our gazes so I know I'm no different despite my desire to disassociate from what I believe to be a flawed genetic pool. In another, my sister Scottie and I in velvet party dresses gaze with adoration at a mall Santa. Finally there's Dad in a Maple Leafs hockey sweater, holes in the elbows, all gangly like a newborn calf, my baby sister in the crook of his arm. In the semi-darkness I connect with their images from memory.

I'm content to stay like this in the silence of early morning. I like lying in this bed. I know something extraordinary has happened to me because the quiet of the room is coming inside me, the barrier of skin and bone dissipating with every breath. Molecules flow in and out steadily, and at long last I don't feel as if I have to get up and do something. Explain. Calculate. Manipulate.

I awaken later to a miserably cold room. The fire died sometime during the night and now cold rain drums on the windowpanes and the wet night air has found its way in, drawn steadily through cracks and down the tin chimney. In socks and a flimsy nightgown I look at the stove dumbstruck, unable to unlock its secrets. Shapes grow distinct in the morning gloom; Phil the visiting dentist is huddled inside his down sleeping bag, a colorful afghan Sufi-wrapped around his head. He doesn't stir as I stand there looking around, expectantly. Too cold to make tea, too cold to be standing here without a coat. A blustery wind is picking up with the rising light, unwelcoming.

Right then. Back to bed.

♐♒♐♒♐♒

The house occupants are still asleep by midday, so I slip out and head into town. We are at the north end of Graham Island, which is the uppermost of two main landmasses in this archipelago. Masset is on the south side of a spit that resembles a crab claw as it curves around a wide-mouthed inlet and sheltered harbor dotted with two-man trawlers. A small collection of modest houses, brown and gray like so many nesting swallows, cluster around the two main streets. With little to distinguish it, the site is strangely barren. Carved for expediency out of heavy, rain-soaked cedar forest, its location was chosen to shelter it from the open Pacific and northern Alaskan wind. The paved main street, wide and deserted, runs in a straight line from the water's edge to dense bush where it abruptly ends.

A few squat pre-fab buildings on the main drag house the co-op grocery store, pharmacy, and a small building supply yard with tall stacks of fresh-cut local timber for sale, sweet-smelling and fresh with rain. Scattered amongst the plain cinder block structures are small, bright signs of enterprise: a chip kiosk dispensing steaming heaps of French fries in a paper cone, a newly painted auto garage, a storefront bakery with a tray of freshly made cinnamon buns displayed in the window. A tiny sewing goods shop displays a sign amongst skeins of brightly colored wool: "Driver's License Renewal Here."

Lined up in a row along the east-west street are the LDB liquor store, RCMP office, and Legion Hall. In the other direction, in a converted cottage, Two Bells Café, and a little further, Daddy Cool's, the town bar. Beyond - each with a Canadian flag hanging limply in the still morning air - the post office, a pink stone Anglican church and newly built town school. No parking meters or traffic lights. The concrete sidewalks are limited to main roads. They end before my street.

I stand on a high point of land and look a mile or so to the west toward the end of the claw where the Haida Reserve lies mostly hidden behind a massive stand of cedar. How odd, I thought when Matty first told me, that both communities have the same name. Both are called Masset. Split in two by Colonial immigrants and resident First Nations, neither giving an inch. Sometimes they are called Old and New, sometimes the Village and Town. Either way there will never be just one Masset again.

I pull my hood up as the grey sky drops down further, releasing a momentary downpour. My soaked shoes are freezing and I wish I'd put on the red gumboots sitting by the back door. Good idea, those boots. I am in no mood to do any more exploring; the slender ribbon of deserted highway that separates the two villages looks ominous and lonely even in the daylight. The cold is seeping inside. Hands in pockets, I look toward the ocean again.

The Haida Village Hall in Old Masset Reserve is off in the distance near the end of the main road, the bold-red oval symbol of the Haida Nation visible across the side. Though noisy and friendly during the party last night, today it is shuttered up against the elements. Behind it, sparse, gravel streets are lined with wooden government-issue houses, no one seems about; only a thin, colicky drift of chimney smoke hints at any activity. An old skiff drifts on a rope along the shoreline - since a much smaller marina has relocated further into the east end of the bay, there no boats in what was once the old Cannery block. Nothing but the rotting posts of lost jetties and the distant tolling of buoys marking the shallows. Beyond is a sliver of gray Pacific, now choppy with whitecaps. An early admonition from Harry comes back to me: *"A dark place, Old Masset. Wouldn't be too anxious to go down there, if I were you. Best to keep away. Not your business, anyway."*

A gust of wind drives stinging rain into the back of my slicker and I turn back, head down, dodging puddles and mud. Walking the three blocks home I consider the boundaries of such a life. My shoes are wet and the leather scuffed - I wonder what I will do if they need to be resoled. There is no shoe repair, no Laundromat, no clothing or bookstore. No hospital. Only two tiny hamlets as distant as if the ocean had intervened long ago and swallowed up the passage between them.

A grey plume of chimney smoke rises up in the vicinity of our house. With two carrots, a potato and a leek from the Co-op thumping inside a paper bag I hurry back to see if anyone is up. Before I have a chance to get my coat off, Matty is waiting to greet me. She solemnly points to the huge seven-foot pile of wood stacked in the mudroom.

A whole winter's worth, I reckon. Yes?

In the next moment I'm outside again in the dripping mist and not very happy about it. Our backyard is bounded by a red picket fence. Beyond is a dirt path, chewed up and muddy, overgrown with clumps of wildflowers, periwinkle, grouse grass, daisy, and ladyslipper. A dark sky drizzles down onto the cedars thick with summer growth. Some of their cones have already dropped with the rain; the next will hardly make a whisper, so thick is the carpet of moss beneath.

The fine dampness coats my face and invades my slicker. I back towards the door.

Over here!

Matty is pointing to something - a twenty-foot mound of lumpy canvas dominating our backyard.

"Elle, let me introduce you to the woodpile."

Oh no, no, no. There must be a forest of trees under that tarpaulin. I stand there looking at Matty, hoping she will go back inside the house.

"We have to chop all of that wood for the winter."

No. Absolutely not! I don't know how to chop wood. I can't do it. Don't make me do it. Oh, Lord, so this is why my rent is so cheap. The few pennies of my life rattle in my pocket, thin and tinny. Bills carefully laid out on the bank counter, less than a deck of cards, my tongue licking, counting off each dollar bill. Now my foolishness: the turnips I must eat to live, the bed of straw I must make to sleep in, the candle I must light to ward off the darkness. Yes, yes, yes, wood must be chopped for the winter.

Matty is holding a small hatchet. It looks manageable. Next to her, stuck into a wood stump, is a huge axe. Paul Bunyan size. "We use the big one for the heavy work," she says, pointing to it. "The hatchet is just for kindling."

Oh shit, not the axe. "Listen, Matty, I don't have a clue."

"Don't worry, I'll teach you."

Inside, Phil has un-burrowed and is feeding the fire. Wood pops and crackles, smoke busily pouring out of our chimney falling in sooty drops to the earth. I hear the clink of cups inside, the sound of a kettle scraping on the stove plate.

Matty eases the big axe out of the stump and hands it over. The pull of gravity startles me and I hang on to what I can. *Watch your feet!* Panting, nervous, I keep my hands wrapped around the handle. The wood is smooth, rounded to fit my grip. I heft it experimentally. *Watch your feet!* Thunk! It meets the ground again. I look up at my roommate. Surely she can see the impossibility of all this. Unflappable, those bright eyes gaze back at me. Crossing her arms she waits in the drizzle, her hair slicked down, a raindrop on the end of her nose.

"Will you show me, at least?" I ask.

She takes the axe and with one hand picks up a large round log. Upends it. "This is cedar, the easiest of all the woods to cut." She points. "See this? It has a lot of sugar sap running through. Makes the wood soft and grainy. If you cut on the grain the wood will split like butter. The axe is very sharp." Steadying the log on the stump she instructs, "All wood is quartered on this."

Then she widens her stance and lifts the axe high up over her head. I step back, away from the power of the stump and the axe. For a moment it seems to have a life of its own, surely to spin off the handle, crashing through the window behind us, shattering glass, somebody yelping, tumbling end over end splitting the dentist's head in two. But instead, she heaves it forward in a powerful arc and with a dull thud it cleaves into the wood, splitting it cleanly down the middle. The two pieces totter for a moment then fall. With practiced ease she cracks the axe out of the stump where the force of her blow has sunk the blade.

In this cold gray morning the wood should be steaming from such power. I lean closer to the two halves, now lying neatly to either side of the stump, pick one up and examine the thin reddish lines of grain running horizontally through it. They are so delicate.

She moves forward. "Here, you try it."

Awww. The axe is shoved into my hands as a bridle on a skittish horse, Matty confident and smiling. She demonstrates again. Arms straight, legs apart, gumboots firmly planted.

I try to lift the axe. Too heavy. I lift it a little further. It wobbles dangerously from side to side. Matty steps away, a distant voice blending into the grayness. My forearms stiffen, muscles object loudly. I drop it, lift it again, this time more prepared. Up it goes. "Keep your eye on the wood!" I can't get any higher than my face, can't lose sight of it, then I aim it downwards, surprised by the force of gravity. Thwack! The log, an impossibly small target, skitters off the stump and the axe continues downward, toward my legs. "Shit, shit!" I yell at the wood, the axe, and my incompetence. My muscles tremble, I am such a wuss. A real piece of work. Curious, Phil peers out the kitchen window.

Staring stupidly at the log, my enemy, slippery and wily, jumping up and away to taunt me. Matty barrels forward like a drill sergeant and as I stand there, sweat and rain mixing, she puts the log back on the stump. Again! And again. I adjust my grip, widen my stance. Slice up and down in the same place over and over. Soon the axe feels less like an alien thing ready to careen out of control, more like power. Yes, a power I did not recognize before. Fixed power, steady and strong, resonant and alive like the wood of its handle gripped in my two hands. Thunk, the wood splits and I turn it sideways. Soon the axe is driving into the stump where it sticks solidly. While Matty watches, I study my logs, the shape of the wood, its density, identifying cedar, ash, spruce. I work the knots, chipping away awkwardly, cursing and grunting.

The afternoon yields three quartered logs and a small collection of kindling sticks, my triumph over the huge woodpile. The backyard is a mess. Wood chip spittle and sawdust mix with grass around the stump. My face is slick with sweat; steamy heat rises from under my sweater. Leaden heaviness in every muscle.

Finally my prizes are gathered up, soaking wet and useless. I protect them under my arm and feel the dismal shame. They are not fit for the woodpile. I hug them closer, smelling the rich, pungent aroma of sap. No matter. They will dry out some day and for a brief moment our house will live because of me.

Matty mucks ahead of me in her big boots.

"We have a saying around here," she says, kicking open the door with her foot, "Chopping wood heats you twice: once when you chop it, and once when you burn it."

♐♒♐♒♐♒

Matty is in front of her dresser mirror applying make-up. This is done with a great deal of eyebrow pruning, face puckering and some very red cheeks. She purses her lips and vamps, laughing. I haven't figured out where to take a shower so I'm quite grizzled; the aroma of smoked fish follows me everywhere. I peer into the bathroom with the hope someone has come during the day to fix ours, broken these last three weeks. The rusting nozzle twists this way and that off its moorings. Nope.

Pat, our landlord, occupies the larger suburban tract house on the leeward side of us. He's been asked to fix the shower but he won the lottery six months ago and has taken to disappearing for long periods of time, louting about in the afternoons. Someone even saw him shooting crows out the living-room window. I've never met Pat and do not care to. The wife and children appear sporadically, picking their way past toys flung in the long, sunburned grass.

Matty suggested bartering for a shower. Quinnie, who has a compact cedar-lined house down on the Inlet shore, offers the use of her shower if I will help her make deer jerky afterwards.

"Join me at Daddy Cool's tonight?" Matty calls as I start to head out, towel in hand.

Tonight she's in a mood. The cocked eyebrow is a clear sign that she is about to break her rule about avoiding bars and the drunken men who inhabit them. The music from Daddy Cools is wafting across the clear night to our backyard and she's in her best angora sweater, slamming the back door, not bothering to wait for a reply. It's one of the things I've had to get used to. People say things and then just go. When you live inside one square mile, they know you will eventually catch up.

A knock on the screen door announces a visitor; the hinge squeaks. All doors are opened at will. We have no locks.

Before me stands Broan.

He is a handsome man with a charming North Wales accent and tobacco-scented clothes. Offered up with reddened hands is a pail of *gow,* a local delicacy made from herring eggs laid on seaweed, eaten steamed with butter and soy sauce. Very expensive in Japan where the market has made a lot of Skidegate sea farmers rich. Having tried and rejected the horrible concoction earlier, this item represents future trade value. The bucket slops a little, filled to the brim. It is a very generous gift.

"Just thought you might like some of this," he says, staring at the falling-away part of my sweater. I hastily clutch it back in place and step aside to admit him. I don't bother to explain I was about to shower down the street. He has *gow* and looks ready to settle in for a visit.

Once on the couch he steals a quick glance in my direction, gelled hair quivering. Reaching up he attempts to pat it back into place and I see for the first time how like a defiant, spiny cactus it is, all whorls and cowlicks. The sun has bleached and burnt it and every bit of exposed skin on his face and arms into a patina of light sand. His nose is permanently peeling and will one day get cancer and possibly fall off. I make tea and study him further. I'm allowed to do this because there is no pretension. Broan has come calling. He's giving it his best shot, grizzled and beaten as he is by the elements and a dozen lost loves. He is the town handyman, busy enough to support his modest needs and a hobby carving birds and small animals from blocks of cedar. Hands, reddened and rough, they deftly articulate the air as if it were a piece of wood to be sanded and shaped.

Last year he and his girlfriend split up and he moved down into a trailer by the Delkatla Sanctuary, a marshy, mosquito-laden habitat for migrating birds. Perhaps remembering some delicious memory of true love and how much better it is than living in a duck marsh, he smiles radiantly at me, then flames into embarrassment. Deep furrows run across his forehead aging him well past his thirty-five years but his brilliant eyes are as blue as a swimming pool on a hot summer day. We regard each other silently, the advantage distinctly mine. He leans back a little, arm on the sofa, looking brave. So?

Ah, no, Broan, not on this dark afternoon. He reaches for the chocolate biscuits placed before him and we sip licorice tea for as long as it is proper.

And so it goes. Every night this week some man or another has conspired to find an excuse to come over. The voices of the lonely ones in Los Angeles come to me, the ones who are spun into cocoons of isolation with dense hearts. They should be here, feeling the warm curious steam on their faces. Such a cavalcade is wasted on me. After a decent interlude of small talk I turn out Broan as I've turned out the others, his abandoned *gow* on the kitchen table.

"They won't give up, you know."

Matty's words come back to me. But she's gone over to Daddy Cools, just over there behind the old sty, back where the sidewalk ends in a tumble of weeds and a hedge of northern blueberry bushes ripe for pie.

I want to pick those berries. In the clear darkness thumping, *"Wild thing, you make my heart sing"* drifts across the neighborhood. I crouch in the bramble, picking a pail full of midnight, a shifting canopy of brilliant stars to watch above. Shimmering, milky, infinitely everywhere. The sky is finally clear, bigger than the land now, the endless traveler. Reedy laughter rises over the music reaching Broan, who is trudging home on slick pavement, cigarette burning in his beautiful fingers, thoughts drifting elsewhere. Like mine, his heart is once again shuttered and mute.

Saturday Afternoon in Masset

♐♒♐♒♐♒

For several hours now we've been playing cards at Colleen's house. The nights have grown surprisingly cold; the dark hour is not the best time to marvel at the extraordinary workmanship put into renovating this old country church. A steeply pitched roof soars three stories above, disappearing into shadowy darkness. Accessible by a ladder are storage lofts, now used for sleeping, joined by catwalks perched delicately between the rafters. Sometimes the walkways lead to blank walls or small, mysterious cubbyholes, remnants perhaps of the days when it had a working bell tower.

Colleen of the dark hair and pale skin seems disinterested in her creation and yet her dreams are visible everywhere in the loving details, dovetail joints, large windows overlooking the marina, pristine bathroom with claw-foot tub resting beneath a geometric stained glass window in deep green and blue. Everything is scrubbed, stripped of its dark paint, a hardy, plain shell bleached and opened up to let in the sun.

Her collection of furniture is meager – typical recycled fare. A few Victorian floor lamps with battered silk shades illuminate the room, but these small pools of light cannot dispel the cavernous gloom. A large stove placed square in the middle of the activity throws off quite a bit of heat, but it is squandered in this vast cavern. It rises straight toward the eaves, disappearing through many unfinished cracks.

"Your deal, Elle." Colleen, Harry, Matty and I are playing Hearts.

"Last time the cards weren't shuffled enough. I swear we keep getting the same hands," grouses Harry.

"For the love of Mike, just play."

"Anyone for pretzels?"

The Queen of Spades turns up in my hand. *Ah, crap.* I'm doomed. She is pushed behind some friendlier cards. Moira, Kim, and a teenager from the Reserve, are sitting out this round. They sit like three birds on a bench watching what I don't know. Occasionally they lean over and pick at plates of smoked salmon and my contribution of Broan's *gow*.

Shy Kim eyes me surreptitiously in a manner that could be interpreted as sexual interest. An ex-forester with a thatch of prematurely graying hair and the complexion of an outdoorsman, he is honored among the Haida for his thorn-in-the-side politics with the Canadian government. For his efforts, he's given free rein to hunt deer on Reserve land for his larder and to forage for a variety of rare mushrooms he collects and ships to high-end restaurants in Vancouver. He has somehow managed to find a place in the social life here without uttering more than two words a visit. He lives in a one-room cabin deep in the north woods and has promised to take me *'shrooming'*, something you do if you want to spend time with him.

He starts up a tentative conversation with Izzie about the All-Indian basketball game scheduled for next week in the Village Hall.

With a small yelp, Oscar the cat jumps up and runs to the curtained-off vestibule. After a thump and much boot scraping, he reappears at the feet of a new visitor. A river of freezing air streams in his wake. Heads turn.

This man I have not seen before. He's clothed in heavy layers of soft corduroy and wool, a big muffler wrapped around and around, thrown over one shoulder. It's red and white striped, like Dr. Seuss' Cat and he unwinds it slowly, looking around. Something unusual about this one. All the more odd since having taken off his boots; the visitor is wearing bright pink socks. Okay. He looks round the room, fixing on me briefly, moving on.

The coat comes off. He's wearing a button-down shirt, red suspenders and a pair of Oxford banker's pants. Fearing exposure I turn my attention back to the game.

"What's up, Jonah?" asks Kim.

He rubs his hands together, taking his time by the door. I notice he has a neatly trimmed beard and thick nut-colored hair with bits of gold and gray woven throughout. His ruddy cheeks glow as he passes by. He leans over and scoops up the cat. One thing I've learned so far is that Oscar hates everything on two legs, most especially if they are male. I fully expect a bloodbath, but much to my surprise he quiets instantly in the man's embrace, turning up a belly of soft white fur to be stroked and the expression on his rat-catching face is quite obscenely contented. We are even treated to a great stretching out as he arches back like a woman in love, his little pink paws quivering with satisfaction. All at once, he is asleep, the last purr dying in his throat.

"Wind's coming up," says the man whose name is Jonah (though we have not been introduced). The others on the couch don't seem to notice Oscar's performance. Instead, the usual talk of weather, rains, and the coming winter. Izzie gets up to make tea.

Jonah eases into a chair and gratefully accepts a warm mug. The steam rises from a big pot of tea resting on our table.

"Play up now, make you're move," urges a voice in our group.

The card game resumes while others sip tea or flip through magazines. Visiting up here is more like sitting. Doing nothing with other people. They come and go. It's the usual thing. Beyond the lighted window a chair is always waiting, a place to settle into, a place to float without purpose, to watch the sky moving overhead, the world shifting on its axis. Voices murmur, then Kim gets up, says his goodbyes, boots thudding on the porch steps where his shepherd, Balto, waits. The hour passes in familiar comfort. I play out my hand to get rid of the Queen. The faces around Colleen's table are lost in concentration, wily looks now and then, cards slapped down triumphantly. We flush with laughter. I want it to stay like this forever, the clink of glasses amidst conversation, the aroma of tea and cake and smoke.

There is a scuffling sound, and Jonah returns with a large box in his arms. Almost at once the crowd closes up as if they know what's coming. From inside the box come flyers, neatly organized with rubber bands. A flyer in hand, Jonah stands in the middle of the room and launches into his speech. "The U.S. wants to build a nuclear sub facility near Ketchikan. To use it American subs will have to pass through our strait." He tries to catch as many eyes as he can. Mine. Colleen throws down her cards and gets up to put more wood in the stove.

"What's the problem?" someone inquires, not too enthusiastically.

"The strait - it's only fifty miles across. If the subs pass through here," he explains, "The fishing fleets could be in danger. Their nets could snag on a sub, pulling them down. Or," he pauses, handing the leaflets around, "what happens if there is a nuclear accident on board the sub? It would kill every living thing in the sea. Our livelihood would be destroyed."

"What do you want from us?" Colleen asks, as she shoves a log into the stove.

"We're going to have a big meeting in Charlotte City in a month, and I need someone to help me get all these flyers out."

I remember now where I've seen this man. He was dancing at the birthday celebration the night I arrived on the Islands. With ash-blonde hair partially hidden under a large, conical cedar-root hat, he came out with the other Haida, a bearskin draped over a red Raven Clan blanket. How strange, I thought as I watched his progress through the dance line miming strong, rhythmic strokes with a painted wooden paddle. He looked more like a Danish Viking than a Clan member. I search his face, made curious by the sudden recognition. He looks back at me. Green eyes flecked with amber, gold eyebrows, puzzled look. His skin is fine, smooth, the color of a snow apple. Expression blank.

"I'll help," I offer.

The others breathe a sigh of relief. They're off the hook. He turns, his attention most suddenly and completely upon me: the bit of eye glue in my lashes, the annoying strip of apple peel stuck between my back teeth, the pins falling out from my hair in a messy tumble. An unwelcome flush creeps up my neck.

"Tuesday, next. Come by my house." He points out the window where darkness pushes in. He doesn't ask my name. "I live that way, on the Reserve," he adds before picking up his box and leaving with not so much as a goodbye to anyone else.

♐♒♐♒♐♒

Today Matty and I cure and smoke two spring salmon. We are putting supplies down for the winter, stocking as much as we can while the boats are still coming in. Their leftovers are cheap and fresh: broken fish or the odd rock cod that the canning factories don't want. Mid-morning is still gray from a lifting fog. Matty, a cloud of huffing steam in a red-patterned woolen sweater and gum boots, crests the hill leading from the dock, her little wagon loaded with an assortment of goods bought for five dollars and some friendly gossip: two salmon, about ten pounds each, some cod, and several whitefish. *"Yeehaa, fish a' comin'!!"*

She shows me how to gut and de-bone the bigger fish. Then we cure and marinate the salmon fillets in a mixture of brown sugar, wine and spices before taking them to hang up inside the smokehouse we share with our neighbors. Rickety and weather-beaten to a soft silvery sheen, it has a door with a simple wooden catch and a tin chimney out the top.

As night approaches I head across to Quinnie's for a shower. Earlier that week she sent her teenage daughter, Stella, to the Mainland to visit her grandmother so the house is quiet for a few days. Quinnie's told me she is worried about her hanging out with the Reserve kids.

"Stella's mad at me because I won't let her drive the car. She's taken to walking the two miles to the Reserve just to spend time there."

"But she's half…" I start, falling into one of the many traps we newcomers do when it comes to the rocky relationship with kids who have one Haida parent.

"Her father is a big wheel in the Village. He wouldn't approve."

"I don't get it."

"Have you met Sgaana?" she asks, raising an eyebrow.

"Not yet." But he's well known in these parts as an influential member of the elite First Nations artist class whose work fetches high prices in city galleries. I'd heard he was Stella's father but he'd been out of the picture for a long time.

Quinnie glances over at a photo she keeps on the bookcase of Sgaana holding Stella as a baby. He is as massive and dark as Stella is tiny and fair. "He's not around much," she muses, "and when he comes here he likes to stay at his cabin on North Beach, rather than with his mother on the Reserve. He sees a lot of truancy, drug use, and some crazy behavior amongst the Reserve kids. He bought this place for me in town so Stella would have some distance from all that." She looks grim. "But they all go to the same school, and right now she thinks they're cool."

"If you can't keep Stella away from all that, why do you stay on the Island?"

Quinnie eyes me sharply. "I'm not about to throw the baby out with the bathwater." Here the conversation ends. She points me in the direction of the shower and then turns to her work with a side of venison ready to slice, salt, and line dry into jerky.

Later, before the mirror in her cedar-lined bathroom, I consider the steamy image it reflects. All angles, serious face, wet strands of hair dripping. Okay, that's enough. This examination makes me nervous. I am better at studying the minutia of each bit of skin, poring over delicate moles or the fine lines circling my mouth. I make a fist. *Grrrrr.* Everything works well. I test each muscle experimentally, feeling new strength in my arms and chest from daily chopping.

Silence. The air is damp, steamy, and clean. No nervous ulcer or other sickness since the divorce. The thought of it makes me genuflect, though I'm not a Catholic, and I look for clues in my facial expression but find none. No one is more surprised than I that the past few months haven't taken a toll on my well-being. I take my health for granted, the strength of my legs, sturdy feet and firm grip. Yes, I'm very lucky.

The silence moves into the room a little more, creeping on small feet.

Where is Quinnie?

Something dark flashes in the mirror, jolting me upright in terror. *What the hell was that?* The fear rivets, freezes everything, jerking my heart into huge thumps, bruising my chest. *What?* My eyes dart about, searching, listening. *Nothing. See, it was nothing!* The mirror is a placid lake, reflecting a tangle-haired girl spooked. Off in the other room is the dull roar of fire in Quinnie's stove. The floor creaks, settling into the earth. A soft growl and a sharp, feral smell. No. My fingers are tingling. I wait. Still nothing. I let out a long, slow breath. It is too quiet in Moira's house. *This is a bad luck place.* I hurry off, wet towels bundled up.

Night has come and I have to get off to Jonah's. With mechanical purpose I down the fish stew Matty has made from the last of the beet greens in our garden. Big chunks of turnip and potato steam in a dark, rich broth. Matty worships black cod, calls it black gold from the sea. I haven't the heart to tell her that I absolutely loathe it. With deft strokes I flick bits of it out of the way.

"How's the fish?" Matty is always looking for new cod devotees.

"Fine. But I gotta go."

"To the Reserve?" She doesn't look up.

"To Jonah's." I start pulling on coat and gloves.

"When you see the boathouse on the beach, you'll find me. Just look to the sea and then you'll find it." No addresses here, just directions with landmarks.

"You know," Matty begins, "I never told you about Jonah." She tips a spoonful into her mouth, eyes closed. I look up at the clock.

"Some other time."

I leave her at the kitchen table, the old oilskin cloth faded and worn, dinner still spread before her, eyes down. The door bangs. Frost on the grass, puffs of steam in the night air.

Jonah

♐♒♐♒♐♒

The road between the town and the Reserve is deceptive. The effort to groom it for civilization is abandoned for those few hundred yards and it feels like miles of nothing, a dangerous emptiness. On one side untamed bush, on the other the sea, dark under a half moon.

His house is just inside the eastern border of the Reserve, directly on the main road. Once the marked boundary is visible I slow down, cautiously scanning the row of planked houses lining the beachfront road. In the darkness they are indistinguishable from one another. Then I find the boathouse and a big silvery barn-like house opposite. It's surrounded by rock and grouse grass, weather-beaten from an endless assault of sea spray and wind. I pull up and get out of the car, boots crunching on the gravel driveway. The two-story house looms above. I turn and look up toward the sky, clear tonight again. A chill wind whips across the road with surprising ferociousness, the sea barely a few steps away.

Crack! Something lands on my car. It skitters across the hood, wings flapping. I stand frozen, holding my breath, watching the dark thing as it finds a footing on the smooth metal and settles briefly. A raven, identified by its distinctive curved upper beak. This is an old bird. Gray pinfeathers line his beak, scatter throughout his head and die away in the blue-black of a worn coat. His claws are huge knobby things, with curved nails spread cautiously on the slippery surface of my car. He turns, looking straight at me, feet shifting and screeching on metal. *Awwwk!*

"That's a good sign." The voice startles us both, the raven lifting off and disappearing into the night. Jonah is standing on the stoop above me. "That old raven has been here since before I was born, I think. He watches over me and my clan." He comes down a couple of steps. "You must be getting cold. Come on up."

I move stiffly, feeling the night wind pushing me onward. Jonah leads the way, pointing to a mudroom for shoes and coats. We are on the upper, main floor, a large open room stretching from one end of the house to the other. A testament to the virtues of his Raven heritage, the clan of creativity and imagination, his home is filled with an extraordinarily diverse collection of objects: sculptures, drawings of all sizes on sketch paper, and bookcases crammed with curios and antiquities. Many of his drawings, a strange mishmash of cartoonish pencil sketches and traditional watercolor Haida studies, are carelessly pinned on top of each other. A box of brushes, coffee cans of water and a drafting table sit off to one side; he is at work on something.

"I baked some pippins," he says, pointing to an enamel baking dish on the stove. The aroma of caramelized sugar and cinnamon from the steaming apples mixes with the steady warmth of burning wood. Motioning me into an old dining chair, he places two bowls on the long table that separates living and workspace. There isn't a bed;

instead a collection of deep-hued Persian carpets strewn about with pillows are tucked into a small alcove off the main room.

The furniture is all old and well cared for. For our meal, we sit at what was once a refectory table. It has spindle legs with lion claws gripping each foot. The tabletop is scored with many beeswax-softened scratches. In my bowl the browned apple swims in a rich butter sauce, its soft center topped with drippings of heavy cream and cinnamon. The sweet apple settles in my belly, drawing down tendrils of cream and sugar liqueur.

Jonah is watching me. His eyes are unreadable. He smiles at my empty bowl. "Did you like the apple?"

"Reminds me of home."

He waves toward the kitchen. "I cook a lot - Szechwan, Cajun. I like my seafood spicy." It's an orderly, well-stocked room. Scrubbed copper-bottomed pots hang in neat rows along one wall; big crockery jars of implements are within easy reach. Swags of savory herbs dry next to racks of salmon jerky strung above a collection of vegetable bins, tinned goods and baskets of bread by the small scullery. A bank of shelves on the far wall display a decidedly strange collection for a bachelor. Among the industrial-sized jars of condiments and spices are sparkling jewels of British gentility: delicate gold-leaf place settings, sterling cups, warming saucepans and ornate chafing dishes.

"Shouldn't we get started?" I ask.

"Of course." He leads me into a cubbyhole office jammed with papers, notices and flyers. Most of the cartoon work is lampooning government policies affecting First Nations rights. "Like I said at Colleen's last week, I need help writing leaflets."

"Well, here I am at your service ... and we haven't even been introduced."

"Word gets around."

"That old raven outside must have told you."

He smiles, teeth even and perfectly white. "Let me introduce myself first, then," he says with a slight bow.

"Jonah!" I blurt out before he can speak.

He laughs. "Well, I guess you speak raven, too!"

I offer my hand. "Liselle."

"Is that a French name?"

"My mother was born and raised in Montreal. My father's people were from Wales. She wanted to call me Madeline, but my father didn't want me to be named after an orphan. They settled on Liselle, and thought I would grow up to be a poet."

Jonah indicates a seat for me to take. "Around here the names we choose for our children are pretty important. Your father wasn't wrong."

"Maybe so, but I don't like it and I'm not a poet, so you can just call me Elle."

He laughs. "Okay, Elle." Then he sits and makes a show of studying me.

"Interested in memorializing me on paper?" I'm starting to go pink around the ears and neck.

Jonah laughs and points to his displayed work. "My portrait wouldn't do you justice – I'm more of a satirist." His output is prolific but none of it looks polished. In fact it's very different from the work of a Northwest Coast traditionalist. Everything looks like it's still in transition, as if he is trying to synthesize a lot of disparate ideas and hasn't quite gotten there yet.

"Interesting stuff, but not very commercial. What do you do for money?"

"I live the old ways," he answers with a sly grin. "I eat what the sea provides and barter for everything else."

So, this man with golden skin and green eyes lives the 'old ways'. Not the face of a Haida. Yet he lives on the Reserve. I have more questions, but leave them for now.

"Sounds like a hard way to get by."

He laughs. "It's a way of life around here."

Looking around at this comfortable place, I decide he is having one over on me.

Abruptly, Jonah turns to the laptop. "Let's get to it, shall we?"

On the wall above the computer is a detailed map of the Northwest Coast with Masset as a dot on the northern tip of Graham Island. Only the narrow Dixon Strait separates us from the snowcapped mountain ranges of the Alaska Panhandle. Most days the forbidding peaks are clearly visible.

"Like I told you the other night," Jonah says, pointing to the map, "the subs will have to come through here to get to the new base they're building near Ketchikan." He rifles through a stack of scribbled papers on his desk and pulls out a cartoon he's sent to the local paper. It lampoons the Americans for destroying fragile wilderness while 'saving the world' from terrorists. "Our prime fishing stock can be found in this narrow area – it's only fifty miles across. I've heard stories of subs catching on drift nets and pulling the whole boat down." He looks up at me with a serious expression, and suddenly grins. "At least, that's what I've heard, and it makes good copy. I've written our Member of Parliament and the Alaskan Governor about this issue several times." He hands me a pen. "But a letter with multiple signatures looks more important."

We work well into the night and then he sends me packing with at least a week's worth of writing chores and a promise to deliver leaflets in town. All this is in preparation for a meeting in Charlotte City, for which he hopes to drum up support. The volume of work is enormous – it's not surprising no one else volunteered to help. As I navigate back home I consider his strange life, the futility of taking on the American industrial-military complex with borrowed postage stamps and handmade drawings.

Later that night I dream of the potlatch. Jonah stands in front of me beating on a drum and singing. A beautiful Haida woman stands off to the side. *I know her*! The woman smiles at Jonah and then joins in the dancing, her oiled hair a dark waterfall. Abalone buttons in the shape of an Eagle. They see only one another. The crowd moves for them, with them. I am caught up in the chanting, the drumming in my pelvis and my chest. The music is inside everywhere. They circle one another. I want to see more. *"Let me tell you about this man."* Matty is blocking my way. A giant salmon in her arms jerks suddenly to life and flips out of her grasp. Where? Where? Heads turn. A raven escapes from the mass of bodies and flies up into the peaked roof, into the shadows above. *No!*

In the uneasy morning I wake early and lie quietly in the dark. Something has found root in my chest. An odd feeling.

Naani Rose

♐♒♐♒♐♒

Her silver wind chimes speak waterfalls in the breeze, high and light. Reminds me of summer. Rose Churchill lives in the house with the chimes; they are like the sound of her laughter from the potlatch. I first saw her as one of a trio of thin, high-voiced old women singing a British war song at Naani Ethel's birthday *doing,* voices better suited to Haida chants and ceremonial solemnity. The enthusiasm from the Ladies' Auxiliary of the First Methodist Church momentarily stunned the men in their headdresses and bear capes, who shifted uncomfortably with one eye towards the strange sound of a reedy a capella version of "Onward Christian Soldiers!" Naani Rose was looking over towards us. "They should feel welcomed." She's old school.

Naani Rose. She is not from one of the important families, nor does she live on the Reserve, so she is, in the social structure of our community, approachable without a formal introduction. Matty wants to send over a batch of freshly smoked salmon and is too busy to go herself.

The walk takes longer than expected; she is on the far edge of town in an area that is so close to the duck marsh it must be infested with mosquitoes in summer. No one is there when I arrive so I sit on the metal folding chair on the porch and wait. Soon a lumbering shape appears from the direction I've just come. An old woman folded down like a crow in human clothing materializes. Black wool coat with a gray lambs-wool collar, solid orthopedic shoes, and a large, black leather purse hung on her forearm. Approaching the bottom of the garden path she takes notice of me and beckons. "Can't find my keys," she says without preamble and offers me the voluminous bag for a try. I dig around until rewarded with a metallic clink. The keys are attached to a pink rubber squid. We move together to the front door.

For her appraisal, I hold up a plastic bag with some of the smoked salmon we have just cured. "Matty sent me."

"Matty's a good girl."

She motions me inside, and allows me to ease her out of her coat. "Hang it up over there if you don't mind, honey."

A wall of coats, cotton aprons, mittens, scarves, one on top of another. Bits of colorful material in a jumbled bag dangling from the doorknob. Clothes are piled everywhere, on furniture, in heaps across the small daybed she has long abandoned. I wonder where she sleeps. The rooms beyond are stacked to the ceiling with old newspapers, books, cardboard boxes, and more clothes. Must and decay seem to lift from the objects with every movement of the air, slowly dissolving into fine dust. I lock onto a faint aroma of black tea, pushing the other smells away. Taking a chair, I forget the salmon I have clutched in my hand.

"Here, let me." She latches onto the bagged fish with startling swiftness. With one fluid motion the package is secured inside her tiny refrigerator, but not before being analyzed, quantified and weighed in the blink of an eye. Purpose accomplished, she returns to her methodical slowness, feet scraping on the linoleum, a sore hip in every step. She takes the frame chair opposite me, next to an over-large wood stove.

"Honey, turn your chair to the fire and you'll be warm in no time." Rose speaks with a rolling cadence, each word pronounced as if carefully remembered, still puzzling and foreign.

She leans over to open the wood-stove door. Her arm can just reach. I jump up to help, but she waves me back. The fire is in that perfect state of suspended animation I have come to admire, still alive enough to leap into flame, yet quiet enough to wait for her return after many hours. The taming of the fire is something I still have not mastered; mine flare and burn merrily but are short-lived. I've not yet learned how to control the elements, to imbue them with steadiness or loyalty. Naani's fire has been waiting for her patiently like an old dog. She feeds it a log and closes the door before the oxygen-rich flame can consume it. She fiddles the damper with a deft touch. I watch hungrily, wanting to understand the damper more, needing to unlock its mysteries. She listens to the air sucking into the stove, her arthritic hands twiddling the knob with imperceptible coaxing to make it sigh for her.

She turns to me, satisfied. The room is a little warmer, just right. She pulls the kettle to the middle of the iron top and gets up to fetch cups and saucers. The kitchen, squared by table, sink and counter, is just large enough for one body, but she puzzles over a multitude of china and hanging trinkets, pulling out sugar bowls and creamers. Her china sets do not match. I watch her expression as she sets one before me, wondering if she does this purposely, the bright purple flowers of the cup clashing with the riot of orange peonies on the saucer. The Haida sense of humor. Always watching you slyly out of the corner of the eye, ready to catch you up. Haw, haw, haw!

Rose folds her hands over an ample chest. "Let's have the tea now." The watery liquid is tepid and something greasy swims on top. She looks hopefully at me as if to ask if perhaps I have brought biscuits. Silence.

"Naani?"

She smiles, her thoughts impenetrable to me, eyes lost amongst soft folds and a thousand creases, each one measuring a day in her old life. "I'm eighty-five years old, you know." She closes her eyes, perhaps from the exhaustion of navigating the Co-op grocery shelves for the herb sprigs, green onions, and tinned cocktail wieners I see in her small string bag. Wanting to be helpful, I go over to it. "Shall I put your groceries away?"

"Oh, just leave them be for now." She cocks her head. "What is your name, dear?"

"Just call me Elle."

"You're a good girl, *Ellie,* to come over with the salmon." She takes her time now to examine me from top to bottom. "So Matty sent you, eh? I knew an Ellie once."

"It's Elle, actually."

She regards me with pity. "But why would you want a name that's just a letter?"

"According to my mother, my name came from ancient Greek and means, 'torch, or light'," I explain, and she leans back to consider this.

Outside, the afternoon is fading. Bits of leaves rustle outside Rose's tiny house as the wind ebbs and flows. Around her still form are the pathways that lead to the small open space around the stove, carved from mounds of bedsheets, old sweaters, fancy dresses from dances long forgotten, dusty bits piled up over months of reminiscing, forgetfulness. Here, life is closing down, room by room.

"Naani, I have to go."

I turn away from the orange peonies and the severity of their bright color on the kitchen table, fumbling for my coat, smiling and reassuring. With great dignity she stands up to see me out.

"Come back any time."

It's a lonely walk in twilight. The boats jostle restlessly at their moorings, disturbed by a coming storm, clouds dark and low. Naani has chosen to live far away from the Reserve. On her side of the new highway bridge, the estuary has gone stale despite the concrete spillways. The smell of the sea is mixed with something darker. The wind picks up in its sudden way as I approach the bridge, momentarily flattening the tall, yellow winter grass, drawing my eye towards a clearing in the trees. On the other side of a stand of *slaal* and thornberry bushes, there appears to be a cluster of blackened lumps. Despite the growing cold and warning sky, I veer off the road and skirt the mucky edge of the pond to get a closer look. There is no path, so I have to push through the thorny bushes before breaking through to a flat area at the western edge of the estuary. Here lies a perfect circle of open land, strangely barren of wild growth despite what appears to be many years of abandonment. Perhaps this is a sacred spot. It feels as if something fierce has pushed down the sodden earth. I can feel it driving down still.

On closer inspection, two of the larger lumps turn out to be the outline of a series of small foundations, each no larger than a one-room shack. A periwinkle plant has twisted its way through the rotting wood, feeding off the rich black decay. The foundations bear the distinctive marks of an intense fire stopped only by the wet earth. Fascinated, I crouch down for a closer look at the timbers. Hand-hewn and very old, some still bear bits of rough nail heads that are distinctly pre-industrial. Haida. But it seems odd they would have put a site here, so far back from the shoreline. The shallows would always have been sluggish and buggy. No place to launch a canoe, the land scrubby and tired. Why would anyone want to live here instead of on the shore or down by the small point with its unhindered vantage of the strait?

The damp cold comes off the distant marsh. The darkness here hasn't the same sharpness as that by the open water; the forest spirits are too close. The little clearing feels like a sentry outpost, the last frontier between this place and *that* place. With a sudden crack the sky opens up with a squalling downpour and forces me to make a run for the road, heart thudding, the hairs on the back of my neck electrified. For a moment I consider taking refuge in Naani's house, but decide to make for home.

The wet state of my clothes and a cold dark house to greet me push away all thoughts of my strange discovery. Instead, I set to work making kindling out back, the dangerous hatchet easy in my hand.

♐♒♐♒♐♒

"This came for you."

Gingerly, Matty holds out an envelope. The paper is creamy, thick, bearing the official seal of the Council of the Haida Nation. And judging from the cancelled stamp, it was mailed from the Council's post box to ours five rows down. With letter delivered, my roommate abruptly turns, pulls on gumboots and a heavy jacket and clumps out the door without another word.

From Jonah, the note has been written with sky-blue ink. "Just when you think you know what you're doing, life throws you a curve ball. I can't stop thinking about those … flyers. Breakfast? Lunch? Dinner? Yes, how about dinner?" His script is open and innocent, like a schoolboy's. I can almost see his features in the letters, generous, full of self-irony and hope.

A formal letter, a formal declaration. Lunch dishes clatter in the sink. I throw my coat on and rush to find Quinnie. You were wrong. You don't know anything about the way things work.

A few days ago Quinnie and I spent the afternoon together looking for interesting objects on North Beach. She collects them for jewelry she makes to sell in Charlotte City. I'd chosen five small white pebbles and one caramel-colored stone. They were old and worn, soft in shape and color.

"Did you have something in mind when you picked up those stones?" Quinnie teased, knowing I refused to have my irises, palms or ear wrinkles read. I closed my hand around the stones. They rolled around in my grasp, heavy and still cold from the sea. I left them in my pocket and later put them inside a crystal inkwell I'd brought from home.

Later Quinnie and I made lunch from the pail of cockles we'd collected, steaming the finger-sized crustaceans and dipping them in butter. They tasted like lobster.

"He won't acknowledge you publicly," she said when I told her about my evening at Jonah's.

I kept quiet, trying to gauge her intent.

Regarding me were eyes of pale amber, shallow-set in a narrow face framed by a shock of thick blonde hair and razor-shorn bangs. She still possessed the last remnants of her once stunning beauty and a lithe dancer's body. Reaching out for another buttery cockle, she gazed at me and then popped the crustacean into her mouth. A necklace of pearly shells and small eagle feathers murmured against her breast. "It's true. He's looking for a Haida wife, and in fact, he just got back from Alaska where he was checking out a second cousin or something in Haidaburg." She lit up a cigarette with long, agile fingers.

"He wouldn't do that to me."

Quinnie laughed. "Oh, honey, you are so naive. He'd do it to you in a second, because he *did* it to me." She took a long drag from her cigarette. "And Matty, too."

"How do you know this?"

Her eyebrows arched.

"About Matty, I mean."

She took a drag from her cigarette and blew the smoke into a perfect circle. "You have a lot to learn about living in a small town."

I tried to imagine Matty with Jonah. Quinnie with Jonah. The images blurred and swirled around into a vortex, limbs and mouths entangled, twisting into lascivious, lip-smacking, steamy something. I sat back, teacup in hand. The stone fetish crackled and grated in my ears as she leaned forward to flick an ash. "Take a close look at him, honey. He's only one-quarter Haida. Everything else, biologically speaking, came from randy sailors and visiting do-gooders." She looked over at me. "A little of this, a little of that. Bingo - you have your boy."

"So?"

"Stay here for a while and you'll figure out just how important it is to be Haida on this island."

"That's ridiculous."

She blew a beautiful stream of smoke, like a horn, out in front of her. Laughed. "You know so little about Jonah. He's not what you think." She gazed at me, trying to read the reflection in my eyes. "You'll be his secret. His bit of sugar. He'll want you all right, but on his own terms."

I rose up and left as soon as I could, not wanting to know any more.

"I won't let that happen," I said as we parted. I'm not like you.

Now I'm on the cedar porch before Quinnie's house, letter in hand. I bang on the screen door, getting no answer. Stepping back I see her chimney, cold and blank, without a whisper of smoke. She is away for at least the day, maybe longer.

With Jonah's public overture, his past with the women here is of no interest anymore. It is not my future.

"Quinnie Sonnensdotter!" A crow, surprised by the noise, flies out of the leafless winter ash tree behind the house, a bit of black breaking off and soaring. I call her out even though I know she isn't home.

♐♒♐♒♐♒

"The moon is full tonight."

It's Jonah calling, a day after his note arrived. The distinctive, rounded-vowel cadence of the Haida is more pronounced over the phone.

I would like to tell him *okay, that's really corny,* but up here the moon is serious business so I sit quietly and listen to the clinking of wood against tin as he cleans his brushes.

"Have you eaten?" he asks after a moment.

I confess not.

Now we are in his sea-house with the raven in the yard, turning, turning before the edge of blue glass where his concoction of yams and pungent herbed fish swims in wine, drunken, winking up from a bed of *slaal* leaves. His finger dips into it and I see his tongue delicately lick the juice. *I'll bet you taste as good as that.* His irises are as open as the moon, white, wide-eyed, eager. We can be read so easily at this juncture; it's all about the slippery sauce, your wet juices, the cracking open of shells. Let me breathe through your gills in this new water, let me soak you up, your curried yams soft and supple.

He gets up from the table. "I think we should go out for a walk."

I can feel my face buckling, making two strong frown lines between my eyebrows. The weather is wild out here at the tip of the Island and tonight it's especially bad, rattling doors and whistling down the tin chimney. What business do we have out there, anyway? Pensively I gaze over toward the large glass window, out to where the sea is foaming.

"There's something I want to show you." He bundles me up, winding the striped scarf around my neck. Still, the air shafts under my coat and grabs at the small of my back. Our pant legs swish together, then disappear into the white noise of other sounds, the rushing sea, papery leaves skittering along gravel, creaking wood. Soon we are at the very western edge of the peninsula and he is leading me down a dark, twisting path.

"Don't worry," he says, "The moon will be out up ahead. You'll see."

He tries to take my hand but the furry leather feels strange in mine. I twist free, stooping to pick up a spiked fir cone caramelized with sap. The dark forest dampens sound, wind. Soon we are out on a wider road that skirts the eastern edge of a small salt-water lagoon, and just as he said, the moon has cast a bright silver wash over everything. Nights like this are called the 'afternoon of the full moon' and in the summer months, when the day ends close to midnight, the sky is never truly dark.

"Only the old-timers know of this place," he says, drawing closer to the water's edge. We stand in silence and I marvel at the sudden quietness, the still, spruce-perfumed air. Protected by a ring of heavy bush, the lagoon is in a world of its own. Then I see why: *Tung'tata-*

skling, the razor's spit, is a thin rocky parapet curving across the far edge to form a natural low-tide barrier.

"When I was a kid we swam here every day." Crouching down close to the water, he describes hot afternoons when the salmon were set out to dry and they'd gone out on the lagoon on inner tubes, floating away the aches that came from hours of heavy work pulling dip nets.

"The rubber was hot, the salt burned my cuts, but I'd bob here like a cork until the tide rushed over the spit and chased us away." He pauses. "It was like a dream."

I can imagine how quiet this sheltered place must have been, the sound of the sea so close.

I don't want Jonah's gloved fingers probing too deeply. "Tell me about Jesse."

He looks at me with some surprise. "Ah, so you know about her."

"She was at the potlatch when I first got here. Everyone was talking about what a hotheaded couple you were, always fighting and making up. Then one day she up and left the Island without explanation."

In the silver light his skin is pale; he turns to me and I see his discomfort. "She outgrew this place. Some do." He glances off, watching the moon's reflection in the tide-pool, and I know he would like to forget and float a little longer in that white light of a summer afternoon, the voices of children not far away. The memories drift over the water like smoke. A frog jumps and makes a big splash.

Jonah turns to face me, a decision set in his features. "The truth is, she left me, and not her people, and she'll come back when it suits her." He shrugs. "Life is about flow, and I'm tired of pushing against the current. I'm trusting in the place it will take me." Then his gaze goes upward. "Elle, look!" A dozen Canadian geese are cresting above us, dark shapes fanning out under the moon. They clatter and call out to each other in a frenzy. "There's a killer whale somewhere beneath them," he whispers, bending close.

"How can you tell?"

"They are warning each other not to come down just yet, even though they are tired and should rest for the night." And as if to agree with him the geese suddenly rise upward and veer off toward the Mainland. "Nothing better a killer whale would like for a snack than one of those geese," he remarks.

I gauge him for signs of the famous Haida humor. I don't know if he's having one over on me. His attention shifts. Pulling off a stalk of pale, hard berries, he strips them into his palm.

"We used the paste of these *salmonberries* mixed with *eulachon* grease to make our hair glossy." The berries smell a little like juniper.

"Must have been good."

He laughs. "Obviously you've never smelled *eulachon* grease."

For a while, we both scan the horizon. The moon is huge, surreal, and obvious in every aspect, flooding the sky with soft pearl brilliance. A universe of stars cannot compete; they are desperate, brittle points of light hanging about the dark edges of a distant horizon.

"When the moon comes along like this, at the tip of Orion, she is close enough to be heard," Jonah whispers.

I know we have landed on Tranquility Base, but what does it matter now? The woman who straddles her is taking shape, her arms and legs wrapped around the glowing orb, robes as delicate as the wing of a dragonfly.

"What is she saying?"

His rough coat and voice brush against mine. "She is very content on this night." He takes my hand and I let it rest there. "When the summer comes, Elle, you and I will float on inner tubes. We'll skin the salmon and then run here like children to float away the last hours of the day with nothing on our minds but how warm the sun is."

I look up toward the woman on the moon for guidance, but she has spoken all that she will on this night. That's the way it is with the Gods up here, certainly in answer to the questions of impertinent city girls who know too much already of the moon and stars they inhabit, whose ancestors came as emissaries and politicians, the smallpoxed thumb of a dead miner, church cardinals, and earnest lovers in search of a more civilized grail. Still, she is beautiful. And furthermore, while she rules, the stars are banished to the edge of the universe, so great is her glory and wisdom.

♐♒♐♒♐♒

"Naani, those houses out by the duck marsh. Who lived there? What happened to them?"

Rose regards me with bright eyes and takes my offering of brownies decorated with multi-colored jelly dots. Her favorite. I've learned never to come empty handed.

"Oh, those were the last places some other people lived." She turns her attention to the pan, fumbling with the plastic wrapper.

"Who were they?"

With a pained sigh, Naani puts down the brownies with a thump, making it quite clear she loathes letting go of them. Then she pulls up her stool by the stove and opens the cast-iron door, stoking up the heat for tea. I have already retrieved two cups and saucers. Purple peonies on china aged to the color of old dentures.

"Just some families that came from our village a long time ago," she finally answers, scraping the kettle closer to her. "Fire took them over sixty years back." Her sharp eyes are on her task. "Why do you want to go stirring up the past, anyway?"

"Just wondering, is all."

Truth is, she's the only one I dare ask. Her teeth are gone and the bark of her soul has been rubbed soft.

"Who were they? Why did they live so far from the clans in Old Masset?"

She fingers the tea box, thinking. "I had your curious mind when I was young," she replies at last, then turns back to the kettle, now boiling vigorously. "I'll tell you a little about it some other time, when I'm not so tired."

When the plate of brownies is unwrapped, she brightens up considerably.

"Some other time, then," I agree.

Later at home I knock on Matty's door, something I rarely do. I may have been careful with Rose but I can't get those black ruins out of my mind.

"Matty, do you know anything about those burned-out houses by the sanctuary?"

She has just finished meditating, and carefully folds the red silk cloth that was her private altar. The faint aroma of patchouli still fills the air. Matty has often told me it is possible to will the body to produce such scents.

"I've never asked," she replies evenly, smoothing her cloth and placing her prayer book into it. "I'm going to give you a piece of advice. You may be flushed with your success at chopping wood," she places the wrapped book on her bedside table, "but no matter how much you chop, or till or bake, it is not about how much sweat you leave in this land, or how much your love grows and takes root: you will always be an outsider. Try to remember that."

Then she sits down on the side of her old bed, and the paisley-covered springs bow beneath her. With her bird's smile and sharp eyes she looks up. "You are fresh and new and an object of curiosity. But don't push your luck. Around here it has a way of turning on those who get too smart too fast."

Doings in Skidegate

♐♒♐♒♐♒

My overnight bag is packed. Toothbrush, jeans, socks. On top, a silky camisole and panties; they glow vanilla under a sliver of new moon. In the darkness I can let my imagination flow, as slippery as pebbles under fast-moving water. His hands, trembling and inquisitive. *Ah, you must help me. Meet me half way.* You are inside. Inside. The house is quiet; his memory, the silk whispering, delicate pieces slipping through my fingers, running over my skin, falling downwards.

The night before we'd been sitting inside the cab of his truck with the motor running.

"I want you to come with me to the pole-raising dinner," he'd said with great formality.

"As a what?"

"You know."

"No, I don't know. And it is wrong of you to assume anything."

The cab windows steam in arcs so I crack open the window. The heat is oppressive. We are stopped at a junction outside of town, the one leading to North Beach, the engine clicking furiously as it cools. I hear the distant roar of the waves; a nor'easter has been kicking up things pretty good the last two days. Leaves fly past along the gutter, then are picked up in a dark orbit and taken away. The road is black and deserted.

"This is the deal," I begin. Jonah's face is ripe with blood, eyes averted. They're unnerving, glowing milky green like a cat's.

"We need to have an understanding," I push on. "I can't let this go any further unless we agree on the rules."

Jonah turns towards me. "I wouldn't do anything to hurt you." His panicked expression gives me a small lurch of triumph.

"Then say it."

He knows what I am talking about. The shorthand of village life, the way your story precedes you so you don't have to say it over and over again in that tiresome way, twisting and turning it around to manipulate.

"Elle, I wish to …" he looks over, takes my hand in his. "I wish to court you."

"Is that so?"

His expression becomes pensive.

"I know, Jonah. About your trip to Haidaburg. The search for a wife."

He sighs. Shifts.

"What happened? I mean, why did you stop?"

"It turned out to be a total waste of time," he says bitterly. The memory seems to take everything out of him and he puts his hand on the key as if to start it up, drive me somewhere, and dump me off.

"I'm sorry," I say, trying to keep the panic out of my voice, and he drops his hands to the seat. "Please, I don't mean to pry, but it's just that I'm trying to understand. It seems if you were so determined to find the right Clan wife, why you wouldn't have just taken one."

He avoids my gaze. "It's not what you think. I had my share of interested women but in the end I couldn't do it." Then he turns to me. "Eventually I realized I was just going about it the wrong way, trying to be someone I wasn't."

For a long breath he sits, lost, eyes roaming the horizon. Reliving past conversations, moving pictures, ghosts conjured up in front of us.

"Elle, I wish it were clearer."

The cab is as cold as a tomb but he makes no move to turn on the heat so I pull my coat tighter. "Maybe you could start by telling me more about where you came from. I know so little about your family."

He grimaces and puts his hands on the steering wheel. "Ah, *that* question. The one that's on everybody's mind when they see the Raven blanket and this fair hair. So here it is: My grandmother, the daughter of a chief, had an affair with a sailor. They say he was from a Norwegian crew. It happened all the time when the fishing was good around these parts. Boats, as thick as a school of smelt, jammed into the harbor and brought a lot of men looking for a good time." His half-lidded gaze shifts sideways. "You know, randy, flush with money and most importantly, white. They could have looked like the back end of a horse and it wouldn't have mattered. Our women liked them because they weren't half-drunk village losers." He keeps his gaze on the logged-out, scrawny bush around us. "I'm told my grandfather was a handsome one. Ambitious, too. The story is, my grandmother thought he was going to take her off the Reserve, but he was smarter than that. He had his way with her and left. Left her pregnant. Abandoned. My great-grandfather took her in, raised the child as his own. She never married. The child, her only child, was my mother, Pearl."

Matty had told me Pearl had refused housing on the Reserve, preferring to live in town. She was a solitary woman who worked as a cook on a fishing boat. No apparent husband.

"I was told your great-grandfather was an important man in the Village," I begin, aware I know very little about who said what or how things unraveled back then. Back then, being Indian was an act of supreme will.

"Yeah, well, it didn't seem to impress my mother, who went and found herself another white guy and had me." He looks down and fiddles with his keys. "My dad left when I was seven. He was the foreman at the salmon cannery, and one day he just packed up and left. Pearl got religion and since then God has apparently answered all her questions."

"Jonah, I need to know."

He looks at me warily.

"Why do you want to be with me?"

Before us is the distant Rose Spit where the high tide has swallowed up the thin bridge of rock. One moment you are on land, the next, it is gone.

"You are like the horizon." He smiles wistfully and searches my face as if to memorize it. "The color of you is like this place. Blue, umber, gold." He turns and picks up a strand of my hair, then lets it fall, his face open with longing. "I can't explain, but I know this is as it should be." He turns back to me and takes my hands in his. "All this searching, it turned out to be futile. I was looking for something that didn't exist. Maybe I'm finally growing up."

"Elle, I want you to come with me to the pole raising."

"Are you speaking of a date, or a courtship?"

"Dammit, don't mock me. I'm serious."

"Okay, is this courtship, then, to be conducted in public?"

He hesitates a moment.

"Of course."

"I won't be toyed with, Jonah."

The release of his breath fogs up the windshield. The ghosts inside are now present.

"I got it, Elle. Loud and clear." He reaches out and takes my hand. I allow him to lace his fingers in between mine. The webs are sensitive. They bend with pleasure, touching his. Then he straightens up, now very formal. "Liselle Marie Owen, I'd like the pleasure of your company at the pole-raising ceremony in Skidegate next Tuesday."

"I accept your invitation."

He breaks into a wide smile, teeth all showing. Well golly gee missy, you've gone and got yourself a boyfriend.

"We have to stay overnight down there." He catches my look. "In separate bedrooms, of course. I'll see if Hugh can put us up." I met

Hugh once. He came up for a birthday celebration for one of the Naanis. He's a bigwig on the Council of the Haida Nation.

Dizzy, I am let off in front of the house. Home already.

I turn to go and he leaps out of the truck, running over and picking me up with a big whoopee! His rough coat and soft face are everywhere on me. I smell his blood and his juniper. I smell his hope, free at last.

"I think I'm crazy about you, Ellie-O!" he shouts, lifting his head up like a wolf to the moon.

Then he's off, gravel spitting, honking fading into the night.

♐♒♐♒♐♒

Skidegate lies a hundred miles south of Masset, a rocky necklace of shoreline assigned by the British Government in the nineteenth century to the Haida as their second and only other reserve. Two villages left out of twenty-four. Dozens more if you count the summer lodges.

One of the first missionaries, the Most Honorable Reverend Collison, painstakingly recorded their encampments on a hand-drawn map, but today, the evidence of most of them is scarcely more than lumps in the green moss. Cedar rots quickly in an eleven-months year of rain. The remaining poles were taken by museums. Smallpox got most of the population anyway; the survivors straggled up to the government reserves in the late 1880s when it became clear who was boss. They were just plum exhausted by then, and the tarpaper houses facing the sea were a good place to sleep until morning. *The long night has lasted one hundred years.* So say the elders.

Word is, the Skidegate Indians did better than the Masset group. Early on they managed to snap up most of the coveted Japanese *gow* licenses available on the Charlottes. Even with its wealth, Skidegate isn't much more than a wind-blown strip along the water's edge. I watch as neatly divided suburban lots come into view, complete with big wood-frame houses, shiny new Broncos and pleasure boats on every lawn. Almost everyone has a satellite dish. Such a contrast to the old, worn-out linoleum up in Masset, rattling windowpanes, pitted aluminum doors. There is much rivalry between Masset and Skidegate. Masset Haidas say the Skidegate group is full of itself; the Skidegate group looks upon Masset as a wild place, full of hooligans and drunks.

I stay out of it anyway. An opinion from white folks can lead to banishment. The Haida don't take kindly to judgment from the outside and they are quick to defend one another if challenged.

Jonah pulls up in front of the Village Hall. Unlike the suburban feel of the new one in Masset, this is a rambling cottage-like structure right on the beachfront, a little worse for wear. The interior is more promising, plank floors and cornices, with a second-floor balcony hung around the outer perimeter, facing the stage. It must have been a dance hall once. It is intimate and warm, rubbed down with wood smoke, French-fry oil, and a thousand banquet lunches. Right now it smells mostly like chocolate cake. Lots of chocolate cake. Two dozen gaily decorated with sprinkles of tiny silver balls, hearts, candies and "Welcome!" spelled out in pink icing.

Jonah has arrived early because he has business to attend to first. He finds Hugh, and introduces me.

"This is Elle," he announces. I mirror his nervousness, reticence.

"You are welcome to stay in my home tonight," he offers gravely.

Then without another word, the two of them disappear together into a back room. It's that way with the men here; they don't go in for a lot of explanation, just get on with it. I'm left standing alone in the hall, coat over one arm. Right, then, look for a vantage point, and search the room. Matty said she might come down. Quinnie too. No familiar faces. No white faces.

The women and their children are busy with their tasks, getting the plates down and putting small paper bundles wrapped in colored ribbons into plastic favor baskets. All the women and girls are wearing starched white aprons, hair tied back, hands reddened from the kitchen heat and hours of hard work. Once in a while they glance curiously in my direction. The hour crawls by. Still no Jonah. The Hall gradually fills up. Others stare more openly at me, alone without an escort. The room is warm; I sit upright in an assembly chair that rattles and scrapes with every movement. The seats next to me are occupied last.

"Well let's get started, shall we?"

A man I don't recognize has the microphone; the room quiets.

Big bowls of vegetable soup are set on the tables. Still no Quinnie, or Matty. I scan the faces again and again. I want to go find Jonah but some instinct tells me this would be a very bad decision. *Not my business, anyway.* Up on the balcony there is a collection of unmarked doors out of which emanate the thud of boots and murmur of voices. Then a movement catches my eye and I see Jonah come out of one of them with Sgaana, the father of Quinnie's daughter and heir apparent to the titular Eagle Chiefdom of Masset. Though I'd never seen him at Quinnie's, Matty had pointed him out one afternoon during a walk on North Beach. He'd been outside his summer home lounging on a deck chair smoking and reading a book. We'd passed without acknowledgement.

He is a head taller than Jonah, powerfully built, his form visible in a red-checked flannel shirt and faded jeans. His oiled jet hair is long and free, dark eyes under heavy eyebrows, skin the color of burnt caramel. Although Jonah seems to be scanning the crowd with mild interest, Sgaana's gaze immediately focuses on me. He takes a long drag from a cheroot and blows it with calm deliberation in my direction as if to cleanse the room of my presence. For a long moment he stares me down, then abruptly turns away.

Suddenly, there is a hand on my shoulder. Jonah.

"Miss me?"

Capricious, playful, he takes his place with deliberateness as formal as a Victorian suitor. His eyes momentarily find mine; then he turns away to make polite conversation with his neighbors. The smell of smoke clings to him, the swaddling comfort of his wool sweater, familiar enough for me to know what it feels like to bury my face in it and feel his fingers digging into my hair, pulling me upwards.

For all his acquiescence to my rules, I am still reticent to reach out and claim him. I stay rooted to the confusion of the room, watching private conversations and plates of food being passed down. They are loaded with barbecued chicken, cream corn, heaps of steaming potatoes. I carefully handle the precious old crockery, portioning something for my plate, pressing the dish onward down the line. My neighbor turns and looks. A girl, perhaps twenty. She takes the cream corn and smiles, her eyes lighting briefly on Jonah. She smiles in the knowing way.

"Are you a friend of Jonah's?"

"He brought me here." I must sound resentful because she rewards me with a triumphant smile. Then she leans forward and gazes fondly in his direction.

"I'm always surprised to see him with a beard. I remember him coming to visit my uncle when I was five years old. He was a grown-up teenager. Very serious. He came every afternoon for a drawing lesson until my uncle said he was done." Her eyes are bright bits of coal, like a raven's.

"He could be a chief one day. We're sure proud of him." She turns away and begins an earnest conversation with an old woman on her other side. They laugh and make a joke about someone across the room, then begin to whisper conspiratorially.

This is useless. So many beautiful young women, daughters of clansmen, fresh out of school, of marrying age. They are outgrowing the confines of this tiny strip of land, yet they will not leave. Jonah, in his red suspenders and peppery beard, grave, serious, of the deep green eyes, is a Raven for an Eagle woman. It can't be me.

"I'm going out for some air."

Jonah turns and tries to reach for me. I push his advances away.

"I'm fine."

The girl beside me is silent. I find the door, pushing outward through a rush of bitter cold to the beach, rocky stones underneath. I sink to the ground, my eyes on the gray waves as they surge again and again toward the shore. So bitterly cold, massed clouds to the north blackening the sky, angry wind that never seems to let up. The sound of the waves becomes the sound of footsteps and then he is there.

"What am I getting into?" I ask.

"I'm sorry. But I'll stick by you if you help me." He pulls me up and we stand shoulder to shoulder in the rough wind. Where am I to go?

We head back in together, thinking our own thoughts.

Inside, heads turn. Jonah has his hand firmly in mine. He moves slowly over to the table and takes out my chair, then sits beside me and takes my hand again.

"For as long as you want, Elle," he whispers.

A figure looms over us and I turn, half expecting Sgaana. "And who do we have here?" It's a smiling, matronly Haida woman in a black overcoat and plastic rain shoes.

"Naani Gladys, this is Liselle."

She turns to me with a certain deliberateness.

His arm comes up around my shoulders. "My girlfriend."

"Oh, darlin'!" She has a gravelly voice. "How dee-lightful!"

♐♒♐♒♐♒

The meal is dispensed with quickly, and then we're on our way to Hugh's. Despite Naani Gladys' welcoming presence, dinner was more of a polite standoff with the community than acceptance, and the effort has been exhausting. I'm ready to crawl into my sleeping bag and blot everything out.

Without warning, Jonah pulls the truck onto a sandy clearing by a copse of tall cedars bordering the sea. The wind is up, howling, buffeting the truck, and whipping the air around in a fury. It is completely black outside, filled with dark shapes moving and bending one into another.

"Why are we stopping?" I ask. The elements seem too powerful here.

Jonah turns to me, his face barely visible. The wind is blowing hard; big chunks of dried grass tumble across the windshield, and outside the roar of the whipped sea is deafening. The whole of the Pacific seems to be crashing up against the edge of its domain, thundering against the rocks, chewing away at the land. It is fearful outside, dangerous.

"Elle?"

I see his irises opening like the petals of a flower. "Can I show you something?" His face and his hands are folding and unfolding. Pressing forward eagerly.

"I want to show you how my grandmother kissed me when I was little."

"Jonah..." I hesitate, head bowed. I don't want this forgery, this incomprehensible memory of something lost, then resurrected. The way of your people. Don't try and do it through me, not now. Not while you are after something.

He pulls away, slowly, watching me. Then, before I can object, he bends forward and rubs my nose with his, laughing.

"You're joking, now!" I chide.

The car shudders, the sea ready to rush over the beach and engulf this land and us with it. I can feel it rise up, steadily pressing onwards, like the secrets I feel all around me. I want to ask about the mysterious outpost, the abandoned places, lost beneath waves of moss, but I dare not. I don't know yet whom to trust. Perhaps I will always be on the edge of that bracken water, looking off to a distant city, full of lights and laughter. An alder before me bends to near breaking, now a skirt of leaves rustling madly. I lean forward and tilt my head. Briefly our lips touch, dry, bright, electrical, brushing. Then we both turn and face out toward the volatile landscape, the blackness of the night illuminated only by our headlights and a great, expectant curiosity.

House of Northern Lights

♐♒♐♒♐♒

I've taken to photographing the landscape. I want to find the shapes and colors I've heard so much about in stories of the wild, untamed north. Stories I listen to but cannot keep. The inky black cloak of **He Who Transformed Himself into a Whale**, the velvety brown marten skin and silver salmon of **He Who Hunted Birds in His Father's Village**. The yellow cedar hat worn by the **Dogfish Woman Who Came Home**. So many things to remember: mouse skin, cranberries, wild clover roots, wild rhubarb, the white tail of a goose.

I begin chronicling the days with a digital collection of found objects, undisturbed and bearing no kinship but to the hording earth. I've spent hours hiking trails through dense wet forest to capture close-ups of succulent mushrooms: bright red with iridescent blue spots, like Alice's Wonderland; lime green beauties no bigger than a thumbtack; toadstools with broad, sheltering tops. I've even collected a few of the ones I know are good to eat, carefully mapping their location.

When the wind is calm I explore North Beach out behind the dunes, where fragrant runners of wild strawberries still yield tiny, sweet fruit. I photograph the many species of beach scrub, some with the dried remnants of summer's flowering. Along the shore a constant breeze ripples across the loamy sand. Young eagles perch on logs, their spotted caramel color distinguishing them from their elders, whose appearance high above me in stark black and white is still surprising. Eagles flourish unchallenged here. They and the raven represent the divided Haida house. Two great families flourishing from the beginning of time within the rituals of life: marriage, birth, loyalty, character. In the past one could not marry within one's clan, so an Eagle would marry a suitable Raven. To do otherwise would have been incestuous, subject to banishment and death. Alliances were carefully arranged and respected, with close attention paid to inheritance lines and class distinctions.

Other than to trade, the societies of this region's first inhabitants did not mix, though the nearby Tshimshin maintained friendly relations and their two clans could intermarry under certain circumstances. Cut off by rough seas and rocky shoreline, the Haida reigned unchallenged for thousands of years on their archipelago, fishing the teeming seas and building great houses adorned with heraldry and art. Less nomadic than other First Nations societies, they were formidable canoe carvers and ocean navigators; their sophisticated culture, ritual, and visible trappings of wealth provided legendary status amongst their northwest neighbors, with whom they warred frequently. They did not take kindly to strangers, considered to be lesser beings. For thousands of years their place in the hierarchy was unchallenged, their position and power base secure.

All this has been upended since the Colonials arrived. The drawn-out, bitter surprise of a world never imagined. I am of this new social order, a sea witch or a bird trapped in a changeling form, unable to mix with the Old Ones. A stranger like me lives in the nether world of the old stories like a vision, a prophesy of wonder, a prophesy of doom. Bitter harvest from their steadfast worship of possessions, class, cachet. How appealing the visitors must have been with their ships the size of sea monsters and their cannons of black iron. Analyzed and welcomed, used like canny currency, finally desperately, futilely rebuffed as the momentum bowled them over. Like the angry froth on the waves, I am one of those still tumbling toward the shore.

Behind me I hear a scuffling.

"Hey there!"

Harry is emerging from the scrub pines, lumbering awkwardly through the deep sand. Today he is wearing a green tartan regimental kilt and hiking boots. He is flapping something in the air.

It is a key, attached to a long, iridescent ostrich feather.

"I'm going to show you my little hideaway," he says, easing his bulk down on a large dune log. "I've been getting the place ready for winter." I peer behind him curiously but there is only a copse of tall beach pines and the ever-undulating waves of scrub grass.

"That way." He points. I think I see something, but … perhaps not.

"Come," he says and heaves himself up and I follow along a small narrow path paved in crushed shells.

"Behold … the Mouse Café."

The sun is in my eyes.

"There!" he points with a flourish.

A shimmer and then I see it! Harry is grinning.

Looking exactly like a gnarled, mossy hobbit dwelling, a tiny house distinguishes itself from the surrounding greenery as if by magic. A trick of the eye. And no wonder: the walls are barely six feet high, met by a low roof that pitches steeply into the dense canopy of a giant cedar. The entire house is covered with cedar bark shakes, except where bits of green moss have taken root in the cracks.

It seems to have grown up from the ground, like a whimsical fungus, forming doors and windows, sprouting cornices and white trimmed flowerboxes filled with buttery glade flowers and pale ladyslippers.

Through a window at one end I can see a large, foursquare bed covered with feather pillows and multi-colored quilts. Beyond, the molten wax of many candles burned down to their wicks. From the bed one could see the channel and the Alaskan mountains beyond. This is a house for dreaming. For being perfectly still.

Harry takes me around to the front door, a heavy slab of cedar wedged shut by a staff of gnarled oak. Creaking, the door opens into a tiny vestibule crammed with shelves of canning jars and gardening tools. Beyond is a small living room filled with antique furnishings, a pair of tall wing-backed chairs by the window, *petit point* footstools placed nearby for comfortable reading. A pewter jug holds dried *saalberry*, a sheaf of red berries set in relief against earth-colored walls. The narrow kitchen leading to the bedroom is filled with yellow crockery. And everywhere, a scrubbed floor made from river stones.

Everything smells of the sea, creosote, the constant wind quieted here behind the dunes. I explore every inch, delighted, fascinated.

"Do you like it?" he asks, grinning.

"Harry, it's wonderful!"

He shakes the key. "I keep this in a coffee can over by the woodpile. Come by some night when the Northern Lights are out – you won't get a better view than from the bedroom windows."

As I head back to the beach, I can still hear the sound of the ocean from inside the cottage, slow and steady like the thudding of an old clock.

♐♒♐♒♐♒

The quartered log falls hard and makes a satisfying sound. Outside in the backyard, Jonah works on my wood. He comes every afternoon and chops enough for the next day. Matty rolls her eyes at the sight of him.

"Dunno what you've done to him." She shakes her head. Earlier we'd had words about his increasing visits.

"Matty, Quinnie told me about you and..."

She cut me off with a raised hand. "Look, I've slept with almost all the available men in this town and Jonah was not much more than one drunken night." Her gaze was challenging.

"Ah, forget it." Then she was off again, hat jammed down over her tight curls, and that was the end of it.

The nightly chopping rang out clear through the neighborhood, and when it began two weeks ago the other gentlemen callers stopped coming around. As Paulie, Jonah's friend and neighbor on the Reserve put it, *"Big contest there to see who was gonna get to chop your wood and Jonah won."* I'd never been a prize before.

I watch him heave the axe and tackle a thick knotty log, the kind I've never been able to split. Like trying to cleave granite. Tough, tough wood. The pierced log sticks to the axe. He picks the whole thing up and pounds it back down, the axe digging deeper. He's sweating, working up an appetite.

Through the window glass we labor in perfect harmony. On the stove, quartered hedgehog mushrooms simmer in butter with steamed chunks of salmon and beets. The door slams and he strides in, stuffing a generous quarter of cedar into a canvas carryall.

"What's that for?"

He smiles, the cold running off him. "Ummm. Smells great!" He puts his head over the steaming pot. "I was thinking we could escape with our bounty and take it to the Mouse Café."

I look at him with surprise. "I've just discovered the place!"

"Things have a way of turning up just when you need them."

It was true, once you understood the Island way. Money for a week's worth of groceries in exchange for a massage. A battered but nearly new alternator salvaged from a truck in the town dump to replace a failing one. Something always came along if you stayed open to the signs.

Finding the Mouse Café in the darkness seems an impossible task, but Jonah keeps a careful watch, finally pulling up before two slender alders stripped of their bark. Our flashlights pick up the mouth of an overgrown path partially blocked by a mass of tangled blackberry bushes cold and bare from winter. "Ouch!" One of the thorny tentacles rips at my ankle. Jonah pushes on ahead, trying to keep the branches out of my way.

Could I have dreamed it? Then the tiny dwelling materializes. In the darkness it is mute and stolid. I find shelter from the wind while Jonah locates the key. Along the pathway, the grass waves and bends beneath us, dry and mysterious. Then there is the clattering of the tin can, the key in the lock and Jonah rushing me into the quiet darkness within.

Once inside I find the oil lamp to light it, while Jonah sets out to tend the stove. "It's huge!" I laugh at the size of the clanking tin burner, so out of place in this tiny cottage, most likely salvaged from the old canning factory. It is rusty and tired looking, but Jonah assures me it is sound. The sea thunders behind the dunes and the wind blows hard across the roof. I'm shivering. Though the fire roars it hasn't yet dispelled the damp cold which has settled deeply into everything.

"I guess we should just get under the covers," he says.

We look at each other awkwardly.

"I'll stay in my clothes."

It comes out from us simultaneously and we laugh.

In the candlelit darkness the large corner window is a fragile barrier between the sea and the bed where we burrow under layers of down comforters and patchwork quilts. Outside, soft light reveals only a shallow world with tall grass bending. Beyond in the darkness is the sea, increasingly wild. The fire roars loudly, fairly shaking the old kettle stove. Jonah has stuffed it so full that the iron sides are almost glowing. Heat fills the room.

"Jonah." He put his finger to my lips.

"Shhh."

It feels strange to be under all these covers still wrapped in sweaters and wooly socks. The pieces still scatter. *Lucky, lucky you.* To want so little. As other unwanted dreams invade my sleep, cowering under a stranger's gasp, pushing inward, so will you. Where will it all end? *Oh baby, feels good.* Distant, repetitive. Dull. Old pain. Please don't say *I love you,* not true, I suspect your prick is talking. But here the courage ends. Same story, night after night, relived like a ghost waiting at the foot of the bed, waiting for the miracle. I've cleanly excised that life out of me, gripping it like a wound, watching with disbelief. I ask this: Either you have a prick, or you don't have a prick. Where is the place in between?

He looks at me, trying to read something there. How lovers do this, I cannot fathom, but they try, bequeathed some strange new power to exercise. A foolhardy delusion.

And yet I look back unable to help myself.

We have never been in the same bed together. It was up to Jonah to keep his own counsel. Keep silent.

"I brought something to read," he says, reaching over to a book on the nightstand.

"Me too."

We whisper like children nestled in a backyard tent. The oil lamp is raised, bringing a steady glow. It reflects back off the glass. He touches my face again, his eyes scanning all of it, rising up over my eyebrows, along my nose, across my mouth, down to my chin. His eyes are light green in this amber wash, flecked with small bits of gold. His mouth seems as mine, softened as lovers' lips are, full of expectation, hope, repentance. I devour his features as he does mine, the perfect line of his nose, flared slightly at the bottom as a Haida's is, skin so close as to be translucent, a hint of freckles here and there. Dark, thick eyebrows.

Both of us are flabbergasted by the other, unmoving.

"Can I get closer?" he whispers. I can feel his hardness fighting through the clothes next to my belly. The rest of him is lushly collecting toward me, finding every ripple and opening, the giving of skin and muscle. Sinewy fiber. I feel everything. So this is how the hands work? This is how the face curves upward, brows drawn, mouth soft? *Life.* He lifts a trembling hand and reaches down under my sweater. I do not stop him. I watch only his eyes and the milky almond there, like cat eyes deeper than anything. Outside something bumps by, caught up in the wind. Light flickers on the reflection of us. Things blur. His fingers find the rise of my breast, delicately resting, holding it as a frightened bird. He tastes his prize; head bent into me he breathes like the wind outside, whistling, beckoning, I can no longer tell the difference.

Suddenly he pulls back. "What is that?" He peers anxiously into the darkness. Perhaps he heard the *kwaagindal,* the killer whale, sounding out at sea. After a moment he comes to his senses, lifts me closer, fitting the curves and angles together.

"Let me have this." With his hand he pushes damp hair away from my forehead, smoothing and smoothing, closing his eyes as if he wished to remember something. He murmurs softly until the words disappear into sleep. Soon the candles burn down to the wick and sputter out, leaving behind the fanning shadows of beach grass to play across the wall. I lie awake long after he has left his body in my care, stretching again and again into the joy, knowing for certain now there is something still alive inside, vivid like the first bit of new green after rain. Bone and blood come to the light, prickling and yawning, unfolding slowly. He turns and flexes like a cat dreaming. I put my hand on it just to feel the life there, to feel his steady breath. Sleep comes.

In the morning the light is blank, winter light, light without color. Jonah has kept the fire going and in this moment, between sleep and wakefulness, his body is familiar. I run my hand up his arm; he shivers and turns and kisses me. Deeply, lesser, forgotten feelings rise to the surface *so this is what it is like*. Jonah looks at me: is this what you want?

Just cup your hand, wrap your arms, pull me here and you have done what I want. This is what I want.

Kitkatla

♐♒♐♒♐♒

Saturday afternoon Matty invites me to a birthday lunch for someone she calls Dobie. "He's a Chief," she offers in her deadpan way, as we stand on the porch tucking our mufflers in. It has turned bitter, but worse the rains come every afternoon and only God has kept the stinging drops from turning into pellets of hail. I pull the hood of my jacket up as we head across our backyard past the woodpile. It's much drier now, courtesy of a new tarp from Jonah.

Inside Two Bells Café, steam rises from all the warming coats, from the mugs of hot chocolate brought to the table. Having gotten the word I'm Jonah's girl, Broan is settling for friendship and has joined us. He observes me with a sad smile, his blond hair stiffened by salt spray.

"How are you getting on?" he asks, taking an experimental sip from a steaming mug of coffee. Before I can answer the door opens and in walks a tiny man, hunched over, face obscured behind the upturned collar of a black leather jacket. Stitched in red on one breast pocket are the words, **Chief Kitkatla,** on the other, a clan crest. Matty looks at me, a wicked glint in her eye.

"Over here, Dobie!" she calls.

"What sort of name is that?" I whisper.

He turns toward us and shuffles over, bow-legged in faded jeans, white socks and brilliant white Reeboks. He stops for a moment at the table and regards me quizzically before a preemptively dismissive wave of his hand.

"Thought it was just gonna be you and me, Matty."

He has sharp black eyes under equally intimidating eyebrows. They are burrowing into Matty like an electric drill. He bears an uncanny resemblance to Charles Manson.

"Sit!" Matty commands, laughing. He grunts, takes off his jacket. For a moment I see the flash of a much larger name patch with his name emblazoned across the back. He seems dwarfed by advertising.

Slowly scraping the chair back, he settles in, gnarled hands accepting the tea Matty has anticipated he would want.

"What'll it be?" she asks. "It's your birthday, Dobie. You can have anything you want."

I try on a friendly smile. He looks over at me and snorts, or snarls, I can't tell.

"Nah, just soup."

Matty tries to coax more, but he stops her with a glare.

"Soup! Soup! That's all I want!"

"Okay!" She puts up her hands and laughs.

The broth comes, along with sandwiches for the rest of us. Broan studies me. Dobie ignores all of us.

"So, Dobie," asks Matty, "have you met my roommate yet?"

He looks over at her, annoyed.

"Nope."

Slowly he picks up his spoon and begins ladling it into his mouth, slurping noisily.Matty jerks her head in my direction. "This is Elle."

He gives me a cursory glance before turning back to his soup. Takes another slurp.

"What are you doing here?"

I open my mouth but Matty cuts me off. "She's just hanging out."

"Seems like a big waste of time," he says with disgust and then swivels around and gets up out of his seat.

"Dobie!" Matty cries, dismayed.

"I'm just goin' to the bathroom."

I suppress an insane urge to giggle. Nerves. He is winking at us, I could swear. When he comes back out, Matty pulls a large jar of canned peaches from her bag and pops it on the table. "Happy birthday," she says, fluffing out the tissue wrapping and garish red bow.

Hand out like a claw, he slides the offering over toward his bowl.

"Nice ribbon."

I hadn't noticed how soft his voice is until now. In concentrated silence he picks up his spoon. At that moment something extraordinary emanates over toward me. I stare at the side of Dobie's head. Like a door opening, a panoramic view. The intensity of it brings tears, sudden and unwanted. I can feel Broan's gaze across from me receding, Matty similarly gone from view. *There is no one else in this room but you and me.* He slurps his soup, bent over.

Get this: I'm not going to turn away. Things around me blur, fragmenting into light, becoming lace, a spider web. I push on. *I saw it.* What, you fool? Something familiar. Alone. Chest tight, I keep staring at the side of his head, splitting open the atoms and finding the interlocking piece. I recognize the loneliness, as clear as any secret language is to the initiated. His head is glowing with the knowledge. He starts talking to Matty, then slowly turns toward me. "How long did you say you were going to be here?"

The sound and noise flood back into the vacuum. Glass tinkling, voices everywhere. Someone laughing.

"Well," I sense this is a trap. I look to Matty for direction but she's banged her knee on the table and is occupied. "I'm not sure," I finish lamely.

He appears uninterested and is focused on opening a small plastic wrapper of crackers. Once crumbled into his soup, he stirs them around thoughtfully. Then he turns to me. "What did you do before you decided to come here and do nothin'?"

"I had a job. Back in Hollywood." It seems like a very long time ago.

The chief takes a slurp from his spoon. "Never met a movie person before."

"Oh, I didn't do anything that glamorous. I just lived there."

Matty snorts. Dobie nails her with a glance. He takes another mouthful of soup and wipes his mouth with a napkin.

"I'm thinking I'll come over for tea," he announces.

Matty looks up, surprised. "I have business in the Village, Dobie."

"Well, then," he turns toward me. "How about you making me a cup?"

I stand up, obedient but confused.

Suddenly he's up, chair scraping. Everyone scrambles, arms shoved in coats, money thrown on the table.

"Oh, you'll like her tea," says Matty, grinning, pushing me between them. "And she just made fresh muffins."

Before I can grasp what is happening we are outside, alone. Dobie zips his jacket, red patches blazing, and starts scuffling down the street. He clearly knows the way.

"You a good cook?" he asks, turning to me. I nod, numb.

Not another word is spoken until we reach home.

♐♒♐♒♐♒

The fire is out. Dobie sits down at the kitchen table, jacket on. He waits, arms crossed, implacable. The room is damp and chillingly cold, as only a fire-dead room can be. I look around desperately for something to make starter while Dobie coughs distantly, eyes roving the flotsam of Matty's life, resting here and there, silently watching me out of someplace in the back of his head. I hustle around, fearful my attempts to get the house warm will fail miserably. *Damn!* There is no newspaper.

Unwanted, the mornings of my marriage come into view: two city dailies spread across the table with cereal bowls and various kitchen implements. The impatient growl of the dog circling his empty bowl while above husband and wife devour the news and avoid conversation. We were well supplied with diversions: an endless litany of liars, greedy cripples, ass wipers, politicians, satirists. All gone now.

Here the big city newspapers come over on the weekly boat, a provincial rag dryly discussing Parliament's latest boondoggle; turn the page, whoops, Tuesday's girl naked except for a straw hat and a corncob pipe. And three days late. Too late. We do not have subscription to a paper with yesterday's news.

Without a subscription we have to scrounge for firestarter, scavenge like toothless Dickensian guttersnipes, leering and salivating over digested throw-aways. I find myself picking up stray bits of the style section as it whips across my path. Peering into empty dustbins, scooping up those desolate few escapees caught in fences, flattened and left to the elements on their crucifixes of chain link.

While I search for something combustible, Dobie gets up and roots around, finally locating our only ashtray, which he carries to the table and sets before him. I stifle apologies, sweating now. On my desk is a pile of letters to family back home that I can't seem to mail – they are soon twisted into a credible firestarter bundle with papery edges exposed for the match. Soon the fire is licking into small shavings of cedar, catching onto the twigs. The smoke thickens and I shut the heavy iron door as the first waft of heat balloons out.

Dobie has made two cigarettes and laid them on the table. I hurriedly boil water and pour dried blackberries into the pot, along with rosehips and a baggie-wrapped potion Naani Rose had slipped into my pocket after a visit. Discovered later, the baggie had a note attached to it, written in spidery hand. I wonder when she could have managed it. *"For you, dearie."* It smells of licorice and new-mown grass. Devil's Club. Good for what ails you. Dobie sniffs the steam rising off the tea, waving it closer. The steam obeys, curving under his old hands and rising up toward his nostrils, splayed wide.

He turns and looks at me briefly, eyes piercing.

"Good tea."

The muffins are consumed quickly. For the first minutes he simply eats and inhales his drink, eyes resting, conserving heat. Then pushing the food away, he pulls the ashtray closer, lights a cigarette, picking a few pieces of fresh tobacco from his tongue with stained fingers.

"I'm an old man," he says, scrutinizing me.

"You're not so old!" I laugh at this notion. He is only fifty, after all.

"My life has been harder than yours. You don't know how old fifty can be."

"No," I admit, hands resting on the table. That same dark void comes again with the cold, still insistent in the room. I wonder dully if my fire has failed to catch but cannot move to look.

He moves his chair closer, startling me. I glance up and find him sitting almost knee to knee, hunched over his ashtray, one hand on the table near mine. He cocks his head, looks over. "I've traveled the world, that's the truth. I was a cook aboard a Navy ship for twenty-five years. That's where I got my nickname, Dobie. They said I was a thinker, like Dobie Gillis on television. Learned to speak French and some Italian swear words. Saw lots of people during that time. Learned to cook a good egg custard too! That was after the schools." He leans back, memory filling up, rushing in the dipper. "Yeah, that school was a tough one."

"You know the schools I'm talking about?"

I nod.

"They sent me there when I was ten. I didn't know any English back then. We spoke Haida. Our language."

I think of the Old Ones who still speak it, how it falls mostly on perplexed ears.

"They made us speak English," he continues, puffing on his cigarette. "And if we didn't they beat us hard with a wooden paddle."

He doesn't say anything for a while. He's lost with Jimmy and Ben and Eddie, running up the Kitimat hills, playing ball away from the ears of the matron. *L'st'aa wanguu.* She is far away.

"Dobie?" His name sounds sweet to my shy voice.

"Huh?" He turns, then taps the ash from his cigarette. It has gone out. *Why me?* I'm afraid to ask. I am at the small center of a skein of yarn being wound around and around. Blue, blue like the sky on those precious days when there is no roof, no rain, no tears.

"Don't mind me," he says to the silence. "I'm just an old man who likes to tell stories." He taps his heart. "Got a bad ticker. Could go out on me at any time." Then he takes off his glasses and points to one of his eyes. "This one is fake." Laughs.

"There wasn't much left when they called me and told me my auntie had died and I was to become Chief of our house." His voice gets slower; something in the lilt is a memory, a gravestone to his old language. I hear it bending back the edges of his words, rolling the spaces in between. A twisted, old path, traveled over and over. "That's when I settled down. Began to think about the place I'd left behind. Remembered the others."

He sips his tea, still warm and smoky. "Had my fill of the world. Saw pretty much what there was to see of it. Time came to go home. Then I remembered I never got married. Hmm! Strange time to think of it, at my advanced age, but some things you don't care about until it's too late." The sigh he gives next is not an unhappy one. "Still, being Chief has given me new life."

The tea has a strong after-bite to it, peaty like old Scotch, and we drink cup after cup, the cigarette smoke curling up toward the ceiling and resting there, tendrils drifting as the fog that had now begun to come in with the evening. He stretches back and begins a monologue. I find myself drawing in his words through every opening. He tells me about his family clan, his mother Ruth who still lives with him in the suburban house they had taken by a small and well-hidden military base where he works as a night watchman. The job surprises me. His frailty.

Suddenly there is a bit of my grandfather. Old Welsh Alwyn, sinewy arms and strong back shoveling coal during the Depression, coughing up seven years in the Cardiff mines before he escaped with his life and twenty dollars passage money. The same punk spirit, bowed legs, wiry frame. *Don't fook wit me!*

Dobie is getting up a head of steam. "The town kids would come around to the marsh, drinking and making a mess everywhere, so one day I picked up one of them and threw his scrawny little ass in the duck sanctuary!" I picture the surprised look on the boy's face, splashing into the reedy marsh and I laugh. *You're one tough little bastard, aren't you?* Ducks squawking off in the distance, curses and shouting in the darkness. "You slimy Indian little shit!"

His eyes are dark and mysterious, even the dead one seems alive. Taking it all in. Then he stops talking and looks straight at me. "Why are you here?"

In surprise my hands tremble, sweat springing from the palms. "I already told you…"

But it's too late; he's drifted inside like the changeling Raven. Drunk up like the river water.

"You running from something?" he asks, cocking his head.

"No!" I'm desperate to change the subject. "Dobie …"

He looks over.

"You spend a lot of time down by the duck sanctuary?" He nods. "There's an abandoned village down there…." I avoid his gaze to gather courage. "Who lived there, anyway?"

For a long moment he eyes me, knowing that now we are both holding on to our secrets. He twists the cigarette around between his finger and thumb and then takes a drag. "I don't suppose I know much about anything, except my own life," he says softly, finally.

"Chief, you're still here!" The door bangs and in strides Matty. She's walked three miles from the Reserve and her face is wind-raw. "Sun's gone down and it's getting mighty cold out there," she remarks, unwinding a heavy wool scarf from around her neck.

The old man rises painfully, testing each joint. He pulls on the heavy leather jacket. "Guess I better get started for home." This is said with a long, theatrical sigh.

I jump up. "Let me drive you."

He smiles, eyes glittering. "Sure, why not?"

"Dobie!" Matty calls after him. "I hear you're making a speech at the big fishing meeting next month."

He nods, and raises the jar of peaches. "Thank you for the present."

On the way home he is quiet, hand resting on the door handle, eyes pensively scanning the empty streets. We pull up in front of a neat two-story house in a small development on the outskirts of town. Red brick with white shutters and a fancy screen door. The base is hidden in heavy bush behind a manned gate and all I know is that it's a joint listening post run by the U.S. and Canada to monitor Russian sub activity. Since the focus has shifted to other enemies in recent years the post has shrunk in size and importance. The remaining skeleton staff does not mix with the townsfolk.

His street is quiet, the house dark. I can picture where he sleeps. In that room above the kitchen next to the bathroom. A plain room with a tray of medicines and his Haida gear stowed safely in the closet. One print on the wall, an eagle drawn by his nephew, the family artist. The chief's jacket resting across the back of a chair, emblazoned in red. *You don't belong there.* My poppa slept alone for the last ten years of his life, wondering why his wife, so much stronger and fuller of life, had gone before him. They put him in his granddaughter's old room with the torn edges of childhood pictures still plastered to the walls, a princess mobile turning, turning in the afternoon breeze.

Before Dobie can open the car door I reach out and touch his jacket. He turns back, face invisible in the darkness.

"That speech, can I come and hear it?"

He pats my hand.

"Sure, kid. I'd like that."

♐♒♐♒♐♒

"Mmm."

I'm at the fading thread of a nice dream, but Jonah's tongue is on my earlobe, licking me to wakefulness. The springs squeak and we laugh sleepily. We're in Matty's bed. She's out of town, down in Vancouver for a weekend of city streets and shopping, so we've got the house to ourselves.

I hadn't had many chances to have Jonah overnight in our house.

"I'm tired of sleeping on the floor," I told him.

"It's not the floor," Jonah grumbled.

"All right, you sleep on two Persian carpets but to my thirty-year-old bones, it's the floor."

"Your bed is out," he counters.

Mine is for pre-adolescents who are less than six feet tall. The comfortable monk's life hasn't lasted long.

Matty is out of town so we both decide her bed is just right. Though I've never seen a man in there, she has created a romantic atmosphere with red and purple silk scarves draped over the mirrors and lamps. There is a collection of poetry books by the bedside, a leather pouch of I-Ching and some massage oil. We tumble in there with guilty pleasure, promising each other we will leave no trace. It is a luxury to sleep like this, entwined, floating.

The morning comes too soon.

Jonah's hand curves under my back, mouth buried in the hollow of my neck.

"Jonah, please, I have to go." He drops away with a sigh.

It's barely light out, a gray drip of light under cloudy skies.

"Think they'll be flying today? If it rains, maybe I won't have to work."

"Forget it." He rolls over in defeat, his erection shriveling. "They fly in hurricanes."

I start dressing, layering long underwear with wool leggings, socks, sweaters, scarves. Thick leather gloves, once pretty, now cracked and worn.

"How much longer do you have to do this?" he growls. "Get up at dawn every day?"

"Till Harry gets back." My neighbor, who does this job for fun, left for a few days to check on his gallery in Vancouver and offered me the chance to fill in and earn a little pocket money. I'm now an airport agent. Duties: make reservations, catch, load and unload planes.

I pull on my gumboots and the last heavy slicker. The sky is spitting miserably but I see no thunderheads so I glumly head off down the hill to the docks.

A distant buzzing signals the approach of the Cessna. Hurrying into the office I grab the empty dolly, thankful there is no mail to load on this plane, and jog down to the floating dock just as the silver and red single engine comes into view, dropping precipitously under a low cloud cover. With practiced ease the pilot skims the pontoons to touch down along the inlet and then, with engines at low, turns and heads toward me. He waves, cutting the power fifty feet out, drifting in slowly. He has a passenger, face pressed against the rainy door window as if he can't wait to get off. The plane nears and I reach out, grasping the cloth loops on the wing to pull it the last foot, guiding it slowly along to where the little railings are installed for departing passengers. The passenger climbs out and brushes past me, looking a little white around the gills.

"Hey there dollface!" Captain Brett bears down on me, a big blustery man with gelled blond hair, aviator glasses and leather bomber jacket. All bush pilot and no brains, except the part needed to be the extraordinary flyer he is. He grins and tries to pinch my bum.

"Piss off you pilot pervert!"

"Aw, come on, you're shure a prettier sight to come in to than that old bear Harry!"

"How's Prince Rupert?" I take the packages he is unloading. Two big, heavy ones for the Army hospital. Assorted postal business with an official seal on the bags.

"Got the lumberjack 'n turkey festival goin' on right now." He leers at me. "Lots of big brawny guys fellin' trees and sawin' up a storm." He laughs, trailing after me as I push the heavy dolly up the ramp towards the office. "And with them coming out of the bush, them turkey's better watch their behinds, I'd say." He breezes past as I push the dolly up the ramp with some effort. Finally I get back to the office, sweating heavily.

"Two passengers to load." I push the manifest over. They are waiting, briefcases in hand. Lumber company foremen. Probably just want to take in a good movie. I haven't seen a movie in three months. Brett is still trying to make a score. "Hey, I can take you across with me today if you've a hankering for some city booze?"

"No thanks." I check in the passengers and jerk my finger toward the large load waiting packages. I give him the evil eye. "Besides, there's a Spruce Goose coming in twenty minutes."

"Okay, your loss!"

The door bangs, and the plane taxies off a moment later, lifting off into the gray skies.

Then I see Jonah coming down the hill with something under his arm. He rushes inside, grinning, long wool coat buttoned up against the cold.

"Got us some breakfast."

The wicker basket is filled with muffins, hard-boiled eggs, bacon. He spreads the picnic on the counter, unbuttons his coat and wraps me in a bear hug. I step back and start to laugh. "You're still wearing your pajamas!"

He laughs too, buries his head in my neck, cold stinging, warm lips mixed in, hungrily biting. "Umm, my version of breakfast in bed."

When the Goose lands we are packing up the silver and licking our fingers. She is an old wooden beauty from the 40s still in service in some northern areas. No pontoons, so when it lands it comes down gently, skimming the surface on its belly like a giant bird, a wash of seawater splashing up over the small round passenger windows. The pilot turns her toward the cement ramp and as he gets to the water's edge, locks down his wheels and rolls up onto the deck. The plane is cumbersome, heavy, but I never fear for her safety. The old girl is sturdy, like an ark. If I fly out of here it will be on this plane.

People stream off, bags and presents in hand. Some of them want return tickets and they crowd around the counter.

"Gotta go," Jonah says, gathers up his things and is gone before I can kiss him.

♐♒♐♒♐♒

"Looks like that upstart newspaper in Charlotte is hiring." Matty is perusing a week-old *Vancouver Sun*. I come over and she points to a tiny ad in the classified section.

Staff reporter position available in The Queen Charlottes. 3 days a week plus car. Contact Judy Schueller.

We have a venerable Island newspaper that's been around for several decades, but last year another weekly set up shop in Queen Charlotte City. This recent competitor is a scrappy, four-page entry owned by a features editor from one of the big dailies back East who apparently has too much energy to actually retire. She took over the storefront offices, archives, and ancient typeset press of a defunct town rag run by one of the logging companies and opened *The Sentinel* for business.

"You could be a reporter," Matty says, tearing out the ad and putting the rest of the paper in the stove.

The idea seems absurd, but up here anything is possible.

I study the ad, wondering if she is right. Up here everyone seems to be able to do everything sooner or later. Just today haven't I been catching planes? Why couldn't I be a reporter?

The next day I send my résumé and what I hope is a clever note down to *The Sentinel*. Part of my last job in Los Angeles involved copywriting for toy packaging. I emphasize this in my list of qualifications and include some samples. As the thick package drops into the post box, I wonder if anyone else will come forward.

"You apply for that job?" Matty asks later that night, draped on the sofa, her quick, bird's eyes watching me. She is back from the Masset Band office, another day gathering research for a project she is doing on a proposed gold mine that will devastate the local river system.

"Of course!" We both smile.

The fire crackles, pops. The room is warm and comfortable. Our looks to one another are those of ancients. Her expression is wistful, caught in a moment, in a certain light, like a rose held close up, delicate, veined, full of secret life. Ahhh, yes. You are porcelain, your ivory love as delicate and brittle as always.

Matty shifts. "Shall we throw the I-Ching?"

She has asked me this before and until recently I have always declined. I am not a believer in such diviners, refusing to have my future read from a dog-eared book thumbed through by so many other hopefuls. At the moment she rises, groaning a little from stiffness. A picture of her ex-husband pops into my mind, unreeling slowly into a moving picture.

She is elusive on the subject of her marriage, but photographs of the two of them together on trips to Hawaii and Mardi Gras are still displayed in the living room. The dusty wedding album, prominent in the bookcase, has the invitations carefully pasted on the front page, the ribbons from her bouquet straggling out, a tangle of pale pink and green. I'd asked her about him only once. We were spending the night at the beach house her husband built and left to her when he fled town.

Named the Temple, it is sacred to her and visited only sparingly. Swooping, red-tiled peaked roof, plain whitewashed walls scrubbed and joined with wood dowels. Clean, simple lines. One window facing the sea.

It had been raining softly when we came for the night. Afternoon dark as evening, buoy bells ringing in the distance. Before us in the wet sand, the Temple appeared, low to the ground as if kneeling in prayer.

I remember the clicking of a latch. There was no key. Something like a cowbell jangled, jarred by the disturbance as we took off our shoes and stepped into the dim interior. The clutter of our house was echoed here too: faded paper fans and bits of driftwood tacked to the walls, faded ruffled curtains on the sole window. A jumble of chipped, patterned china on a shelf above an old-fashioned washstand serviced by a water pump. Piles of books mildewing in the sea air. Two covered foamies and assorted cushions for sitting, lying, sleeping.

The darkness outside loomed large as we huddled next to a cheap tin stove. Despite a roaring fire, the Temple barely kept the night out. All at once I felt the fear that can come from being in such a deserted place. The thin walls seemed no match for the spirits of the wood or the rush of tidal fury.

"Matty?"

"Hmm?"

"What happened with Sam?"

"I don't have a clue." She crouched down by the tiny stove and began feeding in sticks and branches, shoving them purposefully into the bright flames. Then she turned to me. "My feelings for him never really changed."

I knew all at once that he didn't know this, nor had he ever, not in the way she'd wished.

I didn't want to think about such powerlessness. But there were clues in the rooms she inhabited, and they spoke volumes.

"I need to know," I said as we continued to prepare wood for the hungry fire, "that you're okay about Jonah and me."

Her capable hands methodically denuded a pile of small branches and snapped the pieces into thirds. She cocked her head and our eyes met. "I'm not particularly good at anything except finding the irony in things," she confessed, and then gave me a brilliant smile. "And there is something ironic about Jonah's sudden fervor for my woodpile." She caught something in my expression. "Oh, come on, Elle. You'll have to get used to living in a small town where everyone has done *something* with everyone else." She dropped the lid down on top of the stove and opened the damper.

"I have a lot of regrets, but Jonah isn't one of them."

"Did he have anything to do with the reason your marriage failed?"

She gave a harsh laugh. "Hell, no. Like I said, I'm still trying to figure out what happened there. I mean, in the beginning I could have given you full chapter and verse, could have talked your bloody ear off. You know, the usual litany about what an unfeeling, cruel bastard he was. But now, I have no idea what made me cut him off, and my memories seem to have lost their power." She made a wry face. "Anyway, he's happily married now to a very nice girl he met last summer and they've set up house down Charlotte way. I hear she has a bun in the oven."

With that, she pulled out the velvet I-Ching bag and let it drop onto the floor. It made a satisfying clunk, as if full of gold. "Since I have no common sense, I've had to rely on the I-Ching lately."

"What has it told you?"

She smiled secretively. "Many things." Then she jiggled it invitingly. "Come on, give it a try!"

We were in the Temple and there was only candlelight between us. The night loomed long and although I don't believe in oracles, I said yes. Matty shook and then threw the black lacquered tiles down onto the cloth. After studying them, she read the message they revealed.

You are as water pooling in the great river, blocked by stones that have tumbled across your path. A time of waiting.

That's what the Old Wisdom said.

Gallow's Eve

♐♒♐♒♐♒

To celebrate Hallowe'en we are gathering for a costume party on North Beach. Though it is the end of October the weather is still fair. No rain, but a dull cold brought by the unpredictable westerlies. Could change at any moment.

"Whoooeeeee!" As we make our way from the road toward the distant cries of the party-goers, Harry rubs his hands together in anticipation, head lifting at the sound, nose twitching in the still air. He lumbers on ahead, Hawaiian muumuu swinging precariously around his giant legs, a high slit in the fabric threatening to expose his genitals with every step. We are all in costume, mine a concoction made from a lady's corset and frilly negligee over jacket and leggings. Gypsies and skeletons follow behind.

"Let's go get 'em!" he cries, crashing ahead, out of sight.

I can hear drumming now; pinpricks of light dance beyond the forest break to where the crowd has gathered on the beach. A giant bonfire glows through the trees, smoking and crackling. We follow the path marked by shrunken heads nailed to trees. I stare upwards even as we clatter forward, patches of dark, starry sky visible for brief moments. I'm in the slippery bottom, all bits of the universe curving in finite measure around me, forcing my gaze up and out where there is no end, no limit. I rush forward out of the bush and stumble onto the beach, feet sinking into sand.

"Look!" Matty is beside me, pointing. "The Northern Lights!" she cries and then keeps running, voice receding into the wilderness ahead.

Why bother with the obvious? They have descended upon us in layers of shimmering pink and aqua, yellow, gold. Wave upon wave descending like gods of fire, undulating knowingly, floating down toward our outstretched arms, open, dumb mouths, wide eyes.

"Yes!" I say to them. "Thank you!"

In the distance, someone is playing a wooden flute. The grass-scented wind sweeps through me, and I am nothing but the sea and the stones crushed into grains. The earth stands still, waiting expectantly. The sky hums, crackles with electrical current. A melody rises up from the flute and then it comes back. From the west sweeps an iridescent sheet of pink, responding to the call of the music, shimmering across the background of stars like the rainbow glaze of a dragonfly's wing on a summer afternoon.

I'm whooping, laughing, spinning around, then falling to the sand on my back. Off in the distance another large wave of green, wind in a pasture, rippling lazily over fertile stalks, shifting this way and that, capriciously. Seconds later the wave washes over my end of the sky and curves around its lazy way until disappearing from sight.

The sounds of others are far away. Then, something rustles over my left shoulder. Perhaps it is just the wind in the grass. The back of my neck sends a warning prickle and I freeze, straining to make something out of the darkness. There is nothing, only the deep moss and the stiff brambles with the last of the summer's berries hardening, only the soft cedar bark weaving into strange shapes. Then I see a faint glow, the moon reflected back from a pair of eyes. A deer? It seems improbable in all this noise. Something rich and feral wafts toward me, something a hunter would understand. I turn just a little, my hands dug into the sand, feet ready to thrust me upwards. A shape distinguishes itself over there, by the blackest tangle of forest. The moon shifts and then reveals from the shadows, a wolf, crouched. Glowing pale as a moonstone, the familiar white fur! The cold air rushes into my lungs; fear sharpens my senses. His expression is watchful, impassive. My heart is thumping, gasping, muscles tensing to flee.

He's come for me! There is no sound. Dark eyes.

We are both perfectly still. I strain to see his face, to be sure, though I know it must be. Everything prickles, I feel ready to spring, to meet him, to run. Then, inexplicably he sits back on his haunches, thick tail curled around him, crossing delicately around a large opalescent paw. He starts to pant, quietly, patiently. I twist around until we are facing each other, elbows on knees, feet deep in the soft sand. *What? What is it you want?*

A shout from the direction of the road.

"Hey!"

It's Quinnie and her daughter, emerging from the path. The wolf is gone.

Scrambling up I run with them toward the fire until there is no breath left, reaching out for the noise and the safety of others. Jonah is already there, formidable in a dark ski jacket, the striped muffler rhythmically swinging. He is drumming, someone else standing over him on a log, singing. I catch sight of Naani Rose sitting on a three-legged camp seat, a swaddled lump of black wool and her trademark wool hat of bright red pulled low over the ears. She smiles at me, opens her arms.

"Naani!"

She laughs softly like a rose bursting open on a hot afternoon. How warm those petals are on my cheeks, back from the night earth. She touches my face, the sculpted porcelain so long from the fire, and looks up toward the sky. "I knew they would come out tonight."

I crouch on the cold sand, my hand in hers, heart still beating wildly.

"He's a good boy," she says, watching Jonah drum. The beat is strong but soft like the passing of time. He sings a song he has created from the sand, the lapping sea, and the visit of the Lights.

"Naani, are there any wolves on this island?"

She grips my hand tightly.

"You saw a wolf?"

I nod. "And it was white. All white."

She takes my hand at this and turns my palm into hers, warming it. I realize then how much it is trembling.

"We keep the wolves off this island." She gives me a searching look. "They belong to the Tsimshin or the Sitka families on the Mainland. Did anyone else see it?" she asks.

"It disappeared too quickly."

"Well, I don't know much about wolves, but in the land where such things can happen they say that if you see a white wolf, it's very rare and it means you will be given the gift of future sight."

Or it has followed me here. A ghost.

"Naani..."

Her hand disappears back into the folds of her coat, and then she cocks her head. "Don't worry. These are just old people's tales. They don't mean anything."

The Northern Lights snap and pop in a particularly bright burst of color and everyone points.

"Would you mind getting me a cup of tea?" she asks. Her face has emptied.

I think it best not to mention it again.

Later someone, I think it is Kim but I am not certain, jumps onto the tall log by the fire wearing a mask made from crudely shaped cedar, so quickly carved the curve of the trunk is still visible. Pocked and mean, the mask shakes and rolls in the play of the dancer, surprisingly agile on the small platform.

"*Aiiheeee*!" The scream does not sound human. Everyone laughs, amused at this game.

"*Aiiheee!*" the crowd shouts back.

Silence. The eyes are huge holes of darkness, revealing nothing beneath, the mouth open wide, calling. Arms raised. Then with a loud boom three drums start up, someone hoots and calls out. I look for Jonah but cannot see him. The drummers are three men from the Village I don't recognize.

"*Aah, ha, ho, ho*!" the crowd chants. The man in the mask cocks his head, as if listening. Is that Kim? Shy Kim? What the mask does not cover is hidden by a mass of ragged cedar bark hair and a skirt of marsh grass wound around his waist. Even the hands are muddy, as if he has plunged them in something. As the drumming increases the dancer undulates and dips. Everyone claps, watching the fire drift upwards, curling and sparking. Naani Rose leans heavily on her chair and I realize she has fallen asleep.

Matty appears, grabbing my hand, and we join the rest who are circling the fire and jumping to the rhythm of the drums. The sound of wet wood steaming in the fire, heads dipping, feet twisting, the drums getting louder and louder to spur on the dancer who is defying gravity on the circus top of his tiny log, a great beast writhing and jumping with extraordinary agility.

The shouting rises, rebel yells, catcalls. As I go around the second time someone grabs me from behind and spins me around, kissing me hard on the mouth. Broan! I spin away, off balance and stumble out of the circle on the other side, breathing heavily. Where is Jonah? I see several dark shapes in the red tent where tea and cider are bubbling.

Drums loud in my ear, I slog through the soft sand and find the opening to the tent. Three men I have seen at Village *doings* are gathered over beers. Morris, Billy, and a man with dark eyebrows and greasy hair. All drunk. Morris leers at my red corset. I step back, feet sinking.

"Have you seen Jonah?" I ask, keeping my distance.

He is fingering his beer with cold hands. They are like white marble, clawing the drink to his chest so he can balance better and lean toward me. Suddenly he laughs. Billy, though equally drunk, looks shy, apologetic. Morris steps ahead of his friend, reaching out toward me unsteadily. "Jonah's caught himself a good-looking one all right!" Billy kicks him away like a dog, shouting, "Hey, leave off, you!"

I flee out the opening past the mad drumming, up the stone path. Jonah is in the first lighted cottage; I can see his fair hair through the window.

"Jonah!" Breathless, hanging back at the door, all eyes turn in my direction. The other men now materializing in the lamplight are from the Council. Sgaana is among them but quickly disappears toward the beach.

"Hey, beautiful, come on in!" beckons Paulie, who I've met at Jonah's once or twice. He envelops me in an enthusiastic bear hug. "Brother," he growls, feeling the whole of me in his embrace, "you sure won the prize here, didn't you!"

Paulie lives in town with his Haida wife but complains he's henpecked and escapes to the Reserve every chance he gets. With no particular talents of his own he has attached himself to some of the Village elders and often drops by unannounced. Paulie is also the caretaker for River Lodge, a community long house for Reserve meetings or parties. A huge man with sausage fingers and a whale belly, his embrace is like being squashed into a giant pillow.

"We're off," Jonah says, steering me purposefully toward the door.

As we move out into the darkness I point over to the loud whooping and frenzied drumming. "The dancing is getting pretty wild," I remark, but he pulls me close. "Let's get out of here." The fire smoke clings to him, sweet cedar and ash. His body is trembling from some previous excitement. It lingers on him, breath heavy, and it's made him so excited he slips his hand under my jacket and down the back of my pants, cupping the flesh hungrily.

"Come!" We make it as far as the nearby Mouse Café, where someone has lit a roaring fire in the stove. The large corner windows in the bedroom provide an unobstructed view of the light show just as Harry had promised. They suffuse the room with electrical energy, popping and glowing blue, pink and gold waves of color everywhere. We tumble down in their glow, not caring if the door is locked. Arched toward me, his face buried, lapping the warm flush, his muscles still singing from some hidden joy. Bodies entwined, he plays with a strand of my hair, running it across his lips and then wetting it with his tongue.

"I want every part of you," he whispers, warm breath on my ear. I can hear the distant drumming grow louder. The men in the cottage.

"What was going on back there, Jonah?"

"It has been decided that I'll run for Chief."

Outside the joyous whooping seems to come nearer.

♐♒♐♒♐♒

The next week I make the journey south for my appointment with the publisher of *The Sentinel*. Her storefront enterprise is next to the town's only bakery and is infused with notes of copier fluid, dust, and the moist overtones of warm bread. Judy of the stout body and drinker's face is by turns friendly, aloof, and affecting a wearied demeanor. In her hand is my résumé.

"So, you've been a copywriter?"

"Yes, selling toys to kids. I worked on all the peripheral marketing material too." "Toys" was putting it nicely. They were really bits of useless plastic given away by a giant burger chain with little expectation other than their quick demise in the landfill. God knows, there were always more to take their place.

Judy smiles, more like a grimace. I wonder what her story is. She leans back, no doubt wondering the same thing about me. "You have experience as a journalist?"

"To be perfectly honest, no."

"So what are your qualifications?"

"I live here."

We size each other up. She, dyed black mop of short hair, a Harley-Davidson tee under a well-used leather jacket. Portly stretch pants, newly smudged. Me, a thin figure in a blue cashmere turtleneck, worn jeans, leather boots.

Exactly five minutes have elapsed. She looks out the window for one last moment, a gray, empty day. One of a thousand. I can see where her gaze has found the edge of the sea, whitecaps frothing. The highway is silent, deserted. She sighs, then turns, dipping her head a little.

"Okay. I'll give you a shot."

Joy courses through me, our knees almost touching in this small room.

"I have a story idea already."

She squints. "Really?"

"I haven't known who to ask about this but," there is a moment's pause on unsure ground, "a few weeks back I found an abandoned housing site out by the Delkatla Sanctuary. Everything was burned down to the foundations. Nobody wants to talk about it."

Judy leans back and scrutinizes me.

"Have you actually asked?"

"Matty and Naani Rose. They're evasive. Makes me curious."

She picks up a pencil and toys with it, scraping the point over a bit of paper culled from the masses of papers strewn everywhere. They are piled on the old wooden desk she must have inherited from the previous owner. In one corner, *"Sally loves Robbie"* has been scratched and enclosed in a large heart.

"It's natural for people to avoid difficult memories. Heck," she adds with a forced laugh, "I have a few of them myself." Then she puts the pencil down. "That place you describe, I remember hearing about it when I first came here but I knew better than to dig up bad blood. They would have closed ranks and made a quick end of my journalistic career."

"Are you talking about the townspeople or the Haida?"

She stands and pulls at various clothing items that have become snagged in the landscape of her bum and thighs. "Look, it's a good thing you're curious. You notice things we take for granted. But take a bit of advice if you have any long-term plans to stay here." The pencil is in her grasp again, seesawing on outstretched fingers. "I've been around long enough to know one important thing: For the better part of a century, the Haida had to read about who they were in the museums down on the Mainland. That's where artists reconstructed their culture in nifty dioramas created from stuff stolen from Island villages decimated by smallpox. The nice men who were getting their Ph.D.'s in city universities took the last of their totems, carved boxes, mortuary poles, cedar-root hats, and masks, then catalogued them like so many dead butterflies in a display case. Picked 'em clean. Left them with nothing. And I mean *nothing*." She sinks back down into her chair and leans forward, elbows on her desk. "That's how Sgaana and the others found out who they were: plaster mannequins put on display by anthropologists, theologians, geologists and every other do-gooder with a mission. They had to go down to Victoria, pay their entrance fee like every other Tom, Dick and Harry to figure out who the hell they were. So forgive them if they're just a little put off by another curious mind."

I meet her gaze, but it is difficult.

"But how can you not ask questions?" I want to say, what kind of friggin' reporter are you, anyway? "That place *feels* bad. Something happened there." *The wolf.*

Judy sighs. "Okay. Here's what I got. Long ago some Village drunk who passed for the last shaman scraped up enough of what was left of his magic and made that place disappear from view. It doesn't exist. If you try to make sense of it you'll only make trouble for yourself and everyone you care about."

"You said that already."

She turns and peers over her bifocals at me. "Geez, you've got enough worries. Can't you just let it go?"

We look at each other for a moment. She shifts in her chair. "Okay, rumor has it, and it's just a rumor, mind you, that one of the major Masset families had some old shanties there and they burned them down because the government ordered them to."

"But that's nowhere near Old Masset—why would anyone want to live so far away?"

"That I don't know."

"I…"

Her look says the conversation is over. There is a moment's awkward silence. She heaves herself upright. "As for this being the story that you start your journalistic career with, my answer is no. Do you still want the job?"

"Absolutely."

I start out the door. She raises her hand in a dismissive, half salute of farewell. "See you in two weeks."

On the way back from Charlotte, night drops quickly. I'm left to my thoughts on the winding road home. The mossy lumps that had once been a village keep sliding into memory as the road stretches endlessly ahead, a dead, black ribbon. What awful thing had those people done that they had been banished? Why had the government interfered? I had no answers and clearly no one wanted to talk about it. A gust of light rain scatters across the windshield, then moves off like a small tornado.

I could never ask Jonah. The election is coming up in three months, and with it, political change. There are too many secrets within these houses and they are a heavy burden. It would be a good thing to let some of Jonah's generation have more say in the town's future.

My curiosity would not let go. Not yet.

Jonah picks me up at home to spend the night at the Mouse Café. Though only a few minutes' drive from town, it feels like another world. Outside the wind has picked up and a smattering of sea spray hits the big windows. I turn over on the bed to watch it. Jonah feeds the big stove, his expression pensive as he shoves the wood into an already roaring fire.

"You seem distracted."

"Sorry, it's just that nothing ever gets done in the Village," he grumbles. "Just a lot of talk. Useless, political bullshit."

I know he's referring more to the power of the Department of Indian Affairs than to the ineptness of the Masset Village Council. But the problem is not the fault of one over another: negotiations between the two entities are fraught with double-speak, formalized ritual and centuries of emotional baggage. When I try to engage in these conversations it's always about everything being too complicated to explain. Like putting your hand into a bucket of molasses and trying to scoop it all up at once.

Jonah slams the stove door shut with the poker. "Time to take on the Chief Councilor. He's had the job too long, and he's gotten lazy."

"But George is a fixture around town. He seems to command a lot of respect."

"Why should that matter?"

Although I've taken off my clothes and wait for him in bed, he remains by the stove, coat still on. I want to talk about my new job, but I suddenly feel on uncertain ground. Staring out the big glass squares of darkness, Jonah casts his thoughts pensively out to the sea beyond. He turns, and I feel the weight of them pressing on my chest. Then he undresses and burrows into the warm space next to me, hands grasping my inner thighs, kneading and stroking. "Can't we talk about this later?" he asks. His mouth is exploring, and outside the grass and ocean are one. The natural order of things will have its way.

♐♒♐♒♐♒

The week has gone by quickly. Less than twenty-four hours after our meeting, Judy left a message with three story ideas and an assignment to cover an all-Island meeting to discuss lucrative sport fishing contracts in the Strait. Much to-do and grumbling about over-fishing has been building since an American-run tourist outfit began a salmon-fishing operation for tourists on a small island off the north shore. She left me with a gruff reminder. "Get yourself a tape recorder and do some interviews."

I have no money for such luxuries, and worry about it for a few days.

Another message from Charlotte City, this time from Phil the dentist.

"Hey girl, there's a salmon run down in Moresby. You gotta learn how to catch 'em if you're serious about becoming an Islander."

"I shouldn't. I have the *Sentinel* job. Stories to write."

He won't have it. "I'm going with the old man who lives by the Copper and you're luckier than shit to get an invitation. He's a famous guide for presidents and a lot of other rich mucky-mucks. Besides," he adds, "the fish run when they run. You might not get this chance again for another year."

"I don't know."

"You'll need a tape recorder for this new job, right?"

"So?" Damn small town informants.

"I know someone down here who can lend you one. Then you can come fish with us."

Sunday, I'm back with three coho. They are old fish, come upriver to spawn, bright red from their long lives, the taste and memories of faraway seas within. Their blood and their flesh are the same, red on red, seeping out of the corner of their mouths where the hook has torn through. Each one is huge, at least fifteen pounds.

Flushed with my triumph, anxious to share my adventure with someone, I call Naani Rose and Dobie to ask if they will accept a gift of a salmon.

Dobie is waiting for me at his mother's house.

"Big one," he admires with a grunt. In his brown hands the pale wax paper gleams. He shuffles into the kitchen and puts it into the freezer after marking the date with a grease pencil. His house is like any other suburban box. The furniture is Sears-catalogue issue—ruffled sofas and big armchairs with lace antimacassars. Canvas prints of flowers in gaudy gold frames, heavy drapery, everything neat as a pin. The kitchen is painted shiny beige, with a teakettle wall clock and rows of cups and saucers on display. Haida families like to show off their china, and I've seen some magnificent collections. Long ago it used to be blankets, totems and lodge poles, but the craftsmen who made such things died off when the Church forbade idolatry. And though the young Haida have been aggressively reclaiming these lost arts, Dobie's mother is steadfastly faithful to the tastes of her reverend and the cultural guidance of the *Ladies' Home Journal*.

Dobie shuffles around making tea. The sound of running water is hollow, tinny, echoing throughout an empty house. In this over-bright light, everything shines wrongly. All the requisite objects—stove, fridge, small table with four matching chairs, a toaster oven and microwave—are placed here as if in sly mockery of the good life. The tea comes. Beneath my hands, little Victorian children play inside a plastic tablecloth world, lush landscape, well-dressed matrons looking on. The Masset folk are fond of their oilskin cloths.

"I hear you got a job on that new paper." My host lights up a cigarette, pulling a cheap metal ashtray close to his cup.

"I hope I do all right."

He laughs. "Oh, you'll do fine." He taps the cigarette, already heavy with ash. My cup is cooling. Time passes quickly here and sometimes I lose track.

"I've been asked to cover the fishing license meeting on Wednesday for *The Sentinel*."

He looks at me sharply for a moment, then takes a drag from his cigarette. "Be sure to get there by ten o'clock. I'll be making that speech I was telling you about."

The light outside is thinning.

"I've got to see Naani Rose now," I say, getting up.

Dobie gives a short, dismissive nod. When he slowly rises I notice how bowed his legs are. It's getting late and they're shaking a little. "Want to see my room before you leave?"

There it is, at the top of the stairs, just as I imagined. In the dim light of the hallway, the doorway frames a sliver of his world. White walls, the edge of a single bed, neatly comforted. The corner of an eagle crest visible. A plain wooden floor with a tiny rag rug put just in the exact place where his feet will come down when the alarm clock rings.

"I'm late, Dobie." I can't get out of there quickly enough. The screen door bangs. "I'll see you on Wednesday!"

Curving around the streets, their crescent shapes and little cul-de-sacs, I leave him standing at the top of the stairs, hand on the banister. The houses in this neighborhood are all military issue, yellow or red brick, it doesn't much matter, upright with wooden shutters and front porches painted white or cranberry or blue or green. Most people would say Dobie is lucky to have such a nice house and his job on the small U.S. listening post hidden in the forest. There isn't much money in being a Chief.

♐♒♐♒♐♒

Naani Rose takes several minutes to negotiate her way to the door.

"Coming, dearie!"

I'd left the car at home, choosing to carry the gift of salmon and walk past the dark place. No amount of scrutiny has unlocked any of its secrets.

Inside is warm, never smoky, even with a fire going twenty-four hours a day.

"Oh, honey, I forgot you were coming," Naani says, looking a little disheveled. "I was napping," she adds, pulling a shapeless blue sweater over a loose cotton house dress.

I hold out the fish, apologetically. "I won't bother you if you're tired."

"Oh, no!" She takes my arm with surprising strength. "I'm actually feeling pretty good today." She holds the salmon in its wrapper and turns it over, feeling the weight. "I'll bet this one gave you a good fight, eh?"

Suddenly I start to cry. My coat isn't even off yet.

"Oh, chut, chut, chut." She sits me down, wiping my face with her soft hand.

"I had to kill it, Naani. No one told me I'd have to do that."

The fish was strong, even after an hour's fight, when Phil shouted for me to maneuver it toward shallow water. There he picked it up and threw it onto the shore. The fish thrashed vigorously, mouth working. Flesh raw and bright, angry.

"That's one big coho," Phil admired.

The ground shook as it twisted and thrashed on the muddy bank, eyes on mine, not the fish eyes I thought I knew.

"What now?" The rain was pelting down so hard I could barely hear him.

"Don't leave it to suffocate." Phil handed me the stone. "Put it out of its misery quick and crush its skull." My blows were pitiful. It took several before I brought it down hard enough to feel the bones give beneath. Then silence.

The memory is still sickening. "Naani, the sound of the bones cracking!"

She holds the fish out proudly before her, eyes gleaming. Such life. "Did you remember to thank the fish?"

"Yes. I said, *Howa*, thank you for giving your life to me." My tears will not stop. "Naani, I feel such a fool. I didn't want to do it."

She studies the fish, then turns slightly towards me. "Oh, honey, that's the way things go around here. Keep death close to you and life will stay close, too." Then, taking my hand in hers, as she would a child, "It's too bad you learned so late in life." Seeing the look on my face she adds, "It's just easier when you learn this early, that's all. You've been living in a dream world for too long." She puts the fish away in her icebox, an ancient clanking machine with a thick electric cord strung to an outlet.

"I did it for you, Naani."

She smiles. "Oh, child, I hope not."

I can hear the thud of the stone, the thick, slippery skin and the end of life. *Howa, howa,* death in the muddy rain. The whisper of something escaping.

"Naani?"

She turns.

"Can't you tell me anything about the people that lived over the rise, by the Sanctuary?"

At this she sits down heavily, hands on her thighs. "You have so much more to think about." She points to a picture on her refrigerator. "My great-grandson. He got married last month and already they're expecting a baby." She turns back, her eyes on mine. "Jonah is a good boy and he's got big plans. For himself and for the Village."

She takes my hand in hers. "It's going to be hard work with a man like yours."

"Naani, please."

The stove pops with some bit of wood gristle and she uses the distraction to look away, then sighs. "There's not much I can say about the ones that lived there, because it was all done with when I was just a young girl. The Church was my whole life. Being *xaaldaang* used to be so shameful but the reverend showed us that all men were created equal." She gives a wan smile. "That business was over a long time ago."

Xaaldaang? I'd never heard that word before.

The clock on the refrigerator ticks steadily as though mocking the passage of time. "*Xaaldaang*." I try out the difficult syllables. "What does that mean?"

She leans away with a set mouth. "You are a good girl to bring me the salmon, to come here and visit, but I'm too tired now for lots of talking."

"But," I try to press on.

"Better go now. I'm about to nap." Before I can get up to gather my things, she steals one furtive glance in my direction and then closes her eyes. They seem to disappear into the great folds of her face, cascading down into one another, as impenetrable as a sleeping tortoise.

♐♒♐♒♐♒

A big crowd has gathered for the fishing debate at the Old Masset Village Hall. It's been the topic of conversation at the Co-op for weeks. Since salmon fishing is the Island's business, flyers were distributed in both towns declaring all were welcome to attend.

I see the usual collection of trucks in the parking lot: Jonah's battered Toyota flatbed is pulled up right outside the door. In Kim's four-by-four, Balto sits motionless and alert, watching all the activity. The morning sun has broken through, casting a sharp, twangy hue across the bay. Without cloud cover, the air is colder, cleaner. Down by the jetty Reserve children play with their fishing rods. In a flash, bits of silver fly arc across their backs and splash into the water. A dog runs along the beach after a stick and the sound of laughter rises above the sound of the waves.

Inside, chairs have been set up before a U-shaped formation of tables. One side white men and on the other, Haida.

Morris brings the gavel down on his side of the table. "Now, everybody, let's bring this meeting to order!"

On one side are six Council of the Haida Nation committee members, Jonah among them. He's wearing a gray shirt and banker's pants. His suspenders are embroidered with roses. On the other side are two men from The Northern Lodge, a successful fishing operation catering to wealthy tourists. They are dressed in heavy, plain work clothes, short hair neatly combed, hands rough and sun-browned.

Morris, who has been designated spokesman for the Haida contingent, stands, looks across toward the two men with an expression of great formality, and begins the proceedings. "Thank you, Rob and Doug, for coming today from The Lodge."

The men nod, impassive. The one with dusty-colored hair briefly lets his eyes wander the gathering crowd, but in the absence of friendly faces, closes up. It's easy to see why; there are few white faces and all of these are boat owners. The fishermen in Masset, no matter what their heritage, do not want outsiders taking their salmon.

There is a general clatter and scraping of chairs as everyone settles in. With a *frisson* of anxiety, warmth turns to a thin shine of sweat along my neck and up my face. What if the tape recorder malfunctions? What if I get someone's quote wrong and they sue the paper?

Bam!

Morris leans forward. "Today we're gonna find out what the situation is with the fish up there on Cloak Bay."

"Forget Cloak Bay, you leaches are everywhere!" shouts someone from the back of the room. In my haste to turn and identify the speaker, my pad flies off my lap and lands with a messy clatter onto the floor. Bending over to retrieve it I steal a glance in Jonah's direction. His face is set, expression unreadable.

"I don't know who's taking what these days so let's just get on with it," insists Morris. "We want to know what your daily catch is."

The dark one, Doug, I hope, writing down a note to get their ID's later, shuffles some of the thick pile of papers in front of him and clears his throat.

"No way of telling, exactly, Morris."

The crowd murmurs its discontent.

"Now, Doug, you must have some idea."

Rob, the blond one, cuts in. "It's just that we don't require any paperwork other than to insure no one takes more than their limit."

"And, for the record, what is the limit?" asks Morris.

"Two king salmon per person per day," replies Doug.

"And how many fishermen do you bring up here every week?"

"Twenty-five at a time."

There is a shocked murmur from the crowd as they do the math. Most of the fishermen never see that many king in a month.

"And why are you keeping it to twenty-five?"

"Because that's all the boats we have."

"I see," finishes Morris, voice quiet and finely cut like the curved edge of a hook. "But we hear you're gonna expand."

"It's our land!" objects Rob, his weathered face mottling.

There is a loud bang from the audience and we all jump. One of the Village elders has hit his walking stick on the floor. He gets slowly to his feet, an accusatory finger raised toward the two men. "That island and everything around it was my family's for over a thousand years before the government took it away," he says with barely repressed anger, "so I don't think nobody should be saying anything today about who owns what. The way we see it, those fishing rights belonged to us, and the cedar rights too!"

When he sits back down, Doug and Rob exchange a quick glance and shuffle some papers. To my mind they are wondering how much longer they will have to sit there and be civil. There's just no arguing with the Natives, doesn't get you anywhere, so the best thing to do is hunker down and hope to wear them out. Arms crossed, the two men focus on the piles of documents spread out before them, lost in their universe of order, rules, regulations. By the big reckoning, the law they recognize, they do own the land.

In the silence I try to catch Jonah's eye, but he is having none of it. Outside the gulls are gathering as if to bear witness.

Morris speaks again, gazing at the two men and trying to break their composure. "Even at the fleet size you have now, by my reckoning, you're taking out over three hundred king a week." I'm scribbling this down.

"That'll take all the salmon we have!" shouts one of the commercial fishermen in the audience. One of these giants of the sea will feed a family for a week or pay equal value in dollars.

"It's not true," counters Doug, holding up what looks like a data-heavy fisheries report in his hand. "Besides, official counts say the stocks are up this year."

"Bullshit!" yells another of the men in back. Tommy, who owns one of the few Haida fishing boats, has had hard luck this year. Around him is gathered what is left of his life: wife and several children in worn jeans and fish-stink red anoraks.

"I'm just telling you the facts." Doug's reply is even and measured. I know he is also thinking, you can't own the sea. It belongs to everyone. What blind resolve. I try to imagine what it would be like to sit up there, to wade in the field of bitterness.

Morris stares at the two visitors across the table and gets that old look on his face. The others do too. I've tried to remember that look from time to time and I just can't get it right. But I know it when I see it, carved into their features, the deep valleys made from a thousand tears, smoothing, sanding, smoothing, gently caressing, quietly cursing, pushing and pushing. The Haida committee have become one now, their silence an old place to be.

From both sides of the conference table, their expressions say it all. Clearly, there is no more to be said by the Lodge owners, so Morris bangs his gavel on the Formica. "Before we open the forum up to questions, we have some elders who want to speak."

From one side of the hall, Dobie is entering and making slow progress toward the front. He is wearing black Levis, red Nikes with neon running strips, and his Chief's jacket. Once in front of the crowd, he turns to studiously scan the panel before facing the audience.

"Many years ago," he begins, in slow, measured tones, sounding every bit a Chief, "the world changed. And we had no say in any of it. We watched powerlessly as the white man came into our world and destroyed everything that was sacred to us. They told us we would get something in return for our lost lands, our lost villages, and told us our lives would be better."

He pauses, a frail old man in a striped Polo shirt and wire-rimmed glasses. His gaze on all of us is deliberate. "But instead the white man razed the land, and fouled the skies. They left nothing for us. Nothing but *kalikoustla*—smallpox, dark sky and empty seas." The room is silent. On the yellow pad in front of me the words are memorialized. "They have destroyed Mother Earth. They have no shame."

Hey Dobie, that's me. White woman.

♐♒♐♒♐♒

Sunday morning is dawning and will soon be heralded by the incessant gonging of competing church bells. The shroud of blankets is not enough to protect me.

"Matty!"

The wolf is back, as real as the rush matting on my floor, sitting on the far side of the room, a ghostly shadow.

"Matty!"

The wolf raises his head on a scent. I reach out. He growls, showing his teeth.

The door opens and Matty peers in. She seems calm. A yellow glow from the living room pushes back the air and rearranges the molecules.

"There!" She looks to where I'm pointing, shakes her head at the emptiness.

"Matty, I think it was that wolf. The white wolf."

Standing by the doorway she scans the darkness just to prove to me that she believes.

"Naani Rose was right," I babble, "we have no wolves here, but I've heard a Wolf crest belonged to some of the ancient villagers but nobody knows where it came from."

"Perhaps from the Mainland?" Matty asks.

"I don't know!" I answer, frustrated. She comes in and sits down on the side of the bed. In the pre-dawn darkness, only the new fire in the room beyond lights her calm features.

"I know about the *xaaldaang*."

Her face is impassive.

"Matty?"

She leans against the back wall, pulling her knees up to her chest. "All of that was a long time ago. You can't judge them for something that seemed right and just at the time."

I know Matty is reluctant to add to the litany of wrongdoings that seem to plague the Reserve. I've heard many of the stories about incest, drunken brawls, spousal abuse, and social assistance fraud, and they serve to reinforce our unspoken belief that we were right to push them out of the mainstream. Of course we never speak of any of this in front of the Haida, but sometimes alone, the whites do dance around the issue. Always in a sympathetic way, as if to prove to ourselves we do not blame them for it. Yet we do.

"I see how hard you fight against judgment. But here's the thing: Once you see a stain emerge from the surface of many colors, your eye keeps going back to that stain, over and over. Soon that's all you see. You've been here long enough to understand how hard it would be to erase something like that."

I know she's right.

Only then do I realize my roommate is fully dressed. "What's going on?" I ask, struggling to sit up.

"I'm going away."

"Leaving? For how long?"

Her right breast has been kept hidden since I arrived; she's been protecting it with bandages and I hadn't pressed her for an explanation.

"Is it serious?"

"Nothing to worry about. I'm taking the Devil's Club tonic Naani made for me and soon I'll be right as rain."

I want to protest, but it's dark and the wolf, or the other that I cannot define, has been banished for this day, and I am exhausted. Matty gets up and moves toward the doorway.

"Promise me you'll take care of yourself?"

She turns, her smile revealing little.

"Don't worry. I'll come back when the time is right."

At eleven o'clock, the awakening church bells call for worshippers. For a long while I lie quite still listening to the house settle. Matty will have left a fire going, a warm breakfast of sausage and mushroom omelet. I look over to where the pile of notes and tape recorder sit next to the computer and quickly decide I'd rather go to look for beaver. They are much friendlier than wolves, and on such a miserable day they won't be expecting me.

Actually they are not beaver, but otter. They have dams on the Sagan River, a mile or so north of town. I stop at Kim's to pick up his dog. I feel safer with Balto along.

"Careful, he's a crasher!" he cautions, as I bounce off with the dog on the front seat next to me. The big husky sticks his head out the window and licks a streak of something off the side mirror. The moment we are out of the truck my companion strains on the leash, pulling nose down toward the bush. I let him off, only to watch dismayed as he charges into the brambly underbrush and disappears.

"Balto!"

At its mouth the river is quiet, wide, sandy bottomed. Up ahead I can't see much, but surely there must be a bank we can follow. After several yards I realize it is futile. The wild bush strains forward until it can no more. All is chaos and turbulence, choking weeds and roots twisting along the rutted edge, moss-wrapped branches. The endless drenching rain has seen to it that the forest does not need to look to the river for its life. The Sagan River slashes through a living dominance of moss and bush, leaving nothing by her edge but frustration and entanglement.

"Here, boy!"

I hear him in the distance breaking twigs and slapping past leaves, but he sounds far off and getting fainter. A moment later he materializes, tail wagging. He's got the scent, so I snap on the leash hoping he'll lead me to them. The next thing I know I'm holding on for dear life, stumbling over slippery logs, protecting my face from low-hanging branches the dog has powered through. *Damn!* At one point my boot comes close to a cluster of tiny mushrooms the color of lemon drops. Balto jerks me forward and they are squashed into the delicate moss.

Soon we break through the worst of it and meet the river again as it curves west, swifter and blacker now, filled with rich, silty loam. With a watchful eye on his wet undercoat I rein him back as best I can, navigating a muddy incline leading down onto a small grassy half-moon bank. Parallel to the river is a fallen log, leached and bleached by rain and sun, still damp, wormy. I tie the panting shepherd to a bush and leave him to lick at his burrs, easing down onto the log that provides an unobstructed view of the river as it winds past. Soon Balto is asleep.

A patch of sun breaks through and for the moment it is gloriously warm. I feel the steam rising from beneath me, the earth drying as it does here, slowly, leisurely. On the distant bank, light slivers through overgrowth and shatters into small jewels on the backs of trees, blades of reedy grass. The river remains impenetrable, light bouncing back off the blackness, reflecting the currents, the nuances of the riverbed. I wonder if the salmon are running here. Like the ones I caught last week, returning to their gravelly nests, driven by an unknown force to wander a decade in the sea, then come home to reproduce and die. "Open up to them," the old man had said. He showed me how to study the river, to cast my fly in the places where the fish were resting or foraging. The tickle of brushed satin, delicate as a fly's wing, caressing as fingers lightly along a summer's arm. They would see it, dancing against the sparkle of light, high above them, tantalizing. A visitor from another dimension, another world. Waiting for their spindly legs to alight on the moving current, powering upwards, mouth open, the surge of sinew and muscle and bone, teeth wide apart. Snap! Then a flip downwards with prey, back into the cool darkness, the slippery, cool forgotten darkness.

I study the surface, learning the way of it, the gentle undulations here, the tiny flip of undercurrent there, the brush back of eddies further down. After a while the outlines of the shoals reveal themselves; the channels become clearer. There is a place where the river digs deeper right by the bank, maybe an underground cavern, and a flat sandy bar in the middle rises like a whale's back, almost within a foot of the surface. As water flows, the river curves her ways again and again. The sun stretches on. And I watch.

Then a movement reshapes the surface. A splash. Yes, unmistakable. Below, something is disturbing the powerful current, pushing up against it and parting the river. A salmon breaks through, fighting the current as it navigates toward the dam. Not many would have noticed the wood and mud structure. It is small and subtle, barely breaking the river flow. The nursery chamber is on the left bank, the mound accessible only by an underwater passage. Downstream, the salmon encounter many such dams and they find a way over them, as they must. With a strong flip of its back tail, the salmon arches up and over the wall and is gone.

Balto has stopped licking his paws, fully alert: beaver must be near. As we patiently wait, the water begins to change shape, revealing the smooth, shiny back of a small creature as it crests the surface in long, undulating strokes. With ears pricked forward, Balto is equally curious, though he is wisely silent as am I, for the beaver is acutely aware of its surroundings as he rides the flow downstream. The head is small, auburn with dark markings around the nose and whiskers. His eyes, liquid and sleepy from water, are not focused on anything in particular: he seems to be drifting for a moment, drawn as we were by the sun. No other family member appears, none to distract the solitary swimmer, dreaming on the current, listening to the hiss of steam rising, warm and smooth on the top of our heads.

Then, even as we become comfortable with each other, comes a startling splash as the beaver's tail suddenly flaps out of the water and bellies back, propelling him swiftly and powerfully down into the darkness. Too soon! Balto gives me a sympathetic look and drops his head down to sleep, soft dark gums drooping over mossy earth. Some time passes but I don't know how much. I stop watching the river and lift my face toward the sky, drinking in the warmth. Fish go by somewhere in the deep, a Steller's jay calls out from the north and the scolding of other birds answers. High above us on a restless breeze the clouds drift over the sun, obscuring it finally. The gray twilight cools, drawing brackish moisture up from the log and into my jeans.

Damn! I hate this capricious weather, the moorish drizzle constantly spoiling things.

Like this election. Visions of Jonah's wall covered with sketches for his new political posters slurry into view and I kick at them, irritated. The subjects now raised around us seep into the night dreams, the moment before sleeping when precious little is safe.

You cannot know what it is to be Haida. True, but you cannot know what it is to be a woman. We have both endured.

Jonah has never even hinted at the enslavement of his people, and I wonder at the power of these memories, reaching out to the mysterious edges of them as if to a wound. It just isn't possible. I cannot get to the truth. The past here is as impenetrable as this river, given only to subtle signs and echoes. There is nothing for me to do but watch and wait. Judy was right. I take a flat stone and heave it across the silty water, watching it skip once before sinking from sight.

What would Jonah do if they elected him Chief? Lately he has stopped painting humans. Now everything is the Raven, the trickster Raven. Inside the Raven are more creatures: frogs and killer whales, beaver. That is the Haida way, to draw the infinite inward, disappearing one into another as a mirror into a mirror.

"Balto?" He opens one eye.

"Time to go."

With a muddy thrash, he is up lunging toward home, straining at the leash, pulling forward as we try to retrace our steps. The sun is down beneath the trees, more quickly than I had anticipated. The underbrush is dark and scratchy.

"I trust you, boy." Balto will know the way. I let him pull me home.

♐♒♐♒♐♒

Jonah is now officially running for Chief Councilor of the Village. Not unlike a mayor, this Chief presides over an elected council of ten and sets policy on how the annual budget should be administered. On the Reserve no one pays taxes. The funds come from the Department of Indian Affairs, so the Councilor is answerable to the regional DIA agent. The whole thing still smacks of paternalism.

I don't understand why he wants to become part of it.

"You told me you dropped out of law school on the Mainland because you didn't want to be part of the system." We are peeling potatoes. They are homegrown, a bushel traded for a half-cord of beach wood. He shoots me a look. "I can't change the system overnight, but I can learn to manipulate it better."

"Uh huh."

He sighs, breath joining the steam from the wok flowing everywhere like water. "Things will happen." He's right, they will. I look around the kitchen at the collection of china and wooden boxes, the mismatch of things that surrounds him. He worked for every delicate piece, bartering, hauling and carrying, lifting. The crab steams in Szechwan and black bean sauce, roiling up like insatiable hunger onto the wooded cathedral of his dreams.

He stands stiffly, a long spoon in his hand.

"You will never know your father," I whisper.

His face is tender from the warmth of this kitchen and his eyes cast downwards, lost, angry, longing. I kiss his cheek and he turns toward me, slipping his hands around my waist, twisting the strings of my apron. His breath is warm on my collarbone, fragrant hair against my face. He tears the stretchy material downwards until he can bury himself deeper. The spoon drops clattering, and wetness drips down. He licks the fabric, finding the place inside where the pulse of darkness consumes his tears. *Come to me, then.*

"I see you above me," he murmurs, his seed delivered. *I cannot help myself.*

In my dream I am passing Jonah's house, again and again. It's the one by the old boathouse. The moorings creak, birds call in the dark. The car is going too fast; I duck my head down through the window, craning. His house, looming over the street, has no doors. *It's true, there are no doors in front.* Whoosh! It is gone before I can step on the brake. Back there! To turn around would be dangerous. The sea, for one thing, is close by, down there beyond the blades of scrub grass illuminated by the streetlight. Driving in that direction would be like falling over a cliff to be swallowed up by the liquid darkness. On the other side are the faceless, shuttered government houses. The car would curve onto the edge of their gravelly yards and someone would come out, a stranger, and take a gun to my windshield. *Get the hell out of here! Can't you see you're not wanted?* The windows are blank, reflecting the stars, endless nebulae, milky, grassy, awe, awful.

"Hush," he comforts me. "You were calling out in your sleep."

One of the Village Naanis is ailing and I'm taking her a pot of chicken soup. Since last night, Jonah has hung a huge banner over his front window. Raven, taking a stand, crushing the bad creatures below. Paint so fresh it's bleeding red rivulets. I want to stop, but he'll be on the floor, surrounded by discarded paper and stinking of turpentine. The angry window glides by and disappears.

He calls after seeing my car. "You should have stopped by."

It's much later now. Past ten.

"We're getting together at Paulie's in half an hour to play cards," he continues. "Come by and pick me up." The sound of him is a young bowstring quivering. "I miss you in my bed, Elle."

"I guess so!" I'm feeling less sleepy now. The old clock on the stove is ticking in the empty kitchen. It's been terribly lonely since Matty left. On the other end Jonah is breathing slowly, eyes resting on something. These are familiar moments where conversation is only so much noise. The silence is broken by brushes rattling in tin. Something is sizzling in the background, maybe more crabs in the wok.

I feel myself wavering. "Let's talk more about your bed."

His voice is soothing, wrapped around the big Raven banner, reaching out from around the papery thin edges, blood dripping. *I'll put my red hands on you.* "Yeah, I'd like you to come on over here so we can carefully, so carefully, explore all the possibilities."

"I hope you're not molesting the crab!"

He starts to laugh.

"Can't help it, Elle. You feel as good as finger paint."

He growls and growls. I hear paper scattering.

"Paulie's expecting me. Come along."

♐♒♐♒♐♒

Paulie has opened up the River Lodge for our card game. It's a Haida long house on a lonely stretch of Masset Harbor. A cement porch stretches the full length of the front, with plenty of places to gaze at the sea. Sometimes killer whales pod by or an otter will float with the current, breaking open an abalone with a rock on his stomach.

Tonight it's blowing pretty hard, and the cheap aluminum panes are rattling, though Paulie has shored just about everything up that needs work. Paulie, Jonah, Kim and I are settled in to one of the card tables set up in the main room. True to the communal nature of their heritage, this is a combination living, dining, meeting, and sleeping room. It's huge, at least eighty feet long, with high, vaulted ceilings. Original art is too valuable a commodity to be wasted here, but a few pieces by young artists are mounted on the paneled walls. Aside from the folding card tables, a couple of utilitarian couches in an institutional fabric and a scattering of straight-backed chairs provide the only furnishings. When we gather, the metal chairs scrape loudly, echoing off an expanse of bare windows that appear as black voids in the deep night. Small pools of light from floor lamps provide little relief. The others seem comfortable in this perpetual twilight. I am slowly getting used to it.

"What'll it be?" The game is in full swing.

"Hearts," declares Paulie as he pours a huge quantity of onion sour cream dip into a bowl next to the potato chips. He knows my weakness.

"A few gobs of this, Paulie, and you won't have any trouble beating me!"

He grins over toward me and we laugh. I like Paulie. I like his big bullshit. His big, vulnerable bullshit, so easy to step around. Five of us are playing, Paulie, Jonah, me, Kim and his friend, whom he fails to introduce. I think they plant trees together.

A young man from the Reserve comes in.

"Hey, Ronnie." Jonah greets him familiarly, then puts a hand on my shoulder.

"This is Elle."

"Hey." He raises his hand in a salute, then wanders over to one of the couches and sits down. He doesn't seem interested in joining us so we leave him be.

Paulie wins the shuffle for the deal. He gives me a bad hand. Too many Hearts and the damn Queen. I should give up on this game. Paulie smiles wickedly. "Girls against guys, whadd'ya say?"

"There's only one girl, stupid!" Kim snorts, then they all laugh.

"Don't worry, Paulie, I'll kick your butt anyway!" I counter. He studies me for a moment and then decides I don't have the Queen after all.

"Okay, you and Jonah against the three of us."

"You're dead meat!"

"Muffin ass!"

I'm down to three cards and I still haven't been able to peel off the Queen. The game has gone on a long time, interrupted by phone calls and mysterious visitors at the door. Paulie always goes outside to talk to them, carefully shutting the aluminum screen door. Only the frosted imprint of his breath puffs into view. Things are always going on but I don't always know what they are. The backdrop outside is tar pitch, maybe the faint outline of an otter floating by. Never any cops. There's only one RCMP officer in the north end of the Island, and he's always rolling drunks or writing traffic tickets. I've never asked Jonah about these private conversations. No, once, I did. "Indian business," was his curt reply.

I'm about to fold my hand when Sgaana arrives. With girlfriend, Bula, in tow, he acknowledges me with a slight nod and moves easily into the room. I realize I've met Bula before. It was at a downtown Vancouver gallery opening with Harry, back when he saw me as a client with money. Tall and striking in a dress patterned after a traditional clan blanket, she was clearly the star of a group showing of First Nations works. Her paintings, imbedded with found objects and precious stones, took inspiration from traditional Haida designs and established her as an urban tastemaker. When Harry introduced us, she took my proffered hand with vague politeness, quickly melting back into a protective circle of long-coated Haida men. She clearly does not remember the meeting, and eyes me now with veiled curiosity.

Ronnie jumps up and dances around the couple like a popinjay. "Some business you got on the Mainland," he gushes to Bula, who rewards him with a brief smile.

Sgaana ignores him, turning instead to Jonah.

"I have some election material in the truck," he says to him, keys in hand.

"Jonah's gonna beat the crap out of George," gloats Paulie, whose eagerness is grating. Jonah and Sgaana turn and go outside. Making no effort to engage in conversation, Bula settles down on the far end of the couch, takes a magazine from her expensive satchel and starts leafing through it.

I keep my own counsel and ignore this slight, knowing how important Sgaana and Bula's endorsement is to the election. Although neither of them lives here full time, Bula is respected among families who are deferential to the artist class. And Sgaana's clan is one of the oldest, most respected in the Village. His great-great-grandfather was considered one of the greatest chiefs of all time. It was said that over his lifetime he was able to give many *potlatches*, or feasts. His wealth was legendary. Sgaana's great-grandfather also had a reputation as a canny businessman and master canoe builder. By his death in the early part of the previous century, his canoes had all been acquired by museums. During this period of dismantlement everything went south to the cities. What wasn't snapped up by anthropologists was torn down by missionary churches; they took down lodges plank by cedar plank, even moving the dead from raised mortuary poles to newly consecrated graveyards. For many decades, no more totem poles or canoes were created. It seemed pointless. Stopped until the late '60s, when young Sgaana was an eager student of a revival movement to reclaim the culture's lost arts. It was clear even then, he had the innate skill of a master carver. As he grew and matured, so did his leadership skills.

Paulie's shining face says it all: Sgaana and Bula's endorsement, their vitality and powerful Mainland political connections could very well mean the winning edge to a young and inexperienced candidate.

After a while Jonah and Sgaana return, and the two of them join Bula on the sofa. A knife-edge circle of light illuminates their huddle. Paulie is putting on his boots, turning off switches and coffee pots. The cards are still scattered on the table, chip dip hardening in the ceramic bowl. He gives an apologetic shrug. "My wife made me promise to get home at a decent hour." That's right, Paulie. Go home to your wife and children, to your warm bed and the soft flesh of your woman.

Kim is next, with Ronnie following after him into the cold. I'm getting sleepy, but Jonah is deep in conversation with Sgaana so I can only hover around the periphery, lounging in various poses on the couch while Bula studiously ignores me. Eventually sleep comes, their murmuring as mesmerizing as waves lapping on the beach. I want to listen, but exhaustion sets in and I hear only snippets: something about men coming up from the south, lodge poles being erected. By-elections.

In the fog of sleep, I let Jonah's arms encircle me and he carries me to the truck. I can walk, but I let him, let him own me in front of the others, my arms around his neck, face nestled above his breastbone. The next thing I remember he is tucking me into his bed, leaving me alone and resolutely awake, listening to the clink of paintbrushes and the swish of a red sea on paper.

♐♒♐♒♐♒

Back to the paper. There's no more avoiding it. My stories are due in two days and it'll take half a day to drive them to the office. For six hours I write, counting raindrops, and endure a temporary setback when an earthquake frizzles the power, losing two pages not yet saved. Now I'm on a doodle list of possible teasers: **Langara Lost; Northern Lodge Strikes Back; Lodge Crisis.**

Never mind about the damn title. The article better pass muster or I'm out of a job in short order. After a grueling series of drafts, I finally feel satisfied and pile everything into a rucksack, along with two sausages and the bagel my neighbor gave me in exchange for typing his son's English paper. The roads are slick with early winter frost. Black ice, a hazard of tundra living. The frozen ground keeps the road cloaked in an invisible layer of ice, making it easy to lose control if you're not very, very careful. I drive the twisting roads well under the speed limit.

The boilers are working overtime at *The Sentinel*. A rush of warm, bread-scented air hits me at the entrance. Judy is waiting beyond.

"Okay, cub reporter, here's your den." She takes me into a room with a computer and copy machine and stabs in the direction of an old metal desk wedged in the corner. It's partly obscured by a bank of rickety file cabinets.

"Make yourself at home."

Shit, my very own office. I'm glad I've already finished the article.

"I've left a list of possible leads for next week." My boss points to a well-thumbed Rolodex by the phone. Grimy, like everything else on the desk. Whoever preceded me was a slob; I can smell the remnants of bacon, dirty socks, and stale tobacco.

Judy wastes no time. "I want you to call the police stations in Queen Charlotte City, Port Clements, and Masset to see what's up."

"What do you mean, 'what's up?'" I'm thinking rapes, break-ins, murder. What can be going on around here?

"Just dig around for the local gossip," she replies impatiently. "Chat up the constabulary. Get on a first-name basis with all of them."

Several tentative phone calls reveal little more than an alleged bicycle theft and the blow-by-blow account of a skiff broken loose from its moorings, requiring a police boat rescue.

"Why didn't they just jump in and tow it back?"

"Are you crazy? Too friggin' cold for that," retorts Sergeant Tom.

The walls are closing in on me. The computer screen blinks but I don't know the program so I fiddle with papers until Judy comes back in. "Three stories a week," she orders, by way of approval for the Northern Lodge piece. I take in the mess of red scratches and edit notes all over the story. "Good title" is scrawled next to my last choice, **Lodge Wars**.

"Not bad for an amateur," she throws over her shoulder.

"Wait!"

She disappears into the front office and I stay put. Maybe now isn't the time to let her know I can't figure out how to use the publishing software. An ominous whine starts up in the back of the building and then everything starts shaking. I scramble up, scattering pencils and papers everywhere. Earthquake! The only other employee, a gray-haired woman, grabs me before I dive out the window.

"I'm Wilma, and that's just the presses, honey," she explains."Once they get going they're pretty quiet, but running them makes the whole damn building shake!"

Later I ask Judy if she inherited all the back issues of the previous owner's newsletter.

"Yeah, sure, but they only go back to 1960. Before that, the only real newspaper came from Vancouver and it covered all the local stuff. It's probably a fire hazard, but they're scattered in various boxes and file cabinets around here and I'm too lazy to deal with them. I think there's some rare microfilm too, although God knows what I'd do with it."

"Microfilm?"

"Believe me, we're not that sophisticated, but a couple of years ago a film crew came through here and brought copies of research film they'd acquired. Every B.C. publication going back to 1864. They left the material with my predecessor as a thank-you for the use of the offices." She looks over suspiciously. "What do you want it for, anyway?"

"Just curious," I mumble, turning away.

"If you've got any spare time, I suggest you learn to use the software, which I noticed you haven't touched yet." Judy's voice is already disappearing down the hall. "You may end up taking over this whole newspaper, someday."

After my boss leaves for lunch with one of her drinking buddies from town, I try my luck with Wilma, who seems more approachable. She comes in once a week to do the press layout and write up any social announcements from the Queen Charlotte City Ladies' Auxiliary.

"Do you know where the microfilm is stored?"

"In that old file drawer," she answers cheerfully, pointing to a dusty gray lump in the corner of the press room. "But they won't do you much good, because we don't have a reader."

In the dark corner are secrets that I cannot resist, and like the Raven, must find a way to pry open.

♐♒♐♒♐♒

The drive home from Charlotte City is hellish. Snow begins to flurry heavily, so I'm stuck driving the entire way back with a mad rush swirling toward me like the inside of a kaleidoscope. The road is slippery so the drive home is slow. Everyone else is used to this weather and they honk repeatedly with irritation before swerving around at high speed, shooting ahead into the wild darkness.

"Screw you!" I give 'em all the finger. I can't figure out how they can see anything. The headlights only make it worse. It's well past dinnertime by the time the cottage comes into view. Miraculously the flurries have given up, already swallowed by the tundra. I stop the car in front of the house. *How happy is the home with the little crooked chimney*. The lawn is now covered with a soft dusting of snow undulating in delicate waves over tall grass; the perfect prints of a cat circle carefully round the garden. Heart pounding, I sit in the darkened car for a moment, as silent and as careful as the cat that crept by earlier. In the front window one curtain droops a little; beyond glows a faint yellow light, as mysterious as a full moon.

Good news inside: Matty has returned. Her duffle sits in the middle of the living room with a note pinned to it: *"Jonah called. I'm at the Band office until late tonight."* Jonah answers on the first ring. "Elle, they approved my construction grant." I can hear the usual clatter in the background. I wonder if he is ever still. "Come and see the plans I'm making."

I'm out of there in five minutes. I need the comfort of his warm fire so I leave everything undisturbed, even the note, and drive over with a thawed chicken to cook.

Jonah has a big sheet of drafting paper spread over his table, and motions me over.

"Come and take a look."

He has penciled a rough outline of a floor plan for his new house. "I'm going to put a two-story addition onto the house by the kitchen and make the downstairs into a studio and office." The funds arrived as a Department of Indian Affairs home improvement grant, awarded to any First Nations member who has elected to stay on the Reserve. No doubt they were impressed by this Haida's conscientious proposal and neat handwriting.

The plans are grand. His pencil sweeps confidently across the newly expanded rooms, walk-in closets. Breakfast nook with long, thin windows overlooking the beach. I see a bowl of summer peaches warming on a scrubbed wooden table. Roses bursting. Much of the space is still unformed.

He takes my coat and deposits the chicken in a large pan to simmer with bay leaves and garlic. The oven door snaps shut. "I want you to help me," he says quietly. His eyes are cast downwards, fingers nervously on the pencil, once again sweeping across the empty space, an unanswered question.

"It's your home, Jonah."

"Yes, but what you ask from this house matters to me," he replies, color creeping into his face. I sit down and bend my head with his, studying the perimeter of our life, now slowly coming into view on the paper.

"This big space is the bedroom," he points out. The walls show only windows on the seaward side.

"Why not put something in on the other side for ventilation?"

"No!"

"Why not?"

"I don't want the neighbors to see into my house." It seems an illogical argument. The neighbors are a ways back.

"You could put curtains up."

He gives me the *look*—opaque, stolid. The familiar sigh of dark exasperation. "We never put openings in the back."

Bad business, that. The woods were for burials and toilets. "You could use the light," I venture.

He sits frozen for a moment, pencil poised over the back wall in the sketch.

"How about this?" I sketch a wall with high, oblong windows, just below the vaulted ceiling. "You can keep your privacy and still have some ventilation."

He smiles, relieved.

"I like the vaulted ceilings. Like a cathedral." His head bends and lips caress my fingers. "The place where we will sleep will have the sea on one side," his pencil crosses two small areas with dotted lines, "and your vented windows open up high where nothing can reach us."

Oh how you sigh, my love, in hopes of those long fingers probing into secret places. The room, newly jutting and brave, leaps out at us, looming large on the paper.

"And here," he says so quietly I have to bend close, "we can put an extra room for a child."

He watches me now, fueled by this dream of paper and ash. The chicken bubbles in the pot and he lays me down on the Persian carpets, carefully pulling back my blouse and rolling the tips of my undergarments down enough for his use.

"Say you love me," he whispers urgently.

I love your spirit and your hope and your illusion. Your love of me, I cannot say beyond the sound of it transformed into lush singing, high as a bird crowning his territory, wind full under the arc of its breast. Your mouth is as delicate as the sweep of your hand across the table where you lay your future before me with a benediction. In the end I know something more than I did before you called me here. There is no end to the dazzling cock crowing when daylight streams in the long sea windows. Perhaps you are right, the sun is brighter to the south, out by the bay. It is best to forget the vengeance of spirits who have paved your streets and nailed aluminum street signs to the cedar poles that once spoke your namesake, best to shut out the sounds of flickering violence seeping from those doors. Forgive me for what has been done to you.

"I do love you, Jonah." The words are voiced experimentally.

Later I study the plans in the empty studio. Room for a baby. Soon I will be too old for such things, or so I believe, punishment for past crimes. Jonah has gone to meet with some neighbors who are complaining about the lack of proper sewage to the new home sites. Since his candidacy they've started coming around to ask for his opinion on this or that matter. In this respect, much has changed. The house on the edge of the Reserve has captured everyone's interest. Something in Jonah reminds them of their lost energy and verve. Perhaps they are surprised by his intelligence, but I can't be sure. He hides it so well sometimes.

Busying myself with the breakfast things I try not to let my thoughts stray to the sound of their murmured conversation. I want this union. I know his flesh, I can sound its depths like ripe fruit, knowing when it is ready. With a sudden ache I hurry to put my coat on. I don't want to be caught here drifting inside the folds of his clothes where they lie strewn about the bed, the pleasurable scent of him mixed with sausage and eggs. The paper room is plain and the sun is cool white. For the first time I feel I can leave here and something will remain. The house of dreams, drawn for us, carefully traced with places to enter and exit.

♐♒♐♒♐♒

Sometimes Matty exists for me as nothing more than a few scuffling noises and the clicking of the gas stove on dark mornings. I'm still not sure what she does all day. Naani once told me that we know others only by the stories they tell us. And what I do know about the Haida is they were prideful, self-sufficient people with a highly developed sense of place in the world. It was their innate respect and recognition for her Majesty's power that destroyed them because, too late, they realized they could not control them. I wonder if the Raven, even with his magical sight, could have predicted such a great upheaval. The new ones had subdued Shalana, the god of god's, who lived in the Upper Kingdom of Light. *Raven's master*.

On the way to visit Naani Rose's I stop off at the Co-op for some English biscuits, as common as chalk in Canada. Raspberry jam and cream filling. Like the ones I used to have with milky tea after church as the family took time to read the Sunday paper. The Blue Laws in Toronto forbade most businesses from being open on the Lord's Day, so there wasn't much else to do. I can feel their round, fluted shape through the paper package, lined up in neat precision and ready to spill out onto the family plate, sugar granules scattering. For years I searched the shelves in Los Angeles for those raspberry cookies, the sweetness of something to remember, those roast-pork years when life was all crackle and turning fat on Sunday afternoons.

I know what I will do if Rose is not waiting on the porch, cloaked in black wool, as still and as silent as a bird in the snow. I will try and coax her into some tea first; perhaps the warmth of the tea-boiling stove will loosen her joints, and she will pull out the old accordion.

"Rose, will you play for me?"

"Oh, honey, my arms hurt so!"

"Please!"

Her eyes look beyond me, out to where the men came in every day from the sea. "The last time I played good my husband was a fisherman. Died out there in '56. He was hard to live with." The memory of him seems to rearrange the folds of her face into someone younger, full of energy. Perhaps she understands him better now in death.

"What was he like?"

"He was a hard man, so I used to sneak out of the house when he fell asleep." She laughs at this merrily. "Oh my, yes, we had some good old times back then." At this, a flush rises up her cheeks. "I ran to the house of my sister and we would stay together all night, knitting and gossiping." Her voice is mischievous, so I should not mistake it. "Oh, it was such fun, sitting there and telling stories like we did!"

I drag my chair a little closer. She is gloriously shining, bright like a summer day. "Didn't he try to find you?"

"Of course." She is still now, concentrating on that part of her memory. I watch her face, the movement of her eyebrows as they furrow, then smooth. The large, square features, nose too wide, eyes too small. Wisps of thinning gray hair wandering everywhere. She could have been plain. She could have been beautiful. If only I had seen her face then, I would have known. "He'd come looking for me, all right, and he knew just where to go. And when he did, there was hell to pay."

Billy was a white man. I don't want to know any more about their misbehaving white men. Blood flows around us, pushing us forward. The accordion is high above us on a shelf.

"When did you learn to play?" I ask, pointing to the old box. It's crumbling around the edges, the word *Wurlitzer* in faded red letters.

"I taught myself after someone gave it to the church and we didn't want it to go to waste!" Her hand reaches out at last for it so I jump up and bring it down. The box is heavier than I'd anticipated and I nearly lose my balance.

"I told you it was a burden!" she laughs, amused at my clumsiness.

The accordion is red marbleized plastic with black bellows. Dust wheezes out of every opening as it creaks to position. The leather straps have rotted away and the ivory keys are the color of caramel. She unhooks the pleated leather bellows and it wheezes noisily when she tries to pull it apart. Naani sighs. "This thing has seen almost as much life as I have." Her knotted hands are steadier, though I wonder if the weight on her lap will damage her frail legs.

"Where did you play?"

"Wherever I could," she replies, fingers caressing the knobs and tiny keys, the leather full of must and the shouts of a thousand voices. "When the cannery was open I would go down to the bar by the docks. The men came in off the boats or from their shifts at the factory for some beer and good times."

Brave Naani, I would have liked to have known you when you were younger, when the other women lived in fear of their fishermen, raising their babies to more of the same down in the shanties.

"And I played at the church, sometimes," she says softly. "Religion got me through when common sense was scarce." She scrutinizes me. "Do you really think things between men and women have changed?"

I don't like these questions.

The old woman shakes her head, and fingers the keyboard. "It's best not to have your hopes too high—it's not fair to your soul."

"But he beat you, Naani!"

She smiles. Did she hex the sea the day it took her husband?

"Oh, boy, they loved my music!" With this, she pulls the blower apart with surprising strength. Air fills the sac and she starts playing, hands jumping up and down. Just so the polkas, fingers hopping furiously, trembling and slipping over black and white keys, searching, remembering. The music roars around us, right and wrong notes, her eyes wide with surprise and delight.

I think you were a mule, head down, feet dug in. Big Rose, red skirt riding up above thick legs, feet thumping up and down, the merry accordion dancing on your lap; I don't think you broke your heart more than once. *Hey Rose, let's hear it again!*

When the sea took your white man, you figured God had answered your prayers.

♐♒♐♒♐♒

Matty is waiting for me when I get home. She looks tanned and rested. I want to reach out to her sick breast.

"Are you okay?" I ask, looking for signs.

"I'm good."

She moves toward the kitchen in her slow, deliberate way.

I follow. "We missed you."

In the refrigerator there's a new item on the shelf, a big jar of brackish-looking liquid next to the milk. "What is this?"

Matty raises an eyebrow. "Devil's Club," she answers, and disappears into the bedroom. *Ts'iihlanjaaw*. Naani Sandra, the healer who lives up by the bird sanctuary, had told me it was a powerful herb used to treat cancer.

This is alarming news, but since the day I saw her wrapping her breast in cotton, Matty has made it very clear she doesn't want to discuss her "condition." I can hear her in her bedroom unpacking and busily rearranging bottles on her dresser.

Just then, Harry bursts through the door in a bright red muumuu, a magnum of champagne in hand. "We're having a party tonight. Bring something spicy to eat!" The door bangs and he's gone again. I stand before the window and watch him make his way down the street, shouting into the night. Other cries answer him, a chorus from the neighbors. From this view, the darkness in Masset is not pitch black. It is always perpetual twilight, something out of a picture book where the illustration has soft strokes of smoky gray and purple, bits of blue clouds drifting across the top as if they had been put there as an afterthought. Darkness here is always coming, never the prince, never the victor. Kept at bay.

Harry's house beckons from across the street, warm light spilling everywhere, welcoming. I can turn either way and see more of the same. I know where the end of the street lies; I know where the sea begins and the moon hangs every night, where the hawks nest and the ravens rest when it rains too heavily.

Soon we join the flow of people making their way to Harry's. His floors have just been waxed, and they smell of lavender. A big pot of boiling seawater is already steaming up the kitchen; people push past with wine and boxes of beer, cakes from who knows where, buckets of clams and plates of *gow* ready to be steamed. Others are lighting a big bonfire on the beach; sparks fly past the window and get caught in an updraft before reaching the damp trees. Sgaana has come by to check on his daughter, who is roasting a hot dog. His dark beard glistens from the oil of lamps, the smoky light in his cabin where it is said he renews his spirit and reforms the future of the Haida people. He drifts with a group of men into the darkness outside, but not before glancing in my direction. I wish Jonah was here.

"Heads up!" Harry heaves a bucket of crabs toward me. I back away, fearful of their huge claws snapping madly, blindly upwards. "What do you want me to do with these?"

He laughs.

"Cook 'em, honey."

He stops any protest with a raised hand. "You know what to do."

There must be five of them all piled on top of one another, their small hairy back legs scratching each other, claws banging into the plastic. Everything is writhing, clicking. The top one seems to sense it has an opening and it tries to lift itself on the backs of the others to scramble over the top.

"How the hell do I pick these things up?" I ask, fearful of getting any closer.

Broan shows me how to come at them from behind, where their smaller legs can only whisper against my fingers. He hands me one, pale white, slippery and pungent. The tiny black stones it has for eyes dart about nervously, trying to get a fix on me. The flesh inside its shell is like the sea hitting the shore, restlessly confined. Softer underneath. Claws powerful enough to crush bone. For a moment there is a standoff, then suddenly one of its back claws rakes across my palm and I scream, dropping it on the floor. "Oh, shit!"

Everyone starts yelping, *"Look out!"* laughing as the crab scuttles desperately across the floor, moving with surprising speed. It shoots sideways toward the living room, perhaps smelling the sea through the open window. Everyone jumps out of the way until Broan throws a tea towel on top of it and scoops it back up. Whooping loudly he heaves it into the boiling water.

"No!" I'm not ready to see them die.

The claws are still flexing, then it's gone, with two more thrown in. I can hear them thrashing at the side of the pot. Broan is behind me. The sweet smell of crab boiling comes up and up. The kitchen has cleared and we are alone. From my chin he wipes a tear with the dishtowel. "Sorry, but you'll just have to find a way to deal with it."

Howa, I whisper under my breath. Thank you for giving your life to me. I cannot eat the crab and refuse to even look at the succulent pink platter of them brought out and admired by all, instead devouring a plate of cream pastries that soon make me feel quite sick. But I long for the crab, delicately sweet in warm, drawn butter. Damn hypocrite, that's what I am, but I can't help it. And, look, there's some soy sauce and a fresh green onion to provide *yin*.

Crawling into an old leather chair Harry keeps for long reads provides little comfort. The clicking sound keeps coming back. When did some spirits become more important than others? *Howa, thank you for giving yours to me.* Harry turns on the lamp next to me and the revelers outside disappear. I turn it back off. Then the crowd thins and I am left alone.

Outside the fire roars on and someone starts playing a guitar. A voice, singing high and sweet. The beech tree by the window rustles. The sound of familiarity, sameness, is very comforting. It is all right for one to know this feeling, to remember it, if only because it disappears as color into twilight.

"Mind?" It is Ronnie, Dobie's nephew. He finds a place on the sofa, turns on a small lamp and leans forward, light catching the back of his long hair. It ripples.

For a moment we sit there in silence, then he reaches out and pulls a worn, leather-bound book from the shelf. "Wow," he exclaims, "this is the secret Masons book Harry said he found in the attic."

The faded red book with gilt-edged pages looks very old.

"Where'd he get that?"

"The old guy who used to own this house was a grand pooh-bah or something like that in the Masons."

"I've never heard of a Mason lodge out here."

On closer inspection, the cover is made of fine calfskin, with raised gold lettering. The symbol on the front looks strange. Ronnie puzzles over it. "Looks like Arabic or something." He turns it over in his hands. "This book was supposed to be destroyed when he died," he says with a mysterious grin. Running his finger along the tiny script he struggles to read to himself, lips moving.

"Well, what's in it?"

He looks up.

"Ronnie, what does it say?"

"Who the hell knows, it's all gibberish to me. But Sgaana says the Masons have been around since the dawn of time. It's a secret cult of white people formed to preserve and protect what is theirs." Ronnie's voice is calm. We look at one another.

I should tell him my white people were hunted by the Romans and the Moors all the way through Europe until they finally reached the vast shores of the Great Islands and could flee no further. But it's a futile exercise.

Somewhere a window is open, blowing a chill draft through the house.

Ronnie studies the yellowed pages. "There is a logical explanation for why they stayed in power so long," he says, his hand trailing over the words as if to unlock their secrets.

"Dream on, my friend," I mutter.

A shadow of distrust crosses his features.

With a heavy crash, Harry bursts into the room.

"Come on, we're lighting fireworks!"

I flee from the quiet out through the door that leads back to the noise and the merry dance of sparklers. Instead of heading toward the warmth of the bonfire I forge off down the beach, cursing at Ronnie and his indecipherable find.

The shoreline is a dark haven, cold waves lapping near my boots. Above the white noise of moving water, new sounds emerge: the snap of a fin slicing through the surface, restless clicks and soundings as the seascape continues to shelter its mysteries. I find a bit of crab shell from an otter feed and marvel at its cold, pale hue, so unlike the friendly pink it turns in boiling water. The crabs that ended their lives in our pot would have been out tonight, burrowed into the seabed gravel, waiting patiently for unsuspecting prey to come within striking distance. The memory of the scuttling creature, snapping and rearing up, beady eyes swiveling this way and that, is suddenly quite comical. I put the shell down on a flat rock and consider that perhaps the crab, like the wolf, have become my totems, each reflecting a part of who I am, or who I am to be. I bow to the crab, in the sea, and vanquished on the shore. "*Howa*. Thank you for giving your life to me."

Lifting my hands up they become claws, swift and sharp. Snap! Snap! Hunkering down, legs bent, I scuttle sideways, pebbles skittering like shell against linoleum, eyes darting this way and that. I snap my claws, like this, and jab out in the air, practicing. "*Ye-oah*!"

And the crab jumps inside of me, freed from the otherworld of the sea, eyes swiveling in the night air. How light it feels to dance under the moon.

"What are you doing?" Sgaana's sharp voice is as sudden as his appearance out of the darkness. The others are far down the beach, out of earshot. He looks briefly back toward them over his shoulder and then advances a step. "We take our dances very seriously around here."

I am afraid to speak. It's hopeless anyway because we both know my words could misbehave. Betray me. The wind whips around us, stinging and calling out the night spirits that are waiting to rush into any void. I feel as cold as the crab devoured alive.

He sniffs my fear and lets it ride. The bonfire is not so far away, and the world has often got the best of him, so he fixes on me just long enough to savor his victory. Then he steps aside as I run back down the beach, clumsy and awkward, the joy of the dance banished from my soul.Before I'm halfway back I hear a distant clamor.

"Pippi's house is on fire!"

A siren is already wailing in the distance. It passes us on the road out of town. Everyone packs up quickly and sand is kicked over what is left of the bonfire.

"What can we do?" I ask Matty, who is taking some things back to Harry's.

She shrugs. "Not much, I'm afraid. Pippi lives way out in the bush. I doubt the fire truck will be able to do much good. Kim and some others are taking some trucks to see if there is anything of hers they can save."

"How can you be so calm?"

She smiles. In the darkness I miss the subtlety in her expression. "If Pippi called the fire department then she's okay. In case you hadn't noticed, we're on our own out here. She'll rebuild."

♐♒♐♒♐♒

Pippi Longstocking. That's what everyone calls her because of the colorful knitted woolens she uses to trade for food and services. Like her namesake she also has fiery red hair, usually plaited into thick braids.

Pippi fled from an Eastern European city to the solitude of the Canadian wilderness. She has left the judgment of others out of her daily affairs, occupying herself with writing rambling science fiction novels on sheaves of thin onionskin typewriter paper on an old Olivetti with a sticking "p." In her spare time she scavenges old sweaters and picks the wool apart to make her creations. A tiny house in a quarter acre deep in the bush has been transforming itself under her care for twelve years, filling up with an odd assortment of found objects and cast-off furniture. She'd started with a chipboard foundation and had been adding walls and windows as she could afford them. Last I'd heard the one-room cottage had been partitioned into living and sleeping quarters with curtains.

We'd had little social contact, but she'd heard I was looking for some sturdy boot socks and approached me to make a trade: a pair of boiled-wool, red-striped knee-highs in exchange for reading a collection of her short stories. My journalistic credentials would have been suspect in the outside world but here I was the expert in town. It was not a good deal for me in the end. Her densely written stories and bright socks were troubling—haunting my dreams with ferocious Brothers Grimm goblins sliding out from behind dark, twisted gingerbread cottages and descending on small children wrapped up in a red-striped world: the red was everywhere. After a decent amount of time and a quick scan of the pages, I returned her work with some earnest and kind comments. She silently took my notes and knitted her gratitude into a long, violently patterned fuchsia scarf to be left on my doorstep several weeks later. "Thank you for reading my work," she said shyly, the next time I saw her. I mumbled some inane response and hoped she wouldn't ask me again.

Pippi's house was built entirely from scrap lumber. Inside, the two-by-four joists were insulated with bundles of old clothes and newspapers held fast by packing tape. An odd assortment of windows fitted in at odd angles, all colors of the rainbow. Everything was highly flammable and in the end the whole place had burned clear to the ground.

"Get something good on this oddball and her house of cards," Judy admonishes me on the phone. "Don't make it sound like a police bulletin."

Pippi and I meet for tea at the Two Bells the next afternoon. Carrot hair matted and tied out of the way, she is still trembling under a thick gray pea coat that smells of smoke. News of a fundraiser has traveled quickly and a handful of people are already milling around the café buying each other cakes and muffins. Someone is selling small canvas prints on her behalf.

"What happened?" I ask as kindly as I can, opening my little notebook.

Pippi clutches a mug of tea between knobby hands, her thin face drawn and still smudged from soot. "It was the chimney," she answers, humbled.

Since I've lived here I've learned a lot about chimney fires. They are a source of fear in every household. The build-up of tarry resin coating the inside of the stovepipe can catch at any time. We check and clean ours often, watching for telltale sparks and the dull glow visible if there's a bit of fire burning up near the roof.

"Silly thing." She pauses, trying to control her shaking hands. They have a memory of their own. "It took almost five hours for the fire to get out of control."

I can see her there all alone in the bush, the nearest creek two hundred yards from her house. No running water, not even a well.

There is a faint bruise on her cheek and soot peppering her thick hair.

"You mean you knew it was going to burn your house down?"

She looks at me, eyes bright. "My stove was very old."

Some old castaway made of cheap tin, I'm certain. Thin in spots with a dirty burn.

She lifts her head, sniffing the air like a fox. A memory. Beneath the smoky veneer, her skin glows translucently in the lamplight. On her lap, hands work into each other, fingers picking at the threads of imaginary wool. I see the socks and scarf she knit for me languishing in the bureau. She could use them, now. Everything she worked for is gone.

"Anyway," she interrupts my guilty thoughts, "the fire was awfully hot."

In the absence of books or any other entertainment, Pippi told me she was sitting in her favorite chair, alone with her wool and her writing. "I noticed the roof seemed to be collecting a little black smoke and I got up to look…" Her face pinches with the memory and I am pulled up with her, walking over to the stove, eyes toward the roof, curious. "It looked like the wood around the chimney was getting charred." Charred. Changing molecularly, reforming into carbon. Crumbling into dark dust. "I went outside, then, just to check." There is something of the original shock in her telling of this part of the story. Her face is calm, almost serene.

On a cold night like this the stars would be hard above, sharp and clear. We look up into a sky packed full of them, thinking our own thoughts. The smell of wood burning and the fresh aroma of cedar. The hard earth and wizened grass crackling, bouncing back every sound like the taut edge of a drum. Winter coming in, bearing down to a standstill until all that is left is thick, tangy sap and leftover berries dropping as stones onto the frosted ground. Alone in the wilderness in a tiny clearing. A house made from red socks and old news.

"I saw it then, the fire around the chimney." She looks down at her hands as if to ask them why they let her down. I want to reach out to her but there isn't any time. She takes a long drink from her tea. Her eyes look into mine. "I had no ladder, no hose, but I managed to get up on the roof. I used up the tea water, the wash water, then I threw on a pot of chicken soup. Nothing helped." Her eyes are red-rimmed, still raw from tears and smoke. "I slid down the roof and ran inside. It was bad. I barely had time to grab things and run to town."

Only after she'd stumbled into Daddy Cool's had the alarm been rung out and the one fire engine dispatched only to find her house fully engulfed. They'd concentrated on keeping the flames from spreading to the nearby bush.

Around her a crowd of visitors pay for donated food. There is the clink of change as they drop quarters into the jar marked "Pippi's New House Fund."

We consider the pile of coins.

"I'm going to rebuild," she declares.

"But, Pippi, you have no water."

She shrugs and laughs.

I cannot fathom all this building and rebuilding.

A cold rush of air heralds the arrival of Jonah, who now has the stature of someone of importance. He's here like any good politician to show his support for this charitable effort. Pippi gazes toward him vacantly. He has on a big wool coat, with elk buttons and a padded hood. His boots thump heavily.

I catch his eye. "Jonah!"

He gives me that "I've got business to attend to" look, followed by an apologetic smile. He heads to Pippi and bends toward her solicitously with a few whispered words of encouragement. Then he moves on to the crowd at the coffee bar.

Pippi is fading from exhaustion, signaling the end of the interview. Maybe I should return the scarf and socks. In her thin jacket she looks lost. Vulnerable. I take her hand. "You write good stories, Pippi." Then I have to turn away as she blushes with happiness. There is no harm in a white lie; her work has all gone up in smoke. As I move to get up, she reaches out and clutches at the sleeve of my coat.

"Wait. I heard you were interested in the old days," she whispers, "asking questions and the like." Then she pulls a faded log of crumbling newspaper out of her knapsack. "I've had this for years. Others, too." She puts it on the table between us. "As a writer interested in the history of this place, I thought it might come in useful one day. But I needed it for insulation on the back wall." She looks at it fearfully. "I don't know why I grabbed it, there was so little time." Curious, I move it closer for inspection, but she stops me.

"Be careful if you take it. Your house may burn down too." And with that she is gone, off toward the jar of coins and the sympathetic crowd.

I keep the newspaper hidden in my bag because Jonah has taken me home to the Reserve. Instead, I focus on the story I'm writing about Pippi's fire and her crazy bravery. Jonah is sketching a poster idea on the kitchen table. He uses a big, soft pencil, rubbing his thumb to blend the graphite into the gray down of an emerging eagle chick. Soon, exhaustion takes over.

"Come to bed, love."

With a sigh he packs up and comes to lie down beside me. Without undressing he pulls back my thin cotton wrapper and kisses the soft parts until he can find his place. In the last remnants of this day, the threads are woven as tightly as our bodies can allow, all things intertwined, plaited as if by an old pattern known by heart.

In the morning I take my things home. The newspaper sits on the desk, and now that I'm free to investigate it, I stall. *Not yours to know. Not yours to tell.*

Damn them all, they're too invested in this place. I pull out the clipping, and then panic. Some of it crumbles into the bag. Gingerly, I cut the rubber band, unroll it and press it flat down on the table. I can barely make out the tiny print against an aged yellow background.

June 1880

Slavery still amongst the Indians! It has been reported that Dr. I. W. Powell, Superintendant of Indian Affairs for the Province of British Columbia, returned yesterday from a fact-finding journey to the northernmost regions of the province in an effort to determine Indian policy for those coastal regions that fall under his jurisdiction. Dr. Powell has told Governor Douglas he was particularly appalled by the proliferation of slavery still to be found in most of the northern tribes. Despite its illegality amongst civilized peoples and the vigorous efforts of Anglican and Presbyterian ministers, who have ....

Silverfish have eaten away the rest but there is still enough here to understand what Pippi was getting at. There is nothing in the history books about this, no footnotes in the museum.

"Starting over." That's what Judy had said. The silver lining in every cloud. Reconstructing history might have its advantages after all.

The shanty town by Naani Rose's. This is where the unwanted people must have been banished after the government stepped in to free them. The buzzing of flies comes back to me, the stink of brackish water far from the sea. Back then a place like that was only good for shitting in. The fire. How had it started?

The room shifts a little and becomes as a looking glass, all sharp edges and reflections. I slowly and carefully put the fragile bit of newspaper down. It floats on the desktop like the skin of an onion.

I have to see the rest of the article.

The microfilm collection at *The Sentinel* may offer up something.

But first Naani.

The Shack People

♐♒♐♒♐♒

"Naani Rose!"

She takes her time, coming up from the depths of the house, a world hidden as if it were a lost kingdom behind the wardrobe, coming up from behind the warren of skirts and dresses and old mink coats, a lifetime of shirts and ties, piles of forgotten refuse straining toward the ceiling that have come to define her.

She peers up at me, eyes uncertain.

Somehow she knows.

I have never seen Naani Rose nervous. It seemed nothing could disturb her implacable shell, not even the death of her husband on the seas. *I bet you danced on the shore!* Something sharp in the air has made her clumsy. There is no offer of tea, instead stony silence. Lips pressed together, she stands by her chair.

I hold out the open envelope and she peers inside at the fragment of newspaper.

"Naani, what is this about?" I ask, shaking the envelope in front of her. "Were the Haida keeping slaves?"

"Where did you get that?" Her fingers snap at the envelope but I pull it away in time. Two bears glare at each other. Naani trembles. "That's an old thing, rotting away. Don't bring it back from the dead. What business is it of yours to bring it back from the dead?" She shakes her head. "Oh, why can't you just listen to me when I tell you now what I believe is the truth—that all people are created equal?"

I remain standing, coat on in the stifling room. She reaches for the poker. "You should have left things the way they were."

"Naani, you can't just pretend it never happened! Those people deserve more than that."

She leans heavily on the chair and turns away. I feel ashamed now. The old woman sits down, bones jarring, her poker resting on the floor. "Why do these things have to be told?" she asks at last. She is gazing at the fire as if to divine something in the leaping flames. "It was a bad thing and we stopped doing it."

I remain silent because I cannot answer this question, just as I cannot answer why it is that I love her and Jonah and all the others, and yet I am, by my birthright, an enemy. An enemy to their peace and their prayers and to the vision of their soul resurrected into something more decent than I was ever allowed to be. I kneel next to her.

"Naani, I'm afraid. I want to understand Jonah. But I won't be judged for things my people did if he refuses to do the same."

"Oh, child." She strokes my hair and we think about the way of nature, how it gets inside of us all, the wind, the rain and the thunder. There is a storm coming up and she feels where it will be going in her bones so she pushes me to get up. "This has nothing to do with Jonah. Don't make him suffer for our mistakes."

At the door she calls out, arms clutching her sweater close. "Forget the past! It can only hurt you!"

♐♒♐♒♐♒

I can't stop thinking about that newspaper article, the damn red leather Masons book, and the burned-out scar of a town no one will admit existed. But I can't get to the *Sentinel* office for another week, and Jonah is brittle these days as the spell of election fever takes over. He paints day and night, putting new posters up around town, consolidating his support at the Band office.

It's all about secret societies with passwords unintelligible to my ears. Power and ritual. A world order. And now, more grand political schemes.

The sound of a town meeting I'm covering for the paper breaks in. I jot a few lines down, trying to keep my mind on the business at hand: recycling. Jonah's opponent, the current Reserve Chief, George Sinclair, is standing up at the front of the room, along with the Town Council members. When the subject of recycling at the local high school comes up, he addresses Jonah, who is in the front row. "I'd like to know what you think of the idea of creating a separate building for the Haida kids." He looks at the crowd. "Do that, and we'd have to build *two* recycling areas."

George has long resisted the idea of separating the students and has made it clear he wants to continue to build a coalition with the

Canadian government. Jonah knows this question is meant to cause fear with the whites present at the meeting, and he won't be baited. Without missing a beat, he smoothly changes the subject back to plastic or glass milk bottles and the conversation stays on track. I can't help but admire his growing political acumen. By the end of the meeting, he's made several good points with everyone by focusing on the practicalities necessary to fix this one pressing problem. The Island dump is quickly filling up and the smell often wafts into populated areas. As we leave, many from both communities come by to shake Jonah's hand as George glowers nearby.

Back at his mother's house the exhaustion shows as he slumps over tea. His family has gone to the Mainland so we are alone.

"You did well today," I say.

He glances over, brows pinched.

"George thinks he's a moderate but his approach will eventually sell out everything we are as a people."

"Are you including me in that group?"

"You know this subject always ends in an argument."

The clock ticks on the wall and marks the minutes of silence. It's near dinnertime and my mind feels cottony. Outside we hear a lone squawk in the far recesses. *That old raven.* I fumble over my words. "I can discuss it perfectly well."

He snorts and stares into his tea.

"So what is your answer to George's question," I press on. "What is your position on the integrated schools here?"

He looks up, the beginnings of stubbornness shaping his features. "What do you think we should do?"

"There is no real option. Keep everyone together."

He pushes his teacup away with a sudden ferocity, spilling the creamy liquid onto the table. "Haida kids are second-class citizens in the town school."

"Come on, Jonah, I don't think it's as simple as that. But even if you're right, separating them will only make things worse. How will they ever come to know one another?"

He gives me the look. It is a warning I've stopped heeding. "The Haida language is almost dead," he growls. "If we don't start teaching it in the schools we'll lose one of the most important things that make us who we are." I know this to be true: If you want to destroy a culture, first take its language, then its religion, and finally its history. It was so much easier for Naani's generation. They had something to look forward to when the priests brought their fire and brimstone, magical tales and mystery, replacing one passion with another. It was so clear then, the damnation of the old ways replaced with a passionate and forgiving God. I hear Naani's thin voice singing in the church choir, tugging at the accordion and reminiscing about her lost loves and husband who disappeared into the sea. And now the memories of a distant time are flooding back, gathered up in so many stories by a dying generation. To Jonah they are as ghosts, never his to possess, only fearful reminders of a missing link.

"What about optional language classes?" I ask.

With a frustrated grunt, he picks up the cups and slams them with a crash into his mother's immaculate sink. "Always the same old shit!"

We sit in shocked, trembling silence.

"Damn you, Elle," he whispers.

"For what? For wanting us to live in peace?"

"Your peace is suffocating us!"

Then he sighs the giving-up sigh. Always the same sigh.

"You cannot understand." He pronounces each word carefully, slowly. "You will never be able to understand."

"I do understand, Jonah. It's about being whole. But you and the others are made of too many bits and pieces now, and you have to move forward. You have to create something new." I look up at him, trying to find the connection. "My mother's people, who knew a little something cultural survival, had a saying in Quebec: *vive dans le passé, et vous manquez l'avenir*; live in the past, and you miss the future."

He glares at me. "You're trying to make things more complicated, trying to tie knots around the solution."

"So segregation is your solution? I know where this is going, Jonah, and you can't turn back the clock. I mean, who should go from this place? Will you pack up all the townspeople who aren't full clan members and kick them out? Where will you draw the line?"

"I'm sorry," he says. "So sorry."

I try to take his hand but he pulls it away and gets up heavily, and I imagine he is thinking about his posters, the raven within the eagle within the whale. Spiraling downwards into the atomic infinite. I know he believes if he keeps looking into that well, something new will appear.

"Listen to me," I say. "I love you. I love all that you are."

He looks over at me with an expression I can't read, then stands up.

"Get your coat. We're going for a ride."

Gravel spitting, we take off at a furious pace down the road south. The sun is out but dark clouds hang over to the west. I watch the sky because I am afraid to look over at Jonah.

"Where are you taking me?"

He says nothing so I pull my coat closer and turn my attention to the road and cedars rushing past. We drive like this for an hour, until he veers down toward Port Clements and takes an abrupt turn off onto a rough dirt road. I hang onto the doorframe as he shoots into the deepening forest. Nothing can be heard above the thudding and bumping and rocks hitting us like pistol fire. Suddenly the truck shoots up over a rise, and then before we stop bouncing he jams on the brakes and we skid to a stop. Clouds of dust billow up, choking, obscuring. I jump out in a fury.

"Damn you. God damn..." the words dying as the dust clears.

Before me is Juskatla Inlet surrounded by steep mountainous terrain. I've seen it in many photographs before, lush green and blue with a snowy range of mountains in the distance. But something is terribly wrong. From where we stand, there is not a single bit of green left. The mountains, gullies, alpine meadows, river valleys, look as if a nuclear bomb exploded and flattened everything. Gray-brown stumps, twigs, denuded, twisted, broken and shredded, lie discarded everywhere. Stripped of its luxurious coat a naked, a shamed earth huddles with vacant eyes. The entire forest has been clear-cut and then abandoned.

"Take a good look, Elle," he shouts. "Take it all in."

This blackened wasteland.

Our breath is the only living thing left; it whispers out in a cloud toward the cold day where there is no other creature to see or hear us. All else has fled before the chain saw and the stacking machines that crushed everything not worth logging like so many broken bones. A fine ash of sawdust filthy from oil and dirt has coated the earth and choked life out of what foliage remains.

"God, why?"

"Behold the work of the great Unity Forest Co." He points off to the mountains in the distance. "This goes over as far as Yakoun Lake, clear to the other side of the Island. They would have kept going and taken everything on Graham, but we stopped them. Stopped them before they took Moresby and the rest of the Islands too."

We stand apart, watching the sun set on the bald hills, menacing reds deepening into blood and rust like a holocaust dreamed and a terror remembered. The colors are of a distant future come home too soon. They are a vision of a land subdued, tilled and toiled over until, at last, there is no earthly resemblance to the paradise lost when God cast his children out from Eden. "Will it ever grow back?" I ask dully once we are back in the truck.

"Oh sure, in twenty-five years or so. With Unity's so-called 'reforestation' policy. But there is always a danger that aspen, the faster growing species, will crowd out the cedar and the spruce before they can take hold. And without diversity, they'll be susceptible to disease and pests, rusting away like so much junk. We slowly head back to the car in silence.

"The old growth they took," he adds with a vicious grind of the gearshift, "was over a thousand years old."

Looming up as we leave the area is the familiar band of forest, revealed for the veneer it is, a mockery of nature. In the last of twilight I can almost imagine that the forest is as it once was: unknowable, everlasting. The road is a gaping wound now; I have lost the Island, just like the others.

♐♒♐♒♐♒

"Kim, can I come by for a visit?"

My shy friend waits for me outside his small clapboard house, Balto barking somewhere inside. No doubt he is anxious to be free in the bush again.

"If you want to talk you'll have to come with me while I harvest the morels I've been waiting for," he says, turning to pick up his knapsack and gloves. "We'll have to leave Balto behind. He'll destroy the mushrooms."

We pass the small pasture next to his property, where someone from town keeps two chestnut geldings. Today they are standing at opposite ends of the quarter-acre field. They don't bother to acknowledge us as we pass, instead staring off into the deep woods. I've never seen anyone visit the horses and wonder if they're ever ridden. "Ornery creatures," says Kim. "Don't like people very much." I wonder how long they will be left in this acre patch, nostrils steaming, coats dull with dust.

"They look unhappy," I say, hand on the fence, fumbling in my pocket for something edible. Curious, the two animals begin to make their way toward us. Kim seems nonplussed. "Town folk pay me fifty dollars a month to put hay out and muck the field. I don't like to see them penned up like that, but it puts wood in my stove." Abruptly he turns on his heel, and with a gesture to follow, strides toward the heavy band of forest that separates his property from the beach. We make our way down the path that curves toward the ocean. A bit of sun has briefly poked through and it shafts down in front of us, lighting up the old cedars hung with moss. It is silent, save for the muted sea and two crows fighting over a wild strawberry.

"Over there's Crown land," he points out, indicating the acres on the left of the path. "They're talking about clearing the wood and making some pocket change to finance the tourist industry." He spits and picks up his pace, cutting abruptly off the gravel path just as we catch a glimpse of the ocean.

"You mean they'll chop it all down?"

"Yup. But they'll have to take an axe to me first before I'll let that happen."

"Kim, Jonah took me last night to the Unity clear-cut at Juskatla."

He grabs at a branch to haul himself up the steep incline. "I was wondering when that would happen. Unity is a soulless corporate monster bent on shaving this land bare, but we've done a lot to slow the process down." He finds a fallen branch and weighs its value as a walking stick, then strips off the leaves. "I'm sorry he didn't warn you—those hidden clear-cuts are a shock. But we've saved the whole of Moresby Island from the same treatment, and that's over a million acres of prime old-growth forest. Since we started pushing back, the logging companies have gotten pretty wily. They set aside a minimum old-growth preserve around here and send a bunch of experts up to prove their reforestation plans will fly. In the end, they do what they want." He stops by an old cedar towering into the canopy above. "Jonah knows the deal. He's just pushing your buttons." He points to a V-shaped and moss-covered cut on the oldest part of the tree.

"See this axe mark here?" he asks. "This was a test bore made by the Haida to see if the wood would be good for a canoe. That cut's been there over a hundred years." His rough hands caress the old scars. "Some of the land on the south Island is so remote it was probably never ventured into by the Ancient Ones, but around here you can see how much they depended on the land for their survival. They deserve my help to keep what's left." Kim's face, as worn and weary as the last of the old trees around us, looks at me and smiles grimly. "The area denuded by the logging companies helps us more than it helps them when it comes to getting the message out. It's such a mess there's no way anyone can justify getting their hands on what's left."

Then he turns abruptly. "Down this way," he shouts, and disappears into the bush.

I almost lose him in the heavy undergrowth. He bounds on ahead, jumping over logs, heavy boots sinking into the mossy undergrowth with barely a sound. "Look!" He is bending over something at the base of a large tree. The roots are covered in moist earth and there is a small cluster of white mushrooms with heavy-skirted stalks sheltered in amongst the moss. We crouch down and he picks one up in his gloved hand. He has a delicate touch despite the heavy leather. Then he rolls it onto his palm, examining it from every angle, then sniffing at it.

"Is it edible?" I ask, bending closer for a look.

"Don't know for sure." He pulls out a small book, greasy and well thumbed. "I think they're *white matsutake,*" he ventures, checking the corresponding page. "Yup." Together we pick the whole bunch and put them in the cotton sack he has brought with him. "These taste like popcorn," he says, pushing on ahead. We spot more clusters of the tiny orange mushrooms I remembered from my trip to the Sagan River. *Golden trumpets.* "Too tough and stringy," he remarks, eyes searching further on ahead. I want to crouch down and marvel at their fierce perfection. They leap up like bright spots of sun from the dark earth, hinting at some magical miniature world where fairies hide just out of sight.

By the end of the afternoon we have found several more caches: the puffy *prince* with caps bursting like the top of a soufflé; *delicious lactarious,* the color of apricots with caps so luxuriously wide they are like crinolines; and assorted puffballs.

"The morels are this way," he whispers, as if someone might be listening. We are deep into the woods and he takes no care to disguise our route, knowing full well I am completely lost. His morel stash is jealously guarded. "Some years I only get a dozen," he says as we skitter down a soft embankment into the remains of a winter-dry streambed.

He finds what he is looking for almost at once, stopping abruptly at the base of a large, yellow cedar. He holds his hand up as if my exclamation of pleasure will disturb the colony, and then crouches down, mouth working in a silent count. "Almost twenty," he exclaims with awe. I creep up behind him, careful to keep my distance. They are ugly-looking things, with narrow elliptical caps chambered like brain coral, heavy on short stems. The ground around is rich with mulch; nearby a large gray snail makes his way slowly up a fallen ash leaf. The mushrooms look very spongy, caps the color of warm honey. "Perfect," he declares and pulls out a fabric mushroom bag from his knapsack. My companion carefully picks all but the most immature, cradling them in his hand to inspect for the telltale signs that distinguish it from its toxic cousin, the *gyromitra.*

Then he spots something and sits back on his haunches.

"Look," he says, pointing. Over by the edge of the colony, set apart as if in deliberate exile, is a mushroom very different from the others. It is perfectly white, bright and ethereal, glowing in the half-light of the forest floor. Kim edges closer and picks the mushroom up in his gloved hand, holding it for me to examine. "This is a *destroying angel.*" He turns it upside down in his palm. "One bite is deadly, and there is no antidote. See how flat the cap is? And look how the gills turn into the cap before they reach the stalk." So many gills densely packed in unwavering precision, every one perfect as if they had been sewn like silk ribbons above a feathery ring into the most beautiful of petticoats. No creature has nibbled or slid across it; the cap is free of age spots as if death itself had made it immortal. "Just remember, you should never eat a wild mushroom unless you are an expert," he finishes, tossing the white ghost out of harm's way. "As for the logging business, if you're looking for answers, I won't be any help. The need feeds the greed, as my great-uncle the banker used to say. And everyone has a need for something. Even if it's to be left alone."

Then, with a grunt, he gets up and takes stock of where we are before picking a course out of the forest.

Out of the corner of my eye, something glows in the dark mulch. On impulse I pick up the fallen angel, wrap it in tissue and stuff it inside the pocket of my mackintosh before hurrying after him.

♐♒♐♒♐♒

Sunday. The only day *The Sentinel* is closed, giving me the privacy I need to get into those file drawers. I drive the fifty miles in the pre-dawn, hoping Judy answers the knock at her door. She does, handing me a key still sleepy-eyed, the smell of booze sloughing off her nightshirt. She's too hung over to question my excuse to retrieve some computer files. "Aren't you the little eager beaver?" she groans, then shuts the door in my face.

The office is gloomy and freezing cold, protesting my presence with creaks and sighs. I try various light switches, but fail to illuminate the dark corner where the old file cabinets lurk so I have to go out to my car for a flashlight.

Once located, the rusted drawers fail to give way. I pull and push. Nothing.

It's a sign. Not your business.

For a moment I crouch before it in frustration, then I notice a small lock on the upper corner. The key must be here somewhere, probably Judy's desk. With a fearful glance toward the window, I make my way over and ease her top drawer open. Amidst the rubble of broken pencils and half-chewed gum packages are the office keys, duplicates of the ones Judy gave me. Closer examination reveals a couple of smaller ones on the ring that look like they might be for a safe-deposit box or a file cabinet. Discovery in hand I make my way into the back, heart thumping. After a couple of unsuccessful jiggles, one of the two smaller keys works in the top drawer and it slides open with a loud, rusty squawk. A layer of dust coating the files is evidence they haven't been looked at in a long time, if ever. The first batch contains nothing more than pages of provincial history copied from reference texts and a few black and white photos that look like they are from the late 1800s. The last drawer reveals something more promising: two sleeves of yellowed wax paper containing a sheaf of microfilm strips. Across the packet, a large red stamp warns, "**Originals: Do Not Remove from Library.**"

Before I can get back on my feet, I hear the sound of a car approaching. Judy! I bolt up and slam the drawer closed, then jog clumsily to her desk and shove the keys back in their place. From the darkness within I grab the door handle and wrench it open.

"Elle!" Judy looks nervous, unkempt.

"I was just leaving." I hand her back the keys, a packet of microfilm hidden inside my parka.

"Why the hell did you come all the way down here for fifteen minutes?"

But I have already escaped to my car with a cheerful wave.

Once safely home, I shut the bedroom door and lay out the strips of microfilm on my desk. The images are impossibly tiny, useless without a reader. Then I remember my photographer's loupe, and pull it out of the camera bag. Held to the film in front of the desk lamp it will just do. It's tough going. Pages of text reveal standard research material, notes from journals, artifacts drawn in detail by early missionaries, some Haida stories (spelled *Hayda*). The typeface and old English dialect make it difficult to read, as the documents were faded long before they'd been microfilmed. It's weary work.

A building storm and early nightfall leave me isolated under the desk lamp, but darkness and hunger don't seem to matter. After several hours of eye-straining deciphering, I find two things of interest. One is a remarkable Haida fable that may be useful at some later date. The other is the article from *The Vancouver Bee*. The missing piece.

Dr. Powell, it continues, ***has told Governor Douglas he was particularly appalled by the proliferation of slavery still to be found in most of the northern tribes, despite its illegality amongst civilized peoples, and the vigorous efforts of Anglican and Presbyterian missionaries who have made commendable headway with these communities by bringing them to sobriety and the love of God. "The treatment of these poor souls is appalling, "Dr. Powell was quoted as saying in his report to the Governor.***

"Many have been slaves for generations, either captured in battle or traded amongst Chiefs like chattels, with no hope of ever gaining freedom from their masters. "And, he (Dr. Powell) also told the Governor, "amongst the Hayda, I have been told they are still sacrificing slaves into the holes of newly erected lodge poles to bring good fortune to their owners. The slave trade still practiced by the Chiefs and others must be put to a stop!"

Institutional slavery. Generations of indentured families held as property for hundreds of years. Maybe longer. How many forgotten people had lived and died far from their homeland? How many nameless bones were buried here? The hypocrisy of it is stunning.

For a long time the wind knocks outside the window, frantically pushing the long cedar boughs into the west wall. The microfilm sits in front of me on the desk, bits of litter everywhere, my stories, poetry, the cards and bits of love talk from Jonah thumb-tacked in between fragments of my conscience.

Later in the familiar box of my bed I lie awake, unable to sleep, and wonder where the soft darkness went, the palette of deep rose and purple blending into the midnight blue where the moon filters through. Even in nothingness, colors remain long after the light has gone. Now, pulling the sheets closer for protection, the darkness presses onward, through me, far out to sea. The fog bell tolls out in the harbor.

I leave the night light on. Tonight the ghosts of the residential schools are running through the Alberta hills. *L'st'aa wanguu. She is far away.* I dream of the secret red book, where whispers turn to lies and plotters flourish in darkness, their words tooled in gold and etched permanently into the cover. The words seem quite clear at a distance but when I come closer, their meaning becomes elusive and distorted. When I awaken, just before dawn, I realize that I cannot be their judge. There are secrets everywhere.

Turning, I feel Jonah in my bones, feel him in my marrow as if he is already keeping me alive. Loss comes sharply and is pushed away in a breath. Not yet!

"Not your business," Matty warned me. Nothing good would come of digging into things that were long buried. Judy made this clear too. They've made a life for themselves here; they know how to keep the peace.

Morning light folds over the foggy horizon, a shade paler than night. I breathe deeply trying to think, to feel the room as solace again, grasp reason more closely. I have only one piece of information, after all, and precious little proof. Any discussion with Jonah would end in disaster. My questions, my curiosity, would make me a pariah. My life here, over. I can feel the beginning of that old, familiar, lost feeling.

By the time I am fully awake there seems no other choice but the one taken by Judy and Matty, and all the others, too. If I am to stay here I will have to push it out of my mind. I've done worse to keep what is mine. I'm not ready to give it all up. Not yet. Perhaps later I will think of something.

I put the knowledge away.

Witches

♐♒♐♒♐♒

"Quinnie, can you come?" This call is at Matty's request.

I hear the soft things jingling on her breast, her feathers dancing as she laughs. "Of course," she replies, dropping her voice to a theatrical whisper. "On the full moon day after tomorrow."

"Good," says Matty, when I hang up the phone. She's on the couch, picking with little enthusiasm at a bowl of steamed spinach and garlic. Some of her acorn color has come back but she continues to lose weight, and it shows most alarmingly on her face. She appears as a dove now, paler against a bleaker winter day, her subtle layers of white upon white slowly revealing themselves: she seems wiser than ever in her new frailty, closely guarded as it is.

"I consider this to be part of your Island education. Once upon a time there was a real witches' coven here," she adds, picking up a bit of soft garlic, trapping it delicately on her tongue and savoring every aromatic morsel. She regards me with mock seriousness.

"Who was in this coven?" I ask.

"No one knows, or will tell, but it was active in Masset Town for several years—you know," she wiggles her fingers, "with visitors who apparently were attracted to the dark magic of this place. The Haida call it *kuganna*, and they don't like it much."

"But you said the coven here was with white witches."

"Very true!" She laughs at some expression I've pulled. "And misunderstood they were too, as all white witches are. Confused with black witchery, the manipulation of life for dark purpose. Don't worry," she adds, "next week we'll howl at the moon a little and try to stay out of trouble."

So, when the moon reveals herself we will become a coven. Quinnie, Matty and I will ask the rich, transcendental forces around us for guidance. We white folk need something here, something mysterious to call our own. Something Druid.

She leaves me with a book to read, *The Annotated History of Witchery In America*. In the back are several incantations. One for money, one for love, another for a new job. I wonder if any of my colleagues back home knew about these tricks as they were battling their way up to the top. A little nutmeg sprinkled on the intended's hankie, the weaving of stray hairs into a fetish, skewing the universe just enough to move it into their domain.

The morning arrives under a low sky, roiling with fog and layer upon layer of rain-laden cloud. Quickly pulling on an old sweater and pants I make a strong fire and start putting out the breakfast things. Perhaps the weather will improve.

With the darkening night sky, the full moon is revealed and I'm ready, having practiced my incantations all day. As instructed, I am asking the universe to give me enough money so that my needs are taken care of, but not so much the universe will have to take from another. Very egalitarian, this witch business. Makes me wonder what the Puritans were so afraid of. The universe will provide her bounty for everyone if they but ask.

Quinnie has told me, "Tonight we'll pray to the moon and the goddess of the equinox as we reach the midway point between the autumnal and the vernal." The winter solstice is upon us, the midway point between the autumnal and the vernal, so the goddess of the equinox is making her appearance. I don't really know what it means in witch terms, but my guide assures me it is appropriate to make an offering after we go outside and howl. Quinnie, Matty and I bundle up and take candles outside. Stumbling through the woodpile fodder, we are guided by pale moonlight to the lane behind the house.

"Look!" Quinnie whispers, and we stand erect, our faces turned upward. Tonight is unusually quiet. No music drifting from Daddy Cool's or trucks roaring around the corner stretch of the main drag. The sharp cold has even stilled the neighborhood raven.

Thus with faces raised, we stand silently in the rutted lane, candles flickering in the vast darkness that has opened up to welcome us. Nothing but the void, pure and free, soaring into the limitless beyond. It is the place from which we came and shall one day return. One cannot fall upwards into the stars without believing this, without facing God and the mystery of the unexplained.

I believe I can become a witch.

We remain in the empty lane for a long time, watching clouds drift over the surface of the moon, aware as all stargazers are of the gentle and finite curve of the earth. I feel as if everything is upside down; I know gravity is the only thing holding me. I raise my candle. I wish the earth would let me go.

Matty suddenly lets out a long howl and we all laugh.

"Let's get back inside!" someone shouts, and we tumble over one another like puppies, yipping backwards at the stars, drawn by the warmth of a good fire, our candles dropped onto the lawn, their brief light snuffed by the moist earth. Once in the warmth of the living room, Quinnie reaches into her jacket and brings out something wrapped in a silk cloth. "This is a goddess altar," she whispers, positioning it on the kitchen table. It's made of small crystals piled and glued together into a rough pyramid. On top is a small, beautifully carved figure of a woman in white onyx. Matty further adorns it with a pink cockleshell and some small eagle feathers. Then she gives us each a small piece of paper. "Write something on here you most want resolved."

We do as we are bidden, then roll the pieces up and place them at the foot of the altar. Quinnie lights the two small votives on either end. "Oh Goddess of the Solstice," she drones, but I don't hear the rest. I'm picturing my words on the little piece of paper. I'm down the hobbit hole, having tea with Mister Mole, the tea set I lost when I was five, oh damn, where is that tea set, where did those afternoons and those nights disappear to, when did the scraps of those years become lost?

"Bring us wisdom on this night for what we seek," Quinnie finishes, eyes closed.

"Amen," adds Matty. The other two look over at me. Given my drift-off I'm not being a very good witch. "Let's take our questions over to the fire," Quinnie instructs solemnly. We open the stove and gaze at the red-hot logs damped down to slow burn. Matty throws in a rasher of paper and a handful of cedar sticks. The fire flares up.

I'm not allowed to know the contents of the other papers. Mine has Jonah's name written on it, and a prayer for forgiveness. Since our argument two days ago, he has not called. For good measure, I included wishes for enlightenment, peace and the bounty of the universe. Neither taking nor giving at the expense of another. But I've wrapped it too tightly and it smokes uneasily in the flames.

"Come on, burn!" I whisper fiercely. Transform.

Later, Matty pushes open my bedroom door and lets herself in. "I think our first coven meeting went rather well," she says, vigorously brushing her teeth. She's in her long underwear and is brushing the mass of thick, curly hair with her free hand. I roll over from my comfortable reading position on the bed. "It seems so. And I'd love to know, did you wish for something important?" Her expression transforms as predicted into a sly and clever mask. She pulls the toothbrush out of her mouth and gives me a foamy grimace. "Oh, yessss. Very important," she intones, then turns on her heel. Quicker than the time it takes for the stars to reach us her essence is gone, the door to her mysterious universe firmly closed.

Late morning there is a knock on my window. It's Jonah, his face furred by beard and woolen hat pulled low over his forehead. He is holding a gift-wrapped bag for me to see. I scramble up and meet him at the door. He picks me up, opens his coat and buries me inside, the cold-warm, prickling layers, all wool and familiar angles. He holds the bag aloft. "I've just come from Ketchikan, and it was a miserable, bumpy ride without you. Elle, I'm so sorry about the other day. I had to make up for my bad behavior, so I spent an afternoon I should have been in meetings, going shopping." Inside his offering, wrapped in tissue paper, is an emerald silk scarf to tie my hair, a packet of Alaskan salt-water taffy, and a tortoise-shell comb.

"Never mind, I just missed you, is all." We tumble on the bed and I taste the sweetness of him, his skin still cold, his hands colder still. Reaching behind my back, he holds me tightly for a moment. "It's always the same," he whispers, breath like vapor curling around my ears, by the skin of my neck. "When I was in the plane coming home, all I could think about was the color of your hair and how the sea below is deeper than imagining." With muscles relaxing, he falls into my every contour like snow settling. He pulls back a little and looks at me. "I don't seem to have a choice. You are delicious, and my mouth waters when I think of you. I'm addicted." *To my sugar, my sweet, sweet sugar.*

"Thank you for my gifts," I whisper.

He kisses me deeply and the bag is kicked to the floor, momentarily forgotten. His breath is slow and forgiving. He waits for me to open up to him, then he crows softly.

"I've become a witch," I murmur sleepily.

"Hmm, have you now?"

Later I open the bag and find something else, my favorite toothpaste made from fennel, impossible to get here. The licorice taste is like a light-filled valley where spring has warmed the earth and brought out the first small green things. Just like those days when everything is right, when hope springs from the moist belly of the promised earth and tips toward me briefly, joy.

♐♒♐♒♐♒

Today there is a headstone moving ceremony for a Village Grandpa, or *Tsninnie,* who died months earlier. After a proper marker was chosen and carved by a family member, this ceremony for Clarence of the Stevenson Eagle Clan is the final goodbye. Matty asks me to come along.

"I didn't know him."

"His daughter, June, came to Maurice and Sandra Moore's Thanksgiving *doing,* and they're hosting the reception afterwards." At my blank look, she explains, "You ate a piece of June's *saalberry* pie, and even took some home."

The dessert has put me in June's debt. It's potlatch protocol—giving means getting back in kind. Not with objects but with deference. *Respect*. One is bonded to another by how generous one can be with one's possessions. I hardly think a piece of *saalberry* pie is worth an afternoon at the graveside, but protocol must be observed. Besides, staying home quivers with loneliness as Matty turns her back on me and slips back into the bedroom to prepare. The house will be too quiet, like the times my parents tried to pry me away from the television set to visit relatives, only to give up and leave me with the sudden silence and ticking clocks. My roommate has that same way of tweaking my comfort zone.

Minutes later we're in the front seat and Matty slams the car door enthusiastically. I realize this was all about getting a ride. The cemetery is at the far end of the Reserve and my roommate is currently without her bike, having lent hers to Colleen in exchange for a foot massage. She gives me a sly wink and then retreats into silence as we head off to the Reserve. We cross the divide into Old Masset and shortly afterward Jonah's house blurs by, the windows now completely obscured by Raven paintings. I wonder if he misses the sight of the sea churning gray and restless on the far side of the road.

"Cold day for putting up a headstone," Matty remarks into the lapels of her coat, eyeing a particularly large wave as it crashes with a lot of spray onto the stony beach. Then she pats my arm. "Don't worry, there'll be great food afterwards." There is some compensation: The Naani's are wonderful cooks so we can expect a table groaning with homemade fare.

Sandra and Maurice's Thanksgiving dinner had been particularly memorable, a mixture of local delicacies and traditional, Western-style foods. Matty brought me along at the last minute, explaining they had open arms for a stranger without family during the holidays. The Moores were comfortably situated: their large, ranch-style home had been built in the 1960s, close to the end of the peninsula, set back behind a split-rail fence and rough-mowed lawn. Constructed of red brick with white trim, the house had a solid, suburban feel to it. Unlike some of their neighbors', there were no clan markings or carvings. The border gardens were spare, hardy shrubs, and low-maintenance native plants. No trees, although they would have provided some much-needed windbreak. As was tradition, nothing could block the view of the sea. And like every other home on the Reserve, the long backyard was cleared down to short scrub, keeping the forest at arm's length.

Inside, the big open front room was warm and bustling with activity. The gift pies sat on a table in a long row just inside the door as if to trumpet the lavishness of the upcoming spread. Besides traditional *saalberry,* there was blueberry, strawberry cream, rhubarb, pumpkin, cherry and pecan. Because good quality ice cream was hard to get in town and cost the earth, this had been Matty's and my offering. It was quickly taken and stored in the kitchen freezer. Sandra and Maurice greeted me warmly enough, but we were the only outsiders. The other guests eyed me curiously.

There were fourteen of us at a table that stretched from the living room clear through to the open kitchen. By the end of the first course I was so stuffed I had to pick my way through the piece of pie Maurice urged on me. The *saalberries* were small and a little bit crunchy, but the flavor was satisfyingly tart.

As the meal began, Maurice, who was carving up the enormous turkey and handing out platters of breast and thigh, asked me what I was doing on the Island. Sooner or later they all asked. I shrugged. "Oh, just visiting," was my usual response. Someone looked over at me knowingly. I'd only started dating Jonah but it was clear everyone had heard the gossip.

"You know," started Maurice as he leaned toward me conspiratorially, "the first white man to come here we kept for a while." He kept me in his gaze like a trapped bird, the carving knife hovering above a delicately steaming turkey breast.

"Come on, Maurice," chided one of the Aunties. "We're hungry. We don't have time for your stories."

I passed on the potatoes.

"No, really," he went on, his white teeth gleaming as he grinned at me. "It's a funny story, actually. More like a joke." The others went silent as Maurice kept his focus on me. "You see, back a couple of hundred years or so ago, this sailor was stranded on the Island because his ship had gone aground. Seems no one else survived the wild embrace of our neighborly sea." He glanced toward the curtained window as if for a touch point. "This man came out of the water, cold, wet and hungry, so of course we invited him to stay." Then he smiled again. "Kept him prisoner, more like, until we could figure out what to do with him."

An uncomfortable silence around the table gradually gave way to murmured conversation as the others tried to ignore Maurice. Their voices were accompanied by a distinct clatter of silverware as they dug into their food. But Maurice had the stage and I was his audience. He put down the knife and forgot about the turkey, rubbing his hands together as if we were about to share some enormous amount of fun. I wanted to turn away but Matty shot me a warning look.

I should have expected this. How many of the villagers had been humiliated over the centuries, waiting for their chance to dig into these impossibly humorless strangers? I gave him my attention, and

Maurice picked up the pace. "Anyway, once he'd dried off and been fed for a few days the man did something that the villagers thought was pretty amazing! He would stand on the beach and suddenly brush up his leg and a bit of fire would appear on the end of a small stick and then he would light another bigger stick and put it in his mouth. The others thought this was a neat trick so they tried picking up sticks and doing the same thing." He glanced over at me, eyebrows raised. "Of course, nothing happened, so they got really mad and tried to kill him. They said something was wrong with him because he had fire coming out of his ass!" He waited for a second to deliver the punch line. "And that was when the sailor pulled the box of matches out of his pocket!" At this, Maurice sat back and laughed heartily. When the others ignored him Matty gave an exaggerated yawn, burped, and said to the table, "Excuse me!" Then everyone else joined in.

Our host leaned toward his plate, speared a big piece of turkey and raised it to his mouth. "They killed him after they took his matches," he finished. "He couldn't fish or make a canoe so he was just another mouth to feed and they couldn't afford to keep him." Then he turned to me, still congenial. "Our people were much too nice after that. They should have killed off all the whites while they still had the chance." He gave an exaggerated wink just to show there were no hard feelings. Matty rolled her eyes at him and Maurice roared with laughter.

As we near the graveyard I can still feel the humiliation. But my obligation isn't to Maurice or Sandra, but to Auntie June who brought the *saalberry* pie, who pressed it on me after the meal as if by apology, wrapping it in a tea towel and telling me to keep the plate. It is her father who is to be honored today and Matty hasn't forgotten the glass pie dish in our kitchen cupboard.

"Do June and her family know I'm coming?" I ask. I sometimes wonder if Matty enjoys seeing me skewered by the famous Haida humor. The knife edge of their sarcasm sharpens wits and keeps the game in play. We are navigating a deeply rutted road at the far end of the village. The wind is howling by the beach, but as we move into the forest it quiets, dampened by mossy trees and dense underbrush. If Matty hears my question, she chooses to ignore it. Suddenly she points. "Here! Turn here!" The car churns over damp earth down a barely discernable path. I can feel the sea seeping upwards from deep underneath.

"Bodies must rot here pretty quickly," I remark as we pull up to join the other cars. Matty strides ahead, refreshed by the quiet, misty air. We soon reach a knot of people standing around a gravesite. The newly carved marker has been trucked over and placed at the head. The earth is still smudged around the base, marred by big tire marks filled in with rainwater. We are the only outsiders at the gravesite. "How well did you know Clarence?" I whisper to Matty.

"Well enough." she replies, bounding ahead and taking her place reverently by Naani Rose, who has come out for the occasion. Rose is wearing her bear hat, or rather a stuffed toy bear she de-stuffed and pinned securely to the crown of her neatly coifed hair, forepaws dangling above her eyebrows. She smiles wickedly over at me.

The reverend speaks reverently about Clarence, who was a good Christian. Everyone holds hands and circles the grave. The old woman next to me feels like a *murelette,* a little beach bird they used to catch and cook whole. Naani told me they were still a favorite dish. "We boil them good until the bones are soft, then we just eat them."

"Whole?"

"Yes, whole. Bones and all."

Soon a little cloud of fog hugs the earth around us. Somewhere out beyond the forest the sea is crashing and a tempest is blowing. But in this silence I see and hear every one of the dead. They never leave this place. My fate is much less clear.

♐♒♐♒♐♒

Now that an election is coming you can tell how the territory lies. It begins and ends where Jonah's red *Raven Talk* posters have been tacked next his opponent's simpler versions: "Re-elect George." Together they are fixed onto every telephone pole in Old Masset, stopping abruptly at the Village edge, yipping from trees like dogs worrying a vast divide.

Within the Reserve, everyone has taken sides, displaying their choice with silk-screened signs on sticks and in windows. Nothing is gaudy or overdone. *Yahguudaang,* or moderation and ritual observance, is still considered an important quality in a leader. On the other side of the invisible divide that crosses the highway, the signs end. That's Haida business, not town business.

A winter chill has settled in, so the divide seems strengthened by heads tucked out of sight in mufflers and high collars. In New Masset, there is little talk of the Haida election. After all, the town has its own mayor and an elected council who decide when new sidewalks will be built and how to clean up the ever-present trash. The Chief Councilor of the Reserve will concern himself with matters that will have no effect on most of their lives.

Jonah darkens at the prospect of such notions. "They should be teaching more Haida history and our language in the school. There is only one school for the two communities and it's under B.C. authority."

Paulie, who hangs around Jonah a lot, is over at the house again and looks up from his dinner at this remark. He dropped by tonight, being that there's no business at the Lodge and he heard there was good food cooking in Jonah's pot. I still haven't met Paulie's wife but I hear she likes town life. She and the kids don't come around much.

"That's a tough one," says Paulie with a mouth full of bread. He cocks his head, worrying the idea a little. He studies the trio of diminutive hens Jonah has roasted in tangerine sauce. He picks up a tiny drumstick in his huge hands and tears at it with the delicacy of a surgeon. "I'd have a tough time learning it," he adds, then recoils at something he sees in Jonah's expression. He lowers his eyes. "I mean, I'm not happy it's disappearing, but what can you do?" Having taken the safe road, he quickly shifts his attention to the steaming plate before him. The hens are sweet, skin crackling and melting into the roasted vegetables.

We both know Jonah is right in theory. The Haida language is like nothing else on earth. It came to them long ago, perhaps even before they crossed the Bering Sea in their canoes and took these islands for their own. It was the time of the Ice Age, thin dribbles of barren land and little food. In their solitude language came, sounds with meaning and subtle inflection, defining the universe long before they knew their vulnerability, before it was necessary to explain themselves. The word *Haida* means people. I am *Xaadee*. Here is *sqa'anlong,* the sister of my father. And that is *guulaas* (abalone) over here, a *gligu,* digging stick. The sky is one word and the land is another. No more explanation was necessary. Their language can help you understand why a fish jumps, the true meaning of a woman's flow, the hidden seasons of the moon. The sound is like the sand and the sea, separate and fused, endlessly twisting back toward itself against the roof of the mouth, gravel mixing with a rushing onslaught of emotion. Even harder to master are the clicks of tongue and throat, for within them is a cry or a whisper, a howl, a song.

With a quick peck on the cheek, Jonah takes off after dinner, leaving us to clean the dishes. "I guess you and I are the housewives tonight," Paulie observes wistfully before settling into the task, beefy elbows immersed in soapsuds.

Jonah has gone to a war council meeting, preparing for the last round of speeches he will make at various functions. There's a *doing* this Saturday, to honor one of the elders.

"Hey, is Jonah taking you to the party?" Paulie asks, carefully placing Jonah's blue china plates in the drying rack.

"Yes, Paulie."

We finish the dishes in silence, each wondering what Jonah is doing with his cronies while we carefully put the kitchen back to order, hanging the teacups and collecting the food scraps for the compost box.

Kokol from Masset

♐♒♐♒♐♒

"I remember these little baskets. We used to get them at Easter."

"Shhh!" Jonah turns back toward Harold Winter, the guest of honor for whom we are all gathered. The old man's words are soft as he stands in front of the microphone on the stage. "It is a great honor to have you all here to share this day with me." He surveys us all with pleasure.

Small baskets shaped like upside-down hats are handed out with great ceremony, the first of many *kokol*, or gifts, distributed today. Made of woven yellow plastic with small carrying handles, they are so retro I can't believe someone is still making them. Such a basket is just like the one I discovered behind the sofa during an Easter egg hunt at my aunt's house when I was seven. I believed it then to be the most beautiful, precious object ever devised and the idea that it should be discarded along with the violet nesting tissue and pale blue ribbon was just too much to bear. Now they seem like cheap refuse for the landfill.

I put my hand on Jonah's thigh and he shifts uncomfortably. One of the Naanis eyes me appraisingly, motioning toward a chocolate swirl cake. "I think you need a little fattening up, dear," she says, pushing it over. "Jonah, you're letting her get too thin!"

Jonah purses his lips and stares determinedly at Harold, who has the microphone firmly in hand and is reminiscing about his early life and the many friends he's made along the way. It wasn't until I'd gotten to the Hall that I knew the *doing* was for Harold's birthday. I would have asked Jonah earlier what the occasion was, but like many Haida gatherings, internal communication is purposefully obscured to outsiders.

A huge pile of gifts grows even larger with every passing host. Tea towels, more woven baskets, oven mitts, can openers, plastic strainers—some things we both get as a couple, some items are reserved for Jonah alone as a member of the Raven clan. An Eagle is throwing this party so Ravens get more stuff than the Eagles. It makes for a lot of gratitude later on and it's only good when the other side carries the burden.

Being that I'm not of any clan, at least not yet, I get the general giveaways. They pop onto my lap at intervals. The hosts, Harold's children, nieces, cousins, are giving the party and they haul shopping bags up and down the long rows of tables, digging down occasionally to brandish a shiny new aluminum object. I take each offering and carefully place it on the pile next to my plate.

With drumming fanfare, the Rainbow dancers file out onto the floor. One strikingly beautiful woman is wearing a stiff crown of white goose feathers and she carries a large hollow reed filled with clouds of eagle's down. Bits of it cling to her headdress and fall like snow with every shake of her head. It is the traditional welcome to an important chief dance, a great tribute to the guest of honor, and all eyes are on the group. They begin drumming and some of the people get up to do a Raven dance, including Jonah. I know the steps; the right foot goes here and then hands are bent behind, making the wings, then the head cocks, as if to listen. I've seen it a hundred times. I want to join in but cannot. I blush hotly, remembering my run-in with Sgaana.

"Hey, so I hear you're Jonah's girl!" calls a Naani I haven't met. The speeches are done and someone is playing country and western records over the loudspeaker. "He's a wild one, that boy," she shouts over the noise. I know she's referring to me. "It's the red hair," I retort tartly. "You have always loved red hair!" She laughs heartily. It's true about the red hair. The Haida occasionally used to produce a red-headed child, an exotic color usually accompanied by light green eyes. This combination was considered a good omen.

I turn back toward Jonah, who has returned briefly to get a drink. He gives me a quick kiss and gets up to join the informal council of advisors with whom he has lately begun to keep company. Children jump noisily over the downed balloons, weaving in and out of the girls who are now busy bringing out pots of stew and heaps of butter-top rolls.

None of my Town neighbors are here. I search around vainly for a familiar face. The Naanis are alone, their men gone off to some pow-wow or another, maybe to smoke a cigarette or swig a beer outside. Each old woman in her turn eyes me appraisingly. Across the table, Naani Sandra, whom I have only spoken to once before, suddenly looks straight over toward me. She is ancient, thin and very wrinkled.

A blue and red felt killer whale hat balances miraculously over a crown of thick, silver hair.

"Rose tells me you've been taking her shopping," she remarks.

"Twice a week. The bags are getting too cumbersome for the long walk."

She nods, slowly, her hands resting lightly on the table. She seems beyond the need for food, and it sits untouched as a mockery to the days when she had teeth. As with all the ancient ones here, she gives back all that she has taken over the years, as a lizard sheds its skin. Her breath returns now more than it takes, makes the air richer; the land soaks back her buttery smell and the moist air, thousands of tears. "Jonah will be Chief, you know." She need only make this pronouncement for it to be true.

"Yes." I look away to where he is conferring. In spite of tousled hair and the rose suspenders, he has an air of authority. Naani Sandra reaches out with a gift-wrapped dishtowel. "Here, you take this." It's a clan gift and I hesitate, knowing my place. She laughs. "I don't do dishes myself anymore. Lots of grandkids to do that sort of thing, and we have more towels than we know what to do with."

I accept the cloth and fold it into a square. Iron it flat with my hands.

"He's lucky to have you," she says then, watching me neatly place the towel with our other things. "The last one wasn't much for settling down."

I wish she would say this in front of Jonah but I know it will never happen. These are female secrets, fastened tightly into a clean white cocoon spun from many such conversations. A place of retreat and comfort. It is the job of women to wrap each other tightly in these vaulted rooms where glory and wisdom are but impediments to peace, as inconsequential as dreams. When the sea beats down the shore and the men do not return, these dreams are left in place of memory.

Later Jonah wants to make love on his bed of carpets but I cannot forget the basket of objects, now mine. I take them out while he watches: the periwinkle glass paperweight, six kitchen utensils, and an egg timer. I line these and all the rest up on the table, admiring them.

"It's just a lot of cheap stuff," he laughs, unfastening my hair.

I carefully study a wooden spoon while he shakes the thick knot of hair at the nape of my neck, combing his fingers through it down my back. As he buries his mouth to smell it, I watch the light change in the paperweight, deepening the blue shadows within. His hands come around my waist and move upwards, flowing around my ribcage like strong water. I feel the weakness coming on but my eyes cannot leave the soft towels jumbled together in bright colors. He strokes my back, cupping and coaxing water from the deep spring now so familiar.

The objects float before me, sharp edges and soft curves.

"They're all for you," he whispers, rubbing up between the silk folds of my skirt. "All for you." Turning me around, he pushes the hair away from my face. "I know what I am doing."

I see the rising up in his eyes.

"Yes."

Later, when the fire begins to sleep for the night, as fires do when the damper has been turned down just low enough to please the wood, the evening air finally mixes in, drifting in and trying to find its place. "We will live here together," Jonah mumbles sleepily, his breath like young breath against my hair. Soft and regular. When I was no more than five years old I used to spend whole afternoons along Fossil Creek, a bog that ran behind our summer cottage. Somehow the creek's passage to the sea had been long ago blocked and lack of current left it sluggishly trapped in a large circle, finally coming back into itself where it was driven underground. I liked to go back there because no one ever came. The silence was the only real thing I understood.

Jonah stirs. I look up to where the tabletop rises like a high ridge above the valley floor, statuesque in the dark. My objects are still there, lined up neatly, witness to a consummation.

How much of it is mine, truly mine, I wonder.

Fishing

♐♒♐♒♐♒

The salmon are running again and even though I am laid low by a heavy period, I go with Phil down to a secret place just south of the Cumshewa Inlet to fish. Reports are this run is a good one and the big fish promise to put up a good fight. Kim has lent me his rod and tackle, a beautiful set with inlaid abalone handles.

"Lot of people throw them back," the dentist tells me as the truck bumps over an old pitted logging road. We swerve often to avoid overgrown holly bushes and wild brush. "They just do it for the sport." As we turn into a small dent in the bush, I wonder why anyone would want to do such a thing. I have only hunted and fished up here and can't see the point if your quarry doesn't end up on the dinner table.

The Copper River is deep-furrowed, swift. We decamp by the stony shores of one of the only straight-aways, where I crouch and watch the furious current gouge into floor pockets and muscle around large boulders. No doubt they've been pushed down river since the day they fell in. That's the way it is with these rivers. Either they will push you to the sea or wear you down until you are as the sand.

"Watch you don't fall in," warns Phil as he hands me a pair of waders.

"If you do and your boots fill up you'll sink to the bottom and get sucked out of reach before I can help you."

I take a look around. The sun, which earlier had made a watery showing, has disappeared behind a foggy upper rim. Things look like shit in this weather. The trees are soggy, dripping brackish mist, deadened limbs too cold even for insects. The birds are hiding out, probably trying to consolidate supplies for the winter ahead. The ground looks inviting only to snakes; root cords slither under my feet as we navigate through soggy underbrush and black mire. We stop to study the water as we put on our gear. It's churning brown, with foamy patches of dark green from the undercurrent. The fish must have a hell of a time pushing upstream; no wonder they have the strength to fight a hook.

Phil notices me grimacing. "What's the matter?"

"Girl stuff."

He gives me a mock-serious look. "You should have told me you were bleeding."

"What do you mean?" My head is aching now and I'm in no mood to be trifled with.

"The Haida say a woman in menses is bad luck for fishing."

"You gotta be friggin' kidding me!"

"Listen, if I were a proper man I'd tell you to disappear. You may have already put a curse on the fishing today. The Haida keep their women out of important business, away from their tools."

"I'm not Haida and I'll grab your damn rod in a second and fling it in the stream if you don't shut up!" I wish I had some aspirin. An ache in the top of my head is joining the rising chorus of pain now and I'm regretting this whole trip. "You're all just afraid of us." I go on, stomping forward. "We have the secret to God Almighty and life itself down there and you're scared shitless of all that power."

Shrugging, he moves off, putting some distance between us. "Suit yourself," he calls back toward me and then turns his attention to the fish. The river is running very fast. I look over toward my companion but resist asking for advice on where to put my line. If they haven't already, the fish will sense our presence. If focus is turned upwards toward the other universe where the mouth breathers live, they will be too cagy to fall for a dry fly skimming across the borderland.

I cast my first fly, trying to avoid a tangle of dead roots over on the far bank. I know from what I'd learned the last time I'd been out with Phil that the roots mean there is probably a complex trough down there somewhere, a small eddy, a break from the relentless current. The fish will rest here. Maybe eat.

Phil, hat shoved down over his flowing mane, moves up ahead and disappears around the northward bend. What I miss he will catch, reeling in and casting again, letting the bluebottle drift and sink a little before playing with it.

In a sound landscape filled with the rushing and gurgling of the river, I try to listen for the salmon. My bluebottle dances on the surface, a brightly colored sapphire just within reach. For extra security I have smeared it with *eulachon* grease from a small vial Dobie pressed to me before I left. "Good for a bad cold, or to catch fish," he instructed. It stinks like rotting carrion, even though it's from small fish they take by the thousands from the sea and boil in huge clay-lined pits. Just boil and boil it until it reduces down to a small amount of rancid, dense fat. The bottle leaks a little, and already I smell worse than a fish carcass.

I move up slightly to where I can see another shift in the riverbed geography, another promising cavern where they might pool temporarily before moving on. I can't reach the middle of the spot, so I turn to make sure Phil is still gone. Still gone. The spot looks good, inviting almost. The ground is pebbly but firm. I venture in a little, shifting my weight so I can feel each stone. Curl my toes around them. Nothing slips, so I rest. I can feel the full power of the river against me now, pushing my boots flat to my jeans. Cast out, the fly hits the tiny quiet spot where the water is resting between rocks and the remains of an old beaver dam.

Old bluebottle waits. Then something snaps at it and before I can pull back, the line yanks violently downwards and the pole nearly frees itself. But it's not enough, the fish is strong—I get a glimpse of it as it flips toward the surface and then dives. The sudden change of direction pulls the rod over my left shoulder and as I twist around my foot slips and loses its grip on the rocks. Flailing, rod clenched in my grasp, I fall backwards and sideways into the shallow water. A rush of black, silty water shoots up my legs and under my jacket. The cold shock nearly stops my heart. I'm on my ass, boots transforming into anchors. The mass of everything swallows me up. Somehow I'm still hanging onto the pole and the fish takes me down. I grope for the first trough, no bottom; my body is as black as the river now, and I hear someone, Phil, shouting to let go of the rod. Not the rod, the one I borrowed from Kim. The water gags in my mouth, tears at my eyes and I bob momentarily, caught between this world and that, the rushing in my ears like cold blood flowing, trying to get inside my skin. Something strong yanks the rod away from me. I think it's the fish, or the river claiming my folly, but it then tries to pull off the top of my head and it's Phil freeing the rod and the Steelhead, and he's got me by the hair. Shit, you must be strong, I decide dreamily, blackly like my world, the river, made up of the black soul of the earth come to life.

"Ow!" I jerk my legs down and hit bottom, and shove off, trying to move toward the same direction as my hair. Anything to stop the pain. With a powerful thrust I push upward. Legs and arms piston, breaking the surface like a breaching whale, water streaming off the red and the green and the greasy eulachon stains. He gets me by the chest and drags me toward the bank, swearing and cursing in Japanese.

"I told you about the goddamn boots and the goddamn current!" he screams. We tumble onto the dry bank, boots cascading water in big slushy coughs. Then Phil starts laughing and we roll together to keep warm, laughing and shivering.

"Let's get back into the truck."

I look out toward the river, where the fish have won today. "But I lost Kim's rod."

Phil hauls me up. Everything hurts through the bone-chilling sod of my clothes. "Tough for you." He does not mention my menses or the curse it might have put on me.

Later he turns away shyly as I strip out of the wet things and put on a dry pair of thermal underwear.

The ferry captain/fish warden laughs when he sees me, shivering in the truck.

"Screw you," I mouth silently.

"Nothing today," Phil says with a straight face as we roll down the window.

Later, when Jonah caresses my belly I tell him about Phil's warning.

"He was right."

I turn over and start to curl up like a worm in salt. "Jonah, the pain is enough. Do you honestly believe my blood will contaminate you?"

"You can't change a thousand years of wisdom just because it doesn't feel right to you. In the old days women were considered at their most powerful when they came of age and bled. It meant their bodies were mature enough to have children. Her *tagwaná*, or time of seclusion, began: She was taken to a house prepared especially for this event, wrapped in a cloak made from the inner bark of cedar and her face painted. She was made to lie quiet and to fast. It was forbidden for her to lay eyes on any man, or to touch the fishing nets or tools of the hunt. It was then that her *sgaan*, the sister of her father, the woman who had cut the umbilical cord the day she was born, would come and initiate her into the secrets of womanhood."

His hand reaches back around my waist and caresses the taut skin over my pelvis, gently pushing downwards, coaxing the blood to flow. His voice is a sweet whisper in my ear, teasing now. I feel him hardening against the small of my back. "Here in this quiet place, with the sweet smell of freshly cut cedar around her, the secrets of her gender were revealed, the role she would be expected to fulfill as a wife. How to please a man so that he would give her many children. They said her powers were now supernatural and these powers should never be wasted. And so her *sgaan* would sit by her side softly murmuring these lessons, stroking her breast as if to quiet a trembling bird. The knowledge flowed into her body as it had into the marrow of a thousand generations before her."

He runs his hands up the side of my waist and gently turns me over. "Many children are good for a woman's body. The Naanis say that a woman grows healthier with each one and old age is less painful." His hands encircle the warmth and pain, now drowsy and distant. His voice floats somewhere in the darkness and I feel the outside of my skin pulsing. "To me you are beautiful like this. Vulnerable." His face glows in the darkness, lips curving upwards. "Even though my father would turn in his grave to hear me say this, I'm not afraid of your blood. And I have no fear of your womanhood."

We flow on its promise. We flow in its abundance.

♐♒♐♒♐♒

This is an old book, the one I'm gazing at. Deep down in the picture on the second page are colors like attic silks, burnt by time into a mysterious other, indefinable but recognizable. Perhaps it is only memory that plays these tricks.

Our Christmastime street is bathed in the eggplant light of this picture; my eye is drawn to all the fine detail: yellow globes of streetlight misting into the still night, the squares of life in each house, all noise and clatter as dinner is being set, plans made. Holding a plate of mince pies I stand for a moment on our stoop, no, a little further out, where I can see all my neighbors in one slow sweep, watching for them each and separately, breathing their oh-yes-come-eat-now, it-does-smell-good lives into mine. I have found this memory at last.

"Coming?" Matty is bundled up like a bag lady, bits of cotton tubing slinging dangerously close to the chocolate cake she has refused to cover. The neat cylinder of my prized pan has produced, under her care, an object tilting off to one side, winking at me from one of the hundreds of silver balls sprinkled, poked and spilled onto the goo she calls icing. She turns and her boots crunch on new ice, the evening's work of three slushy, mild days.

"Jesus, don't slip!" I cry out.

She ignores me. Out on the lawn in a tentative trailing of blue-patterned china, with each doted-upon offering in kind, we come like great kings bearing local delicacies. I follow well to the rear, watching for hidden obstacles. The moon is fully out; we have not repeated our witchery. Perhaps not all of our wishes came true. But then I think of Jonah, who will surely be waiting in the warm rooms, and blush at my good fortune. The goddess has granted me some favor these past weeks. Since his return from Ketchikan he has been hungry, but not too greedy. I am reminded of the Babylonian word *shappatu*. The quieting of the heart.

Boots stored, I wander through the crowded kitchen made hazy with steam billowing and pots sizzling. Harry hands me a dishtowel. "Get that coat off so you can help me with this mess." Matty bears my plate onward to the dessert table. "Lovely!" he remarks as it passes by. He winks, and for some reason I think of the bath I took there three days ago when I was as scruffy as a street dog and needed pampering. His tub is as big as the sea, green water floating toward green walls. White towels like the soft backs of swans all folded up and waiting for me to wrap and wrap forever. The scent of lemongrass clinging somewhere close. The aroma is still clinging to my hair.

I labor now over his collection of dishes, each one different yet part of a whole. The plentiful colors blend into one another along with heavy industrial utensils and big cooking pots. Guests stream in bearing food and disappear into the front room to socialize. "You look settled, Ellie," sighs Harry. I glance fondly at his ruddy profile.

The green plate is dried and then the yellow, and the tomato red to follow. I want them to last and last, all wrapped up in the smell of thyme and bubbling lemon sauce, braised pork chops so tenderly small they will fit into my mouth in one satisfying bite.

"You can go," he whispers as he spots his latest muse, a mustachioed nurse all done up in a salmon parka and wooly socks. I hand the new visitor my dishtowel.

"Your turn."

Not long after I am into the food Jonah arrives with Sgaana. He is wearing a brocade vest, a gift from the Mainland. His shirt is crisply ironed, curved around a mauve silk tie. He looks big and prosperous.

"This is for you. I have loads more but this one couldn't wait." He folds a small box into my palm. It seems like a dream, this Victorian room all done up with garlands of cranberries, paper hats and Christmas crackers, candy corn trains and silk poinsettias. The deep-blue box in my hand, the man before me in finely woven threads from the city. He guides me over to the big leather chair, now nestled between the fireplace and a big blue spruce festooned in lights and tinfoil angels. The fire pops a little, then groans, letting go of a log. Falling down, settling as quiet ash.

I open the box. Inside, lying on a small gold square of China silk, is a pin. A woman's face, the color of sweet cream, all afternoon and buttery. Thick masses of russet hair, floating on what looks to be a blue wave crossing through. The eyes are wise and watchful.

"You made this?"

"It's you, Elle. The woman who looks over the horizon." His hand is warm and certain, there by my elbow. I feel it wanting to caress, to remember.

I take the pin out and clumsily open the back. His initials are carved into the fired clay. J.D. He pins it to my sweater. A totem for the impossible clan found between this and that, the somewhere and the nowhere. I look toward his eyes, the nose of ancestral memory, not so very much like a Viking nose after all. Everything is so mixed up and crazy, so serenely falling into place, but wait, oh do wait. Rest a while.

He kisses my forehead and moves off, now tethered safely in the engulfing room.

"How beautiful!" They all admire my gift over the small canapés of smoked salmon, the thick dreamy slices of marinated nor'easter scallops, the roast beef and *saalberry* compote. We live richly.

Jonah and I pose for pictures, sandwiched between Naanis and laughing children, their eyes reflected in the flashbulbs, hands full of whirligigs and toy soldiers, balsa-wood planes soaring. Later Jonah folds my gift to him, a handwritten poem, into a carved box he keeps by his bed.

♐♒♐♒♐♒

The daily grind of trying to create print-worthy stories out of Town Council meetings as interesting as watching paint dry is starting to get to me. So far no drunken holiday revelers arrested. Maybe on New Year's Eve someone will shoot a gun off into the inlet and piss off the neighbors. One can only hope.

I lie in bed and cast about for something to focus on for next week's issue.

Judy calls on Tuesday to discuss our story options. I've been out harvesting beached scallops and lobster traps torn up by this morning's strong nor'easter.

"I want you to do a piece on Moresby," she says. "The government is beginning to get their backs up over the Watchmen's refusal to let them administer the park."

"Listen, Jude, this is a really sticky situation for me."

I can hear her stabbing her pencil into the desk. "Sticky or not, I want you to get in there, use your political connections and find out what's really going on." She is referring to a radical manifesto released by the enforcer wing of the Council stating, unequivocally, the Watchmen were prepared to restrict access to the park "at any cost."

"Okay, whatever you say." I hang up the phone and shove it under a sofa cushion.

Outside my window the trees are bending. Oh, God, this is a political nightmare. I wonder if I'll be able to write anything that doesn't offend the Haida Nation and still maintains some semblance of objectivity. I should just stay out of it.

After a long, torturous delay I finally call Sgaana, who is the official spokesman for the Watchmen. He is surprisingly gracious on the phone. "Come by my house tomorrow," he suggests. His cabin sits on an isolated spit of land north of town, and very few are invited to visit.

That night I bring the pail of scallops over to Jonah's for dinner. I pry one open and sever the abductor muscle to release the top shell. It looks good and plump, as big as my palm, round, smooth and milky white. Under the experimental prod of my knife it draws inward sharply, trying to pull itself closed. I caress the muscular surface and feel it give beneath my touch, rippling and contracting, searching for safety.

We shuck and split them into quarters, browning the pieces in butter and lemon. They are poured in a steaming bowl of black squid-ink pasta, as black as the new urgent signs Jonah is painting and nailing up around the Reserve: **For real change! For action!**

No visitors are invited for dinner so we eat until we can eat no more. Later, Jonah washes the stiff, salt mist from my hair and curls it up in rags.

Two days later I'm headed down to the office. Fair weather for traveling; the morning slipped in like a lamb and light rain melted the last of the ice and made short work of the remaining snow. The sun makes a brief appearance, even as the air is taking a cold turn. The day can change fast here, with fog, sleet, wind. My commute to the paper is fifty miles and today there is not another soul on the road. I glance at the tape recorder on the seat beside me and consider my options. The threat from Sgaana is on there, plain and simple.

He kept close to me as we sat in his living room the afternoon before. Though modest, his cottage had no wasted space—all available surfaces were fitted for the purpose of study and work. Haida art and sculptures hung on the walls, or sat on display tables. What appeared to be a comprehensive collection of religion and philosophy books, many of them old and well used, filled the floor-to-ceiling bookcases. Two large, unadorned windows on the west wall provided an open vista to the shoreline beyond. On this day the sea was blue, the sky clear. If there was a stove, I couldn't see it in my brief scan of the room and a chill hung in the air. There was an *au naturel* feel to the atmosphere as if its occupant wanted to stay in tune with the weather outside.

Upon my first question about the validity of the issue between the Haida and the government, he set the tone. He cocked his head and looked at me quizzically. "I don't know how it could be any clearer," he answered. "We stopped the logging, now we want everyone to stay out."

I tried another tack. "Yes, I understand. But is there any compromise possible between your two positions?"

He leaned back and stared at me. "Why is it that you white people always talk about compromise when you really mean we should give in?" Then he smiled pleasantly, as if to show he wasn't bothered by such naiveté. His dark hair and oiled beard smelled of patchouli, and as he draped his arm across the sofa back between us, it was with pure muscular grace. "As far as the Watchmen are concerned, we are through negotiating." He lowered his head a little and regarded me with an ease that made me feel like prey.

I focused on the tape recorder, determined not to let the interview get away from me. "I want to know more about your organization.... Not everyone on the Island understands its mission. Can't you request a joint venture with the park rangers?"

"Ah, yes, this matter of the Watchmen needing *permission*." Though his smile remained, his expression was impenetrable. "As you well know, the Watchmen have begun a campaign to document all the valuable sites on the Islands and it is our right to protect them as we see fit. And since our partnership with the Canadian Government hasn't been particularly helpful, we're not waiting for permission anymore."

He turned and pointed to a collection of coffee-table style volumes on a nearby shelf.

"You see those beautiful books? Our history was stolen from us and published by outsiders. This will end. The Watchmen will protect what is ours, and that includes all that we were and all that we will become." He swiveled back so we were facing each other, as in the moment before battle. His presence seemed to fill the small room.

"Our stories are our history, and they belong to us alone. We reserve the right to tell them in the time and manner we choose."

The hairs on the back of my neck rose up. Could Naani Rose have said something about my shack people questions? Surely not Matty? I felt a weak relief at not ever having brought it up with Jonah.

He took a deep breath and leaned toward me. "Do you not agree?"

"Without analysis, history becomes subjective."

"Isn't all history subjective?" he replied, glancing back to his book collection. "In your world, past events are subject to the sensibilities of current values and morals—whatever is popular at the moment. Their value changes accordingly." He drew a slow circle in the air. "But our timeline is endless, and I prefer to think of it as a living thing, folding back into itself in ways you could never imagine. Our lives and the earth that sustains us are full of magic, mystery, and immortality." He leaned back and crossed his arms. "And that's something you people have never understood."

In the silence that followed I broke free of his gaze. I'd gotten nothing useful for my story.

He reached his hand out and it slid along the back of the couch toward me, resting a whisper away from my shoulder. "I know you have a job to do," he said, "and I'm very glad you came to discuss the subject of the Watchmen with me. As we move forward I appreciate the trust that will build between us and caution you to be careful not to misrepresent the truth. Or dig around into matters that have no relevance to our lives in these challenging times." He stood up, signaling the interview was over.

"Thanks for taking the time to see me."

He smiled. "My pleasure. Perhaps, when you have finished the rough draft of your article, you could let me review it for *inaccuracies*." And with that, he took my elbow and steered me toward the door. "I know you are trying to be as fair as possible."

Once home I played back the tape with growing dismay. Was I asleep? There seemed to be long silences in between his answers, and my muted questions were impossible to make out. The crackling of shifting movement, and a strange hiss of unknown origin obscured what little Sgaana did say. Even so, none of the substantive questions in my notes were asked, or answered.

Judy will be expecting some momentum on this story and I don't know what to tell her. Making the long way down south to the office, my mind starts to drift, searching for an opening sentence to an article that will compensate for the lack of overall substance. Just then another car appears on the flat horizon, coming up toward me. I tap the brakes, unconsciously, and the car starts to fishtail ever so slightly. Before I can do anything else, the oncoming vehicle gets bigger, filling up the other side of the empty road. My back end is swerving now back and forth, crazily out of control.

Everything that happens next is in the muted and quiet trance of an animal caught in the jaws of death: Careening sideways, the car dives head first into a big deer ditch and flips end over end, then rolls over. The car and I, for we have become one, crash into a row of bushes. Bits of glass shower down on me, then the car flips sideways, hits the soft embankment and then tumbles down into a salt chuck, bouncing once and then coming to rest, right side up in the black water.

Sound rushes back into the void. The water is silty and freezing cold. I'm still buckled into the seatbelt; everything inside looks untouched. The radio is quiet. I unbuckle and clamber onto the hood of the car, looking around. I'm alive. Somewhere distant, a woman is keening, high pitched and open ended. It gets louder just as I slip into the water and wade to shore. Her head bobs into view above the broken bushes and freshly gouged earth.

"Ohmygodohmygod!" she keeps wailing over and over, staring transfixed as I clamber up the steep, muddy pitch, hands grabbing onto whatever vegetation I can for help. I heave up and over the edge.

She finally gains her wits. "Are you all right!? Is there anyone else?"

The air is freezing; she seems oblivious to my wet clothes and the danger of hypothermia. Maybe she's in shock. I move toward her. "I need to get somewhere warm!" I say urgently. The woman backs off a little, then turns to look at her car. She is not wearing a coat either. "I'm on my way to Masset to catch a plane," she stammers. "I..." Her expression is wild. "If I don't go now, I'll miss it."

At the same time, we hear a sound and turn toward a distant truck, belching black smoke. Clearly relieved, she jumps onto the road, arms waving wildly. It's a garbage truck. Honking the horn, the driver downshifts and then I see the black ice on the road. I pull her roughly back. "Watch out!"

We skitter back and the truck slides by us, gears grinding. Bits of refuse whirl in its wake. We run over and I open the door.

"I've had an accident. Can you get me to a farmhouse?" I ask the driver.

Behind me the woman stands silent, white hands still tugging at the sweater across her chest. He looks at me, then her, then reaches over and pulls me up by the arm. The door closes. The woman disappears from view. In the rearview mirror her car is a small gray dot on the horizon.

At the house where the garbage man leaves me, an older couple supply me with warm clothes and the use of their telephone.

"Jude, I'll be a little late." I'm still shivering. She grunts and asks nothing.

Jonah answers his phone on the first ring.

"My car's totaled. Come and get me at the paper," I say and hang up without another word. Later I find out he took a convoy of RCMP down to the site and surveyed the damage and found the soggy remains of my backpack and purse. By the time he collects me I've rewritten two smaller stories and dried my clothes at the local laundromat.

"You're shaking," he whispers, cradling me in his big coat.

My hands in his are bits of salted leather.

"I let Judy down on the Moresby Park story. I didn't have enough material and I lost all my interviews." The tape recorder is now buried at the bottom of the salt chuck, Sgaana's threatening words lost. I wanted to have Jonah listen to the tape, hear the danger. I wanted him to ask me, finally, about the things we cannot talk about, to open the door just a little.

He says nothing, and I can't read his mood. The trip home is driven carefully and in silence. We turn into the Masset road and the sea is there before us. He stops the car, leans forward on the steering wheel, breathing deeply. I see now he's been terribly afraid. His face is gray and aged beyond his years. "I don't care about the goddamn story right now," he says. "I care that you're alive."

With some distant bell tolling I realize I may never have another chance to ask what I need to ask. "My work is important. I'm trying to do the right thing," I say, taking his hand in mine. "Will you stand by me?" He rubs my hands to warm them, looking at them and turning them over in his.

"Yes," he answers finally. "I trust you. I want to trust you."

With his coat still on, Jonah sits by the tub Matty has filled with hot water and a comfrey tincture to reduce any bruising. I peel off my clothes and ease in, feeling strangely vulnerable. A cup of warm tea is pressed into my hands and I sink back, Jonah's hand in my hair. He sees something and points out a small triangle of flesh torn from the lobe of my ear.

"You didn't get away scott free," he whispers. "You've finally left something behind."

My grip is like death.

"Don't leave me tonight!"

He takes off his coat and I sink into the steam, floating away like a leaf into the endless current. That night Jonah encircles me. His chest is massive and comforting. Tenderly he pushes matted hair away from my face, strokes my cheek. Tears flow unchecked into his river and he buries his face in my hair and sighs, taking my breaths as those of his own.

"It's okay to want," he murmurs. "Have faith in me."

In the darkness he is all. The cold memories cannot reach me here.

He moves his head to look deeply, in the way only lovers can look at each other. Unashamedly. Vividly.

"Elle, if we were to have a child, he would be extraordinary."

I pull away. To have him trust me is different than what he is asking for now.

He leans over and kisses me, deeply, hands and body cupping, inviting. His body seems so perfectly together in this purpose.

"It's what I want," he goes on. "To live here together, and have many children and be wildly making love in this bed until we have no juice left."

High above the flood plain, high above the mad rush. This can't be true.

I twist and turn inside, trying to find a place where I can accept his words. Trying to find the thinnest edge of trust.

His mouth kisses the edge of mine.

"I'm afraid," I say to the darkness.

"This is meant to be," he answers. The words are drawn out through a thousand breaths and I accept.

Afterward he lies in wonder, stroking my belly. "Be strong. Be brave."

His life flows into mine.

♐♒♐♒♐♒

The election has come at last. By week's end we shall know who has the gods on his side, who shall lead and who shall follow, who shall have the power, who shall harvest the bitter fruit. No one would choose for this to come to pass; in such a small place the victor must rule over his neighbor, the vanquished. Plenty of time to stare across the divide, to worry an idea or drop well-placed criticism—such slow poison is the legacy of every Councilor. Then there is the next election.

Jonah has turned as stiff as a cat's whisker on these winter mornings, determination and resolve as formal as his heavy gray topcoat, which he affects with a bright red muffler and wool gloves of startling periwinkle blue. He leaves each day promptly at half-past eight, visiting with the elders, the invalids, the unsatisfied, murmuring promises over and over. What these promises are I've become less and less sure. They are becoming like a secret language, one forged with as much disdain for outsiders as a lover's shared endearment.

There's been no more talk of politics at the dinner table. Sometimes Paulie joins us, but even his innocent probing is met with glowering silence as Jonah oversees the evening meal.

Nights are spent in lamp-lit solitude at the house, where I try to work on the week's articles. I find other things to keep me occupied when visiting Jonah, who paints with increasing conviction and solitude of purpose. His humor escapes him during these periods and it is best to let him be. At the end of the day, his brushes are deposited in pots of water next to a large stack of blank newsprint, always looking as if they will never again rest. He has taken all of his other artwork down to make room for the new paintings. The larger ones line the hallway leading to the front door, rustling and flapping every time it admits the sea breeze. Increasingly they have begun to resemble a visual gauntlet with their intense slashes of black, bold circles and deep red. Always red. It's a strange thing to think that one or the other will win by as little as two votes. I've seen George in the grocery store several times and he is always polite. I wish him good luck, but I want Jonah to win. I want Jonah to have this power, this acceptance, this validation.

The night of the election we gather at Paulie's long house. The weather is calm and clear. Without clouds the air has turned sharply cold and there is ice once again on the beachfront.

"It's colder than a witch's tit, but everyone will get out to vote, at least," remarks our host, stirring a large pot of chili. A platter of white bread and a pot of butter are laid out on the tables, but no one seems especially hungry.

There is no music. Without card playing and laughter, the big room echoes and reverberates, the silence broken occasionally by coughs and scratching, dampened murmurs spilling like cold light onto the porch. I tentatively test the lino floor with stocking feet before retreating under a comforter and the solace of a book. I am the only woman here and my presence is barely tolerated. I turn away and concentrate on my reading, an Edwardian mystery. It is none of my concern if they are unhappy with me there.

Ten o'clock comes. The votes are being counted now and soon someone will come from the Band office to give Jonah the results. With people moving about restlessly, I shut my book and look over in his direction. For a moment our eyes meet. *Tell me it will be the Raven that opens the box at last.* He looks away quickly, guarding his privacy from the others.

"Jonah, you've won!"

The shouting can be heard even before the door is opened. Men rush in and before long the place is filled with them and their smells, the coldness streaming off them, the sea and the smoke. Soon the chili is bubbling again and there is hot tea all around, along with joking and admiration.

Jonah is all smiles. He takes me in his arms and swings me around while the men laugh, drinking and eyeing their new Chief with new respect. "You had a good margin, too," says one of the men who counted the votes, and they open a case of beer to celebrate.

The hour is late before the last stragglers leave, all except Paulie who is stacking dirty dishes. Though he is intent on cleaning up, he keeps glancing over at Jonah even as he says good night to the last visitor. "He's an important man now, Elle," he says with reverence, "and you're his woman!"

Jonah comes back in, picks up the bear drum lying on the sideboard and goes out onto the back porch. There he drums a thank-you song to the startled otters drifting by on the Inlet. After a while I fall asleep on the couch.

The moon has gone down before we make it back to his house. We stand for a moment on the muddy lawn where the backhoe has already begun digging out the new ground-floor level he is adding in the front. The earth is hard with winter frost, all grass gone beneath the scars of construction. Behind us the sea mills restlessly, jealous when we stand too long with our backs to her, but Jonah takes no notice of it tonight. I know he is dreaming about the days to come when visitors will begin to call on him for his help, guidance and intervention. His features soften with the dream, his longing finally surfacing.

The ground is stiff beneath my boots, and the unfinished house unfriendly, even forbidding in the darkness. Bare cement foundation walls with blank squares for doors and windows rising up to meet the hill behind. Monolithic. The sea-wind rushes up from the shore and we hurry inside. After the fire has been stoked and teakettle set to boil, we face each other cross-legged under the light of an oil lamp wicked low. Jonah looks pensive.

"Are you all right?" I ask.

"I left college in Vancouver after a year." He looks ashamed, defiant. "Your schools were not for me."

I lean forward and touch his hand. Sometimes it is best to say nothing.

A week after the election Jonah's uncle suddenly takes sick and has to be airlifted to the Mainland for treatment. I find him at his mother's place, rushing through papers and packing a suitcase.

"Lionel had a recurrence of an old cancer," Jonah tells me matter-of-factly as we drive to the seaplane jetty. There was a snow yesterday and the roads are not yet plowed so he's flying out to Prince Rupert and catching a connection to Vancouver, where he will stay with his uncle in intensive care. With his hand in mine, Jonah waits patiently on the jetty, heavy coat firmly buttoned, scarf neatly tucked, suitcase in hand. He's packed himself away. We do not embrace, but stand shoulder to shoulder watching the plane land and taxi toward us. His uncle was always so strong, so capable. Beneath the calm, I sense Jonah is frightened. Lionel stepped in to raise his sister's son; he and his wife gave their charge a house full of cousins to play with, a love of pinochle, and wit.

Later, when the plane has long since disappeared from sight, I wander back home and fret by the television. People on a game show dressed like chickens smooch, jump up and down; numbers flash and jingle. Jonah has not told me how long he will be gone.

I play my phone messages.

The first one is in Judy's usual clipped tone: "Jude here, Elle. The Congress of the Haida Nation is next week. Let's talk about coverage."

For my boss it is a simple matter. But no white reporter will be allowed to sit in at the Congress.

Dammit. I'll talk to her, and then if she insists, I'll do my best.

♐♒♐♒♐♒

The abandoned Christmas tree has frozen solid in a pail of ice on the front porch. Bitter cold wind roughs up the trees and rattles the windows, reminding me the woodpile has shrunk alarmingly since the last time Jonah had a go at it. Matty and I are packing tinfoil angels and whittle-stick ornaments into a small box for attic storage.

She turns to me. "What happened with the Moresby story?"

"I tried to be fair."

My roommate snorts. "Well, look at it this way, only about ten people took it seriously."

"What the hell do you want me to do? Really, Matty, I'm not up for this right now!"

It was true that earlier in the week, I had contacted Sgaana after all my notes were lost in the salt chuck. It was his interview too, I'd reminded myself. I needed his help to reconstruct my original story, and once I'd pulled another version up on the computer, it was woefully incomplete.

When my interviewee came over to the house, he stood on the porch steps, his fierce demeanor masked behind a look of concern. "I'm happy you weren't hurt the other day," he offered solicitously, as he waited for me to invite him in. I stepped aside, and as he passed, the faint aroma of hickory smoke followed. The pleasantness of it made me dizzy. When we sat at the kitchen table, he seemed even larger than I remembered. With cool efficiency, he took a pen out of his jacket and began scanning and marking the hard copy of my story.

"When does this article go into print?" he asked, after a moment. It was hard to pull my gaze away from the bare typewritten lines, the brashness of my opinion.

"Whenever it's ready."

"Good." He bent down again to the task of rereading the material, making editorial notes in the margins, sometimes eliminating whole phrases. "We don't say things this way," he remarked at one point. For an hour he x-ed and deleted, wrote new text. Then he pushed it over toward me. There was very little left of the original.

"In two weeks, the provincial government is sending a representative to discuss the Watchmen," he said, putting the cap back on his pen with an efficient snap. "If you run the story next week we can use it to stir up public support." I nodded without speaking, carefully folding the paper into halves. I felt a little dizzy. My visitor rose, scraping the chair back to accommodate his large frame, and smiled. His hair fell in luxurious curls around his head. An enormous, powerful surge of sexual perfume filled the space between us and I hurried to the door, anxious to see him leave.

As instructed, I handed the story over to Judy the next day. She gave it a cursory glance and sent it to be typeset without comment. I felt a tremendous surge of relief.

I'm not to be so lucky with Matty. As she shoves the last of the ornaments into the box and tapes it shut with a vicious snap, she turns on me. "I'm sorry this is an inconvenient time but I'd like to know, just when did you become the propaganda arm for the Watchmen?"

I move away from her and sink down onto the sofa, pulling the red blanket onto my lap. "What the hell, Matty? You work with them, so what do you suggest I do?"

Her stare is unnerving.

"I don't need to be objective. You, on the other hand, have a difficult choice to make about whom you serve." With a weary sigh she moves slowly over to the stove to attend to a pot of soup.

"Is that all you're eating today?" I ask.

She flips me off. "If you're going to change the subject I suggest we talk about the shrinking woodpile, because I'm leaving tomorrow."

It's obvious she has been losing weight steadily since last month. Her small frame is purposefully obscured by layers of mismatched clothing.

"Where the hell are you going?"

"Haven't you heard?" she retorts. "My friends all got together and gave me a ticket to some holistic treatment center in Victoria." With the self-absorbed concentration of a cat she turns her attention from the soup and burrows into the couch, where she pulls out a large purple blanket she's been knitting since September. Examining the wooly mass, she fiddles with it for a minute as I stand above her, hands on hips.

"Matty!"

Sighing she puts it down. "Seems like they felt an intervention was in order. Lots of iris reading, meditation, stuff like that."

"Are you…?" From her sharp replying glance, the subject is clearly off limits. Nose pinched, eyes small and hard, she attacks the wool pile with determination, knitting needles clicking furiously. I put on my mackintosh and go out to deal with the wood, axe in hand. After a time, there is a knock on the window. Matty rubs a circle in the foggy glass. "Jonah's on the phone," she mouths.

His voice sounds distant, tinny.

"How's your uncle?" I ask.

"He's been stabilized. By the way, I saw your sister tonight." He had promised to pick up a watch I had left with her for repair in Vancouver. "We had a good visit. I brought some paper snakes for the boys to play with."

What must she have thought of this formality, the gifts and the strong hot tea offered along with biscuits and smoked salmon in his hotel room?

"Oh, Jonah, you needn't have gone to the trouble."

I wonder how he found the time to organize this nicety. He sounds distracted, pensive, and something else that is worrying. I carry the phone into the bedroom, leaving Matty muttering over her project. "Will you be coming home after the weekend?"

"I can't."

In the ensuing silence I wait for some explanation.

"I'll be back by the time Congress starts," he offers finally.

"I'll see you there. The paper has asked me to cover the meeting."

"Elle, you can't get in."

"Why not? I'm with you."

"That's totally beside the point."

I don't know what to say to this. The territory is slippery. Dangerous. The admonishments of Matty and Judy come back to me. "Listen, Jonah, the Congress is of interest to the entire Island, maybe even the Mainlanders. Besides, it's my job to cover the news. I can't just say no because you can't see why I have to be there."

More silence. I can feel him working up to something. "I'm just letting you know that our relationship puts both of us in an awkward position sometimes," he finally says. "Word's gotten around you've been snooping into some very sensitive things from our past and I'm asking you to take a step back."

My heart tightens.

"Jonah, I've done nothing wrong."

"What do you plan to do with any information you've obtained?"

"Plan? I have no plan!" I hadn't counted on having this conversation over the phone. "Can't you trust me on this?"

I can hear him checking himself on the other end, taking a deep breath. "You're going to undo a lot of good we've accomplished so far. The damage will fall on you. On us."

I know I'm on shaky ground and don't want this conversation to continue on the phone. "Look, Jonah, I'm just curious, that's all. I have no agenda here, no ulterior motive. And besides, I wouldn't talk to anyone else about it before talking to you first."

"I've got to get back to my uncle."

"You can trust me, Jonah. Please believe that."

"I apologize for leaving you without enough wood for the week," he says with stilted formality, flowing away on a distant sea.

"Let me come see you when you get to Charlotte City," I ask softly.

"I do miss you," he says, before hanging up.

Outside I attack the wood, splitting it cleanly, avoiding knots and the kinks that are hidden as wounds within the wood. These malformations are brittle scars from some earlier trauma and will not yield to the axe or be cleaved. They are eventually discarded. With every quarter split comes the memory of those first damp chips, held close to my breast. A few months ago I knew nothing about wood. Now I have mastered it. Now I burn it.

♐♒♐♒♐♒

Matty leaves the next morning. She hands me a key to the Temple, along with instructions for paying the rent the following week. A true Islander, she departs without a forwarding address. Leaving this place is like leaving the world. Any emergency is too far away to do anything about. Like Pippi's house, it is simply the unfolding way of things.

"I'll be back in two weeks," she whispers as we embrace. Then she steps back and heaves her duffle bag up over her shoulder. She is still strong.

"Don't piss off the landlord," she advises with a wink.

The house seems too empty, as if she has already left the earth. I follow her clumping steps out to the car and picture her traveling down the road, getting on the airplane, arriving at the *ashram*, eating vegetarian food, getting better, sleeping well.

Later that day, Naani leaves word through a neighbor that I'm to come over to share a pot of rabbit stew. Transplanted earlier this century by European settlers, she considers these mild creatures quite a delicacy. Freed from many of their natural predators, their numbers have multiplied and they are easy to trap.

She greets me at the door in a faded green gingham wrapper under a sagging lemon yellow sweater. The wool is threadbare and dirty around the cuffs.

"Can I wash that for you, Naani?"

"Oh, dear, no." Each word is accentuated carefully. "I like my clothes to be comfortable." She points out a patch: a small red heart. "I stitched that on just last week. It was a gift from my niece." It is then I notice other baubles attached in various places—a black rabbit's foot, a quilting square of flowery cotton, a tiny gold key on a ribbon.

"What's that, Naani?" I ask, pointing to the last object.

She smiles mysteriously. "The key to someone's heart." Then she laughs. "I don't know where that key belongs. I pinned it there in case someone could tell me."

I have begun taking down the tea things; Naani watches from her favorite chair. From the collection I choose a pair bright with pink rosebuds, two saucers matching, green vines curling down toward the inside as if from a secret garden. Her china is cleaned in tepid water from the iron kettle on the stove; there is always a thin slippery film on everything. It is my habit to pour the brew and then take only a sip before distracting her with conversation. The room is warm, suffused with the sweet smell of herbs and stewing meat.

"Who gave you the rabbit?"

She points to the west window. "The nice man from down the street brought it over."

It's probably Duncan, the transplanted Swiss hunter of the forest who still wears lederhosen and gathers much of the Village's supply of medicinal herbs. "He brought me some wild rhubarb root too, for my neighbor, Jean."

Naani holds the baggie up in her hand. "Poor woman's bowels are stopped up because of the baby and she asked me for some medicine. Can you help me prepare it?"

I empty the pale root into a pestle and begin the work of grinding it down to a fine powder as she has taught me. Not long ago, after I quizzed her about the Devil's Club Matty was taking, she began teaching me some of her ways: how to mash boiled fern roots for a poultice to treat a broken bone, how to apply an ointment of burnt fruit and *eulachon* grease for burns. And in some of the jars she told me were the ingredients for charms, talismans, hallucinogens; even a remedy for ugliness.

After Jean's potion is prepared, any left over will be carefully scraped into a clean Nescafe jar with the Haida name marked on a piece of masking tape and stored for later use. Rows of similarly marked jars have been rescued from the garbage can, labels gone from many washings. What once contained peanut butter, pickles, and fruit cocktail now house skunk cabbage root for skin rash, wild parsnip to boil in a tea for irregularities of the bladder, hemlock bark for acne, and licorice root for coughs and sore throat.

"Naani?" The root is breaking down into stringy pieces; I have to grind hard. The pestle pushes down on the hard surface of the stone mortar, then there is a twist at the end. Grind and twist, grind and twist. "Is there something here for a troubled heart?"

"I know of some. They come at a price," she answers. "Not worth the trouble." She checks my work and puts a hand on mine to slow the pace. "You know, when Jonah was a small boy he used to come here on errands from his *Tsinnie*." She closes her eyes to concentrate. "His mother's father was one of the last Chiefs who remembered a time before the villages disappeared. When he started coming by I said to myself, 'This boy is too small to be out so far from home.' But his grandfather told me his mother spoiled him too much so it was his job to see that he got strong."

The rhubarb root is giving way now. Soon I will be able to remove the pithy strands and concentrate on the softer marrow. Naani's voice continues on behind me. "Jonah looked a lot like his dad, the big boss at the cannery. What a lot of curly blond hair he had back then, and wide, curious eyes. Always asking questions. In a lot of ways, he was starting out just like his dad—a thinker and a dreamer. But that father of his was a wanderer, always up and going someplace without any notice. Made his mother a little crazy, I think, and that's why she turned to religion the way she did. But Jonah got something else from that good-for-nothing. His father was a real good artist and it rubbed off on his son."

The stew pot begins to boil and Naani takes a quick peek to assess it. "One day Jonah's dad left and never came back. Back to the Mainland, they said, but no one ever heard from him again so who knows? That's why his old *Tsinnie* sent the boy across the bridge to see me. I guess he wanted to find out if young Jonah would come back home, or just wander off the way his father did. I'd give him a bit of sugared spruce-gum and the medicine he'd come for, and then I would stand on the porch until I saw he'd made it across the highway. He would stand on the edge for a long time listening and looking down the road, then all of a sudden run real hard right back home like he was supposed to."

She looks at me. "Did he tell you his grandfather died before he turned six?"

"We don't talk much about his family."

"He stopped coming around then. I bet he doesn't even remember." She checks what I'm doing with the rhubarb. "That's enough grinding, *scundula*! Too much and you'll take the life out of it." She waves toward the stove with her hand. "Lift the lid and check our dinner, there's a good girl."

As I maneuver around to the side, she opens the stove door with her poker and makes a few expert jabs at the hardwood burning smartly inside. The pot is bubbling now and I gingerly lift the lid with a tea towel. When a great waft of steam clears, the entire skinned rabbit is revealed, milky eyes staring heavenward. My stomach churns. Naani expertly tears some of the flesh from the creature's back, slides it into her mouth, and gives a satisfied nod. She pulls the bowls over with a clatter and I spoon some of the greasy broth into them. I fill up on biscuits, begging off the stew with a promise to take some home. When I leave her for the night, she is hunched over the tiny kitchen table delicately continuing to strip her rabbit clear to the bones, eyes half closed in the comfortable warmth of the fire.

♐♒♐♒♐♒

The first week of March heralds more bitter weather: low clouds obscure a weak winter sun. The world seems to have resigned itself to a peaty darkness, the cold assault of snow and ice. Ribbons of cold fog, heavy with salt air, shroud the restless ocean and blanket the forest. I have taken to wrapping myself in long johns and a heavy sweater, not venturing far from my room. Preferring the electric bar heater by my bed, I've abandoned the axe and the hungry wood stove until Matty's return.

This morning I wake up feeling unwell. Not sick, exactly, just queasy. I remember the rabbit and roll over to push the image from my mind. When I finally get out of bed, the wind has picked up alarmingly, rattling all the loose shingles and driving a thin spittle of icy rain onto the windows. Bowl of cereal in hand, I turn on the computer and start to work on three stories due by Friday.

My insurance agent calls from Los Angeles. It has taken some time to settle the final disposition of my car, now a "boat anchor" as he so eloquently describes it. Before we'd hauled it to the dump, someone stripped all the tires and even took the ruined radio.

"Where should I send the check?" he asks.

"Mail it up to Masset."

Quinnie arrives at my door just after lunchtime, a not unwelcome intrusion. I turn off the computer and take a ride with her out to North Beach, where she is contemplating the purchase of some land. Her little red Honda is a rat's nest of loose papers and stinks of wet dog. As we take the highway north, I burrow into the mess and take shallow breaths.

"Have you heard from Jonah?" she asks, watching for slippery curves.

"His uncle is doing better."

We pass over the Sagan River and I strain to follow its course through gritty windows. I roll mine down and then quickly retreat after a blast of cold air pulls at my hair ribbon.

"He's at the all-Indian games in Prince Rupert," she remarks. I look over at her with surprise.

"What's he doing there?"

"Not sure." She is driving with marked determination, her focus on the road. I look at her hands, smooth and plump, with lots of rings.

I don't know why she is asking these questions, neither sly nor inquisitive.

"Out with it, Quinnie."

"Okay." She avoids my gaze. "I got this from a friend of a friend who lives in Rupert who doesn't know you. Her brother is on the team and she went to the playoffs. She called me this morning to gossip about something she'd heard." She pauses.

"What?"

"It's just that, well, Jonah, whose search for a wife has been public knowledge for a while now, told a friend of my friend that he was finally making plans to get married."

"Well, well!" I lean back into the old upholstery, ridiculously happy. "He's a sly one."

Quinnie seems distracted. I glance over, curious.

"You don't seem pleased."

"Don't be ridiculous." She watches the road for a bit as if trying to sort something out.

"It's just that my friend didn't mention your name."

"Oh, come on!" Everyone is always trying to make trouble. "Quinnie, someone was just trying to stir it up. You know they've been at it since Jonah started taking me to the *doings*." I look over at her. "Now I'm not sure he said what she said. He's only been gone for a week and he'd hardly leave his uncle for a trip to the games."

She sighs, hands on the steering wheel, her face a map of sun-bleached lines, swept brow freckled and worn. "I guess you're right," she finally admits. "They'll always see you as an outsider, no matter how long you stay." The truck noses into a small dirt clearing.

"Here we are."

The piece of property my companion is looking at is half an acre and lies beneath an undulating sea of mosses, mushrooms and poison ivy. The sun cannot break through the heavy canopy of cedar. In the middle is a small gully.

We stand in silence. The ocean is muted, but still discernable. It might be possible to clear a view to the water, but the property across the way is overgrown and blocks the sea air and view. A light rain is beginning to fall. I don't like the feel of this place and Quinnie can sense it. The memory of my last conversation with Jonah is now starting to weigh heavily. I miss him and want him back home.

"Come on, let's get out of here," she says, squeezing my shoulder. "This land won't be going anywhere soon."

I'm all too happy to oblige. It is Thursday, the boat is in and I have shopping to do.

♐♒♐♒♐♒

My body has wanted a child since I came of age. A body should be allowed to go its own way. Otherwise, there is war.

I pick up the pregnancy test on the dresser and consider the deepening blue lines. Mine is such a cunning body, so perfect in its ways, without conscience, without fear. My belly feels soft like a summer peach with a secret, hard pit inside. I contemplate the double blue lines and let an unfamiliar flush of joy reach down to my womb. Marvel at the precision of my ovaries, their shrewd ability to excoriate what is left of my safety.

I have not lost my chance after all.

I stare intently into the blue sea, my second life, the infinite receptacle of my desire, and sing for the gift, yelping and dancing about. The walls vibrate with whoops, becoming kinder in their old age. The pressing memories, retribution will find no host for this my cross, I shall be spared at last the public scorn due me for giving into the fear and the terror. Cradling the test, I get down on my knees and ask the Celtic gods, the God of Israel, Buddha and whoever else might be listening to spare this new life the burden of my sins.

The image of Naani's skinless, potted rabbit jumps into my head and I fight the urge to gag. Everything smells bad now. The moldering wood of the house yaws and cranks its decay into my gut, the old egg-fry smell seems to have permeated every niche in this dusty, over-laden trollop of a vessel. I can pick out with sickening clarity the strong smell of fish oil that has been in the cutting board since last month when we last had smoked salmon, the seaweed we dried on a string draped in the back hall before stuffing it into plastic bags. I follow my nose around the room, willing the nausea to let go of my body. There may be months ahead of such turmoil so I grab a piece of pickled ginger and start chewing on it.

It's the best I can do for you. Just not get in your way.

The phone rings.

"Elle, it's Jude."

"I'm not feeling well." There is silence on the other end.

"Unless you're down with spinal meningitis I expect you to bluff your way into the Congress session tomorrow and get me some news coverage," she barks.

"But they'll just kick me out!" I daren't tell her of my conversation with Jonah. The urge to throw up is overwhelming.

"I need a story, and that's the end of the discussion." She rings off abruptly. I know her long-suffering patience is wearing thin. Now I'm pregnant by one of them, for God's sake.

For the rest of the day, I'm alone in the house, knocking around, bouncing off walls, full of excitement, afraid to tell anyone. I practice writing certain phrases on a piece of paper. "I'm having a baby." "We're pregnant." Now what?

There is a banging noise at the door and I jump up guiltily, nostrils flared.

It's Quinnie.

"I'm leaving in ten minutes for Charlotte City." She looks at me with pity. In the mysterious way information gets around here she seems well aware of my task ahead. "Thought you'd like to share the ride." I fight down the sharp memory of her doggy-scented car and accept. Notebook and tape recorder in hand we take off. She is driving very fast, heat blasting.

"Hold your horses before I puke!" I moan. She takes one look at my pale face and we exchange knowing looks.

"Either you're sick, or you've got to be frickin' kidding me. Oh, hell, are you sure?"

"Believe me, I tried the test more than once. I'm planning to tell Jonah when we get to the Congress." The timing makes me uneasy but how can I contain the news when we meet? I long for the quiet plum-colored shade of his house, the place where such dreams are conjured up and rightly consummated.

"Yeah, I guess you can't just sit there and say nothing," Quinnie says, reading thoughts that come across clearly when the space between us is as small and silent as this car. "Do you want it?" she asks, her expression unreadable in the dark.

"Of course!" I slouch down in the seat, unwilling to say any more about it until I've had a chance to share the news with Jonah. I am suddenly and painfully aching for his calming presence, the *chee chee* noise he makes when speaking to my belly. I want to feel his hands caressing there, coaxing life to begin.

"Well, here we are."

The lights inside are fairly blazing with intensity, pouring out the high windows along with the noisy mix of voices and cooking food. A few dancers in blankets and ceremonial headdresses stand outside smoking. Quinnie pulls the car into the Hall parking lot and indicates for me to get out.

"Aren't you coming, too?"

"Hell, no, girlfriend. Last time I looked I was white." She leans over and yanks the door closed. My belly feels like it has bloated out to the size of a basketball. I feel my pant waist cutting in as I lean over and try to lock onto her face, pleading. With a sigh, she rolls down the window and I lean in as far as I am able. "Where are you going, then? When will you be back?"

"I'm just picking up my dry cleaning and a pint of Haagen Dazs," she replies, looking grimly towards the Hall. "I figure you'll be booted out in about fifteen minutes so that should be enough time. Then we'll go have dinner."

The massive front door of the Hall is shut, signaling the proceedings are underway. She leans over closer. "My advice, go around to the back door and just ooze in. They'll be too busy working themselves up into a lather about how we destroyed the planet to notice you." Before I can object she takes off, spitting up gravel. The dancers stub out their cigarettes and look over curiously. I slink back into the shadows before realizing how odd it looks. Then I start forward, brushing off their advances.

"Hey there sweetie," one of them coos. I veer off and head for a small square of light spilling out of the back door. From inside comes the start of rhythmic drumming and I move closer to have a look.

A respected Canadian political activist from the Mainland steps onto the stage. Though not Haida, he is wearing a heavily decorated ceremonial blanket, a gift from the clan that adopted him. When the drumming stops he is introduced and then begins a long speech about the evils of the white man and their contribution to global warming. No doubt he flew in here on a jet spewing pollution. Tuning him out, I try to find an agenda on one of the tables. I'm more interested in any news regarding the Council's outline for a Moresby Heritage Site, the expanding role of The Watchmen, and any other plans they are developing for the Islands. I've heard they've stopped using Canadian passports to travel and issued their own Haida Gwaii documents, challenging the resolve of the federal government to deny them free passage.

The young men in a group standing next to me are all from Masset families. We've spoken politely at events, shaken hands, shared potluck feasts. Under the purple neon glow of Daddy Cool's, they would lick my neck if given half a chance, and fight to get my favors, their shirts moving in soft folds as they reach across the table to hold me in their gaze. Now they seem not to see me at all. Though their attention is fully elsewhere I cling to their drowsy warmth, and this familiarity provides a slim measure of protection from the mass of belligerent, angry men and women as they get up onto the stage and rail against the Western world. There is much posturing, shouting, and fist shaking, but up here in the back, most are content to just watch the action while they eat. All around me families are unwrapping sandwiches in wax paper, lining them up next to jars of pickles and soda cans on long tables already littered with pens, paper,

Styrofoam cups, balled-up napkins, mustard containers—the flotsam of two days.

Judy's voice barks inside my head and I know I should be paying attention to what they say but I cannot. The words blur and disappear behind the nearer rustling of clothes, the murmurs of women and men engaged in private conversation, objects opening and closing.

Then someone grabs me from behind and pulls me outside to the cold darkness.

I'm spun around to face Jonah.

"What are you doing here?" He must have wound his way from the head table down below and is sweating with the effort.

"I told you!" My arm is twisted backward and I stumble to right myself. He backs off and squares himself between the door and me.

"You're lucky no one noticed you," he hisses.

"Why?"

"You know perfectly well that this meeting is only for the Nation."

"Do you have any idea how ridiculous that sounds?" His response is to pull me roughly into the shadows of the parking lot. Music starts from inside, and no one notices us. I try to shake off his grasp. "I asked you a question, Jonah! What the hell are you so afraid of that you can't even allow freedom of the press?"

With a fierce glare he answers with deliberate slowness as if I were a child. "I've already told you. We will have our right to express our feelings without fear of retribution."

"What do you think I'm going to do to you if I'm allowed in there? I'm not out to get you. I don't have that kind of power!"

He leans away from me, and as if by a trick of the light, his features rearrange into those of a stranger. Familiar, yet not.

"Don't you realize how all of this looks?" he asks, his grip on my arm painfully tight. "You coming here, expecting to get into a closed meeting?" He steps away, dropping his hand from my arm. "You're trying to undermine my credibility!"

We stand apart, looking at each other.

"Where's *my* credibility?" I snap back. "My boss expects me to do my job."

His body is rigid, fists balled at his sides. "This is a delicate situation—I've barely made it onto the Council. I asked you with all due respect to honor my request."

"Where does it say that you get respect and I don't? Tell me, please, why does it have to be one way or the other?"

Without responding, he turns on his heel and walks stiffly away.

I shout after him, "People on this Island have the right to know what goes on in your meetings—you can't live like the world is your enemy forever!" He gives no sign of hearing and closes the door to the Hall behind him.

Fifteen minutes later, Quinnie pulls up and finds me standing at the edge of the parking lot, huddled under the shelter of a tree. She doesn't ask any questions, but pulls off into the town's only restaurant. The tiny diner is oppressively hot and smells of sweat and wet wool. Once her meal has been delivered, Quinnie focuses on the food, sniffing appreciatively at a fair-sized chunk of aromatic black cod. She takes a bite, stabs her fork at me experimentally. "Screw him." Then she snorts. "Oh, right, you already did that … Fat lot of good it did."

Quinnie is happy to eat while I sit in stony silence.

"Aren't you the least bit hungry?" Quinnie asks this only because I'm ruining her meal. "Will you stop looking at my food that way?"

I must have been grimacing. The cod smells like it's been reducing down to its essential oils for weeks. I am reminded of the dozens of salmon bits drying on a laundry line in Jonah's basement, the strong aroma wafting up through the furnace and making everything smell like the inside of a shoe. I want to talk about this shithole of a mess I've gotten myself into but it wouldn't be any use.

"I don't feel well."

Quinnie squints at me. "It's just a fight. You two will work it out." Her features soften. "Besides, that man is crazy about you."

I'm just too tired to care about what she has to say. She chews her fish and tries to read my expression. Neither of us wants to start the conversation. "I just want to go home." I push off from the table and retrieve my coat.

"Hey, I haven't finished my dinner yet," complains Quinnie, grabbing her keys. She curses me all the way to the car. The lock is frozen so I wait outside until she cracks it open from the other side.

Janice Joplin is playing on the radio.

During the ride home stones flick into the windshield, collecting one by one inside my heart until there is no room left for blood.

♐♒♐♒♐♒

The next day I start for Naani Rose's for some much-needed tea and comfort, but somehow end up on the highway with the idea of hitchhiking to Port Clements. I have no transportation. One car is in the town dump; the other is making rattling noises and is being examined by the Town mechanic.

I just have to get out. Walk about. Think.

Three people pass by during the first hour. No one stops. The spiky trees, stiff in the cold afternoon breeze, bend and sway just like the ones at our cottage on Lake Sinclair. There were secrets in that wood, visible only to a ten-year-old with nothing better to do than live wild in the tangled underbrush.

My mother's words come back to me: "You're getting underfoot. Go off and find someone to play with!" But there was never anyone. I would set off, the blacktop hot and shimmering beneath my rubber flip-flops, destination uncertain. Once in a while a car would roar by in the flat, constant heat, exhaust and tires spitting gravel, and I would jump into the ditch to hide. As they flew by there would be a glimpse of blowing hair, white shirttails tied high under the breast, tanned skin, silk scarves of aqua and yellow fluttering and snapping.

The power of their passing lingered—the fading radio and aroma of aftershave mixed with hot asphalt.

Now it is winter. Seasons have come and gone. Always the same.

A big truck full of Haida guys passes at full speed. Somebody hoots over the sound of a country song blaring. Silence settles back down.

The road has a powdery dusting of snow on it. I walk around in a spiral, carefully making sure the pattern is even and unmarred. The spiral goes around one full revolution. My boots have a lot of ridges on the bottom and they make a perfect pattern on the asphalt. I make more patterns. I'm afraid no one will stop for me on this road. It has too many memories, the way the blacktop travels over land in a straight line, the way the sun and the wind find a body here and keep it so still, keep it too from moving off into the unknown. The deep, tangled forest of fear, gnarled and old, the thorny, knotted mess of it all.

Slogging back to town, I am nearly blown off the road by a semi. It screeches to a halt, air brakes squealing, and Matty's head pokes out from the shiny aluminum cab, suspended what seems like a hundred feet in the air. "Shit, girl, what are you *doing* out here?" I run towards her with great gasps of laughter and clamber up into her embrace.

Once in our house, I want to roll inside this fresh, new Matty. I wait patiently as she unpacks her things, watching the careful way she takes out each folded item and presses it once with her hands before putting it in her drawers. I want to be one of those soft, cotton shirts, the color of the sky on a warm spring morning, the cool blue of promise. She moves with fluid grace, her warm aroma finding its place back in her room, filling up the damp emptiness. I let it wash over me, sitting on the edge of her bed. I wait for her until the last small thing has been taken out and put back, every sock and scarf, even the velvet I-Ching bag. No words are spoken for almost an hour. She is aware of my gaze, like a bright bird perched on a wire, ever so curious.

My roommate makes a pot of tea and we sit down at the table. She has a small present for me, wrapped in violet tissue paper. "Open it!" she says, eyebrows raised with delight.

I want to hold her and feel her bones, know she is all right, still whole, or more whole than when she left. But that is not permitted.

Inside the tissue is a small egg-shaped stone. Deep red, almost purple. Perfectly smooth, it has been milled by the sand and the sea. I enclose it in my palm, where it fits very nicely. "What is it?"

"I think it's a bit of garnet. Or maybe it's just a bit of tumbled wine bottle. I found it on the beach. Pretty, isn't it?" She takes a long draft from her tea and lets the steam waft over her face, eyes closed. I want to ask her how the treatment went, who she met, what happened to all the bits and pieces of her. I want the reassurance that the tumor has gone, but instead hold the stone against my cheek and think about precious things that might only be glass.

"Has your wolf come back?" she asks gently.

I shake my head. This and all other totems once visiting me have melted back into the shadows. "Everything's a mess," I whisper into her shoulder, above the place where her own war is being waged. I feel the ropy cicatrice beneath my cheek and I know it hurts her to hold me there. But I cannot think about her troubles right now, and I am truly ashamed of my selfishness.

K'yuust'aa

♐♒♐♒♐♒

The Congress has wrapped up in Charlotte City, so the Reserve residents will start trickling back. Jonah left a phone message with a rambling, emotional apology, and promised to see me as soon as he could. He doesn't have a cell phone so I must wait to sort things out.

The wind has picked up, and although the sky is clear, the day is uneasy with change. Under bits of scrappy clouds high up the whole of the world is revolving, moving from one place to another, taking whatever is loose with it. The grass, stiff from cold, bends this way and that. The beech trees around our property creak uneasily, letting go of dying leaves to whirl in small tornadoes around fence posts and into foundation grates.

Outside, a bit of loose siding beats a steady rhythm in the wind, and I'm forced to go out with a hammer and put a nail to it. Matty is off on some Reserve business so I have to search for her tools. Outside is warmer. The house is little more than temporary shelter from the seasons, holding on to winter's cold and damp well into spring.

The shower is still on the fritz so I head to the bathroom with the idea of bashing one of the taps so the landlord will be forced to deal with the flood. But I'm distracted by a brown house spider that has begun an intricate web from the top corner of the wall down to the water spigot. The phone rings and the machine answers. Jude has left several messages, each one increasingly irate.

When Matty bursts through the door after lunchtime, she is full of purpose and energy. Emerging a moment later with a duffle bag she's stuffing with clothes, she announces, "You, clearly, need something to do. I'm going to *K'yuust'aa* and you're coming with me." She picks up my coat and shoves it in my direction.

Captain Brett is waiting with his Cessna at the dock. He looks at me gravely. "Nice *Rasta* hair you got going on," he remarks, opening the elliptical door to the plane. "Maybe I should just throw you in with a bar of soap when we get there." I stumble past him to the back seat. Matty whacks him on the back and he gets in without another word. We take off into a strong cross wind and bob about like a cork in water, wings dipping and swaying this way and that as the plane struggles to rise above Naden Harbor. I peer out the small window to my left and watch the forested shoreline drop away. Something picks us up from the back and almost flips us over.

"Whoaaah!" Matty's voice roars up over the machine drone, the sputtering and yawing of the engines as they bite through the wind. Below, the waves are choppy, broken only by a cowlick or two of foam. The gray sea reaches out toward the horizon, where it is met by a darker shade of gray. A squall drifts off in the distance. As we round the western edge of the Island, I can see Langara off in the distance and the small lagoon Brett has indicated as our landing place. After a quick descent, we bump and skim along the shallow water until we are close enough to shore.

My boots fill with cold water after I jump from the pontoons. It's freezing as we stumble gasping onto the beach, brown, gold anemone-hued shells crushed into jagged pieces. I turn back, but Brett has nosed back out for take-off without so much as a wave goodbye.

"Storm's coming," yells Matty as we slog toward the tree line, shivering now with cold.

"What about our wet clothes?"

She points into the bush where I can just make out the outlines of a newly constructed long house. Once inside the damp, frigid stillness we strip and change quickly into the dry items in our knapsacks.

"Why am I here?" I mumble, stamping my numb feet.

Matty pulls on her jacket and shoves her wet things into a plastic bag for retrieval later. "I need you to help me pack some gear out of Rediscovery Camp." A summer retreat on the wild side of the Island for Haida children. "The trip back will be rough; we've plenty to carry." As we emerge from the long house I notice for the first time it's on a small rise surrounded by a ring of deep, moss-covered depressions.

"This is what is left of K'yuust'aa," Matty says, pulling on her gloves. "Back when smallpox finally overtook most of the Island, Naani Rose was told by her mother that some of the families from

Masset fled here, thinking it was more isolated. But when it came, it decimated the entire village. K'yuust'aa was abandoned."

Despite the nearness of the beach and the comforting drone of the sea, very little light penetrates the dense canopy of cedar; the air hangs heavily. It seems a fierce place, but without the big-planked houses and the village totem poles, what's left is a dark mystery. Only the square outlines of the great lodges remain, edges softened by waterfalls of moss. "Back then so many were dying, they were putting the small children into canoes and sending them to Haidaburg in Alaska to save them."

"Did they make it?"

"No. The parents put their children out to sea and they died. Those who survived buried their families and left K'yuust'aa to rot."

The moss has won this village back. I study the holes silently for a time and then step back, away from the edge.

"Are we responsible for this?"

Matty looks over at me pityingly. "Stop trying to understand everything and just keep moving." She gives me a push. "Let's go." Without another glance she hauls her pack up and starts off down a narrow trail leading inland. I pick up my share and follow after.

She strides quickly, with surprising strength, stepping nimbly over roots and pushing branches out of the way. Sometimes the trail branches off and she takes a fork without hesitation. Once we are far from shore, the air hangs as thick as the moss, damp and heavy. The spirits are walking today and they are making their presence felt. Something skitters along the path in front of me and I jump, but Matty forges ahead and I have to hurry to keep up. Soon the sound of the ocean on the other side is discernable, increasing in pitch as we reach the mouth of a small stream emptying onto the beach.

Once out of the cover of trees, a surging wind knocks the breath out of us. On this side of the peninsula it's fierce, howling down through a clear sharp sky past the humped shapes of treeless islands on the horizon. I double over with exertion. Brown creek water rushes past my gumboots, the noise of the wind and the pitch of the waves, the waves are up above me, higher than the beach, the sea roiling and bubbling and spraying like nothing I've ever seen. My hair ribbon tears off behind me; everything is streaming, the air alive, so alive, pushing me forward while everything else rushes back. We hug the cliff, black with algae seven feet up. A big wave comes from a hundred yards away, a three-foot wall of water. I freeze, terrified.

"Look out!" Matty screams.

The wall breaks onto the sand and crashes into me, surging forward toward the rock wall. My boots have sunk into the sand and they keep me up as the sea drags backwards, swirling around me, pushing to claim me, but I hang on, Matty's voice like a gull, screeching behind me. When the wave finally gives up and retreats I run for a safer place, my breathing loud and ragged.

We get to the camp and after a few hours of cleaning up and packing away the stores Matty leads me to sit together on a log by the water.

"Listen," she starts, eyes cast downwards. The wind is noisy and we huddle together. She takes a deep breath. "Dammit, Elle, we have to talk."

There is something inevitable about bad news, about wanting to get ahead of it so you can make it a memory and then snap it shut so it can't hurt you.

"What is going on?" I don't want to lose her, I don't want her to talk about death, I don't want to…

"Jonah is marrying someone else," she blurts out.

For an agonizing moment we just sit there. Then I round on her, just as she expected. "How do you know? It was that person at the all-Indian games, wasn't it? Jonah's only been gone for a week. This doesn't make any sense!"

I know Matty would like to be anywhere else than on this log with me, but to her credit she forges on. "I couldn't let him sandbag you with the news. She's Haida, Elle. From the Mainland. He got back from the Congress yesterday and came by the Band office this morning. I don't think he knew I was there. I heard him talking to the others."

"You're wrong!" I lift my head to the wind and join its wailing rush. The wind tells me to run into the bay where the water rolls in like tidal waves onto the flat sand, where the green and white foaming wall meets the rock face with force enough to crush bone. I crouch there, and water comes and again until I am knocked on my back and Matty has to drag me up and away.

♐♒♐♒♐♒

The house is cold and dark when we get back. A fire is quickly built and Matty puts a bowl of peas in front of me to shell. I obey her. In K'yuust'aa she dried me off, changed my clothes, and got me back on the plane to Masset.

We both jump at the knock on the door. We exchange glances and then I move over to the big armchair we keep for visiting Naanis. Matty waits at the table for a moment and then gets up, stopping to damp down the fire before opening the door. Jonah comes around her, big wool overcoat streaming off the night cold, his hair cut very short. He looks older and grayer. "Not much left, is there?" Matty observes, and disappears into her room.

As I sit with my arms laid flat, hands gripping the carved wooden lions, my feet on the floor, I remember one of the Naani's stories recounting her protestations of a marriage at fourteen to a man twice her age. She was horrified at the prospect of being with "that old man" and she begged her mother to stop the marriage. "*He's a good man, y'a Eyt, high class, too,*" her mother told her. And she let go of it after that. Just let go. Fifty years later when he died, she missed him very much.

He takes off his coat, draping it over a chair where it looks ready to jump back up at any moment. I sit and wait. He comes over, finds a stool and pulls it close. "I have something I must tell you."

I squeeze the chair arms, thrust forward. "Jonah, there's something you should know. I'm pregnant."

He stiffens, expression frozen, hands in his lap. The big bravado from the Council meeting leaves him like so much hot air. *We have done this.*

And then with some extraordinary force of will I do not understand, he takes a deep breath and presses on with his mission. "Elle, I came here as soon as I could. I've..." he drops his head for a second and then looks me straight in the eye. "I've had to make a very difficult decision."

It is the abrupt and formal way that he says it and I know he has come to tell me out of a sense of duty to some long-forgotten way of things that he's draped on himself like a Raven blanket. The trickster Raven slashed in red against the black void of a world gone mad. In a last gesture of futile triumph, I steal his secret.

"To marry someone else, you mean. Someone you've known for three days."

Jonah looks surprised, then nods miserably. "I'm very sorry." He tries to compose himself. "I seem to have made a mess of things. I blame myself. I should have been clearer about my future."

I feel brine in me rise like a tide, bringing with it a thousand images. I have lost my footing just as I feared on Rose Spit where the seas meet each other in raging fury. I struggle to stay above the churning water, not sure why I am making the effort. Perhaps it is just habit.

The man I thought to be good and fine has pried his way into this house. He is bleached by fear, still resolute. He has become a stranger, merely a sketch of a human being. He turns to face me. At such fortitude I confess a dark marvel.

Finally I break the silence. "Would you please explain what the hell happened to the person I knew?"

In his downcast, wordless response, I am lost like Dobie on the hills of Kitimat, unable to speak my own language anymore. I run and run as fast as I can, fearing the sound of another coming up over the hills and calling me back to my punishment.

He tries to be reasonable. "Elle, I won't desert you. I'll look after the child of course. And you."

"Are you kidding me?"

He looks at me with grim stoicism. "Elle, I…"

"What was all that talk, then, about building a house and making a life together? What about your promise to stand by me? Am I going to be another one of those women in town who takes what little I can get from the messed-up father of my child?"

"I'll come back when you've calmed down," he says, pushing the stool over and backing away. I stay in my chair. I think of Naani Rose sitting in her regal way, rings flashing. Her soft voice. I turn and watch him steadily as he reaches the door. Goes out.

He hadn't told me the name of the woman he's marrying. I'm sure he wouldn't have anyway, in some perversion of honor to spare my feelings. I have protected him, nurtured him and loved him as I knew best, and now I see my devotion for the fraud it was. Was I not just as considerate to my husband when his time came?

A raven flies into view. Landing on the fence, he hops down to the garden and regards me silently, head cocked. *I have come back*. You are the old raven of a woman I saw the wintry morning I set out for school. I was eight, and you passed me on the path, your dress and bags of dark stuff; your gait was of a bird unable to fly. You did not look up as you passed, and yet I was stopped as surely as if you had spoken to me. I stood quite still for a moment, a powerful feeling in my breast as if I had reached the crossroads too early in my life. I turned for reassurance toward my home and saw only the distance from which I had come. The sky was the white of frozen clouds, the ground put down for the winter. In the end there was only you and me on this path and my heart stopped then, perhaps forever. I am wolf and I am raven because they have claimed me, but I have none of their courage or their wisdom. Perhaps I am nothing more than the sum of a hungry hunter and a harbinger of death.

Days begin and end just as they always have. But something is coming apart in me that I can no longer thread together. Thousands of stitches, minute in their aspect, unraveling quickly as an unseen force pulls them apart. Beneath are the earliest maps of love, long before the time of men. Alone on the beach with seagulls wheeling, the longing defined me: bands of playful children had spun themselves away and never returned; images jumble together as I sift and sift for something true that will keep me from going down to the place where I do not want to go. I see those faces over and over. And in between are the long, blank stretches of time when my life was lived in the spaces, watching and knowing the inner secrets of the living as only a spirit could.

Why? It has something to do with imagining. I think of the stones I used to make the path to the tree house I discovered when we built our cottage, the white stones I collected so carefully and how they led a welcoming path to my door. Those stones were of marbled quartz; worn smooth and bleached by the sun and the wind, they stood out against the black mulch like the teeth of a skeleton. I took warmth from those stones, I stroked them and knew their every facet. My heart cried out to share this extraordinary beauty, but I saw only the empty lawn of grouse grass and heard only the buzzing of cicadas as my reply. And so I said nothing. I took and took from those stones until they glowed with life. I took from nothing else that summer, and the summer after. In the end, I simply faded from view.

The fruits of imagination. They'd gotten mixed up somehow with fear and never quite got unstuck. A dark future come alive.

My dreams are of striated hills, generations of heavy stone, sand, wind, the bones of my ancestors compressed into thin lines of color, each memory clearly visible but crushed under the weight of so many others. My grandmother loved her man for twenty-five years, the bastard, but she took him back again and again, and I watched her sink into his lap and caress his hair from the stairs where I was hidden from view. I don't remember much about him except he played the violin. Then there was Aunt Ellie who married the vicar. He turned out to be as mean as his thin-lipped portrait. Poor thing. She hardly knew him. And the uncle, who slept on a cot in the hallway because his parents couldn't spend the night in the same room. So much anger.

What had I done but repeat their failures as my own? And now the final punishment for seeking shelter in marriage as dry and as safe as paper, for trying to fix the rutted everything without passion, the pointless drumming marking time in years waiting for a sign, dribbling away the soul of a man who gave me permission, and so sealed his own fate. What was it about me that turned the kindness I was shown into a penance? I reach out for his memory and realize that I have only an epitaph. And so the bitter tears come, the dark days with them, and I accept their vengeance. When was I cursed to be so wrong?

♐♒♐♒♐♒

The failing winter days pass outside my bedroom window, ice turning into a thin spittle of rain daily scratching on the glass. The sky comes up gray and leaves the same way. Matty brings me soup in the afternoon and we sit together while I consider the white china bowl, steam rising. In the jacket of my housecoat is a little plastic bag. The destroying angel mushroom has dried out now, withered into a hard string of white leather. I keep my hand on it from time to time. I need to know it is there.

"I'm too tired to eat," I protest.

She says nothing, but her soup smells good and she coaxes me into taking small spoonfuls, her gaze soothing, empty of all judgment.

"What have I done?" I ask, looking at her deeply.

On this day, she takes my hand and lifts it to her cheek; I feel the faraway sea in her blood and see her home down by the lime grass with the wind all a' blowing and she is there too by the rustling chimes, all smiling and welcoming and so at last I know the joy and the love of it in her breath. She looks at me steadily, her touch a true thing between us. I feel her willing what is left of her own life energy into me. My fingertips hum with it. I love you so much I give what is left of my life to you. And to the child.

We sit like this until the sun goes down and she has to turn on the lamps. When I wake up later, she is in the kitchen steaming cockles brought up from the beach. Butter will be melting in a little pot set out on the wood stove. The kind and familiar sounds gradually fill the emptiness.

"Is there enough for two and a bit?"

She turns in surprise, then smiles. "Those turnips need peeling. And after that you can fetch some wood." We stand side by side in the kitchen, hands busy, the warmth of the stove our security.

"Tell me everything," I ask, as we peel and scrape, wash and chop. "I want to know who she is, where she comes from, and when the marriage is to take place. I want to know it all."

Later that night, Dobie arrives at the door. He is wearing his chief's jacket over work clothes, hands in his pockets, knapsack over his shoulder. "I've come to chop some wood for you," he says to me without preamble. He sheepishly glances at Matty.

"I thought you was still in Victoria."

I realize that besides our trip to K'yuust'aa, Matty has not left the house. She dismisses him with a wave. "I've been busy, that's all." Then she disappears into her room.

He opens his bag and pulls out a bag of China tea and a small vial of eulachon grease.

"I heard you had taken sick," he says. I nod. He picks up the axe and heads out for the backyard. "I'll get some wood put in for you, then we can have tea." The eulachon reeks but I put a small drop into the strong, black *Oolong*. The two flavors blend together in the steam.

Dobie sits down after putting a fair-sized load in the back porch and leans forward with authority. "I'm coming to the house to take care of things for a while," he announces, then takes out his cigarette fixings and rolls a couple, hands steadily turning the thin paper, twisting it just so for a good burn. He refuses the couch, instead taking up a position at the table, upright and watchful. I know he is looking out the front window and I oblige him by leaving the curtains open. Even when I go to bed he stays, leaving long after Matty and I are asleep.

In the morning I get up at sunrise and dress. Dobie has left his knapsack by the table, neatly zipped. From it he has removed his ceremonial button blanket where it now drapes fully displayed on the back of the couch. I pick it up and examine it closely, surprised by its weight. The eagle on the back is beautifully stitched, with abalone around the edges and around two strips of black on the sides. His name is stitched in tiny, iridescent buttons. Kitkatla. I bury my face in it, breathing its smoky aroma, before carefully putting it back.

♐♒♐♒♐♒

Naani Rose accepts my unannounced visit with aplomb. "I'm glad you're coming. Can you take me over to the Wallace's later? I have to pick up some medicine." We get in the car, she in her Sunday hat and best black coat, I in mine.

"Naani, there is something I must tell you." I'm certain the families have been talking but her expression reveals nothing. "Jonah has broken his promise to me. He is marrying another and leaving me with child."

She nods, reflectively, eyes watching the road leading out of town. "Oh, my dear, he's making a terrible mistake," she says softly. She sighs, remembering things. The way of things when the houses had rules and the clans enforced them.

"He's always been young, that one. Never grew up."

"I don't think it's that, Naani. He's marrying a Haida woman because he's ambitious."

"Maybe so." She reaches over and pats my lap. Her hand stays on the seat, halfway between us. "When I married my husband they told me I would have bad luck because he wasn't one of us. I never believed them. But he was a stranger and no one knew how things would go in a marriage like that. Oh sure, we fought some. But I've forgotten most of that over the years. In the old custom, they would have married me off to a nephew because a widow couldn't live alone. A *levirate,* who would have been obligated to stay with me until I died. Nice for me, having someone to chop my wood, and pull my slop to the back toilet hole, but not so nice for him, being young and all. Times have changed—I like my freedom, and I don't like the idea of someone deciding who should take care of me. I made my choices. My children and grandchildren visit nearly every day, and that's what keeps me alive. And," she adds with some satisfaction, "I have a house of my own to see visitors like you whenever I like."

Leaning back with her purse on her lap she observes the forest rushing by. "He may have not been the best man, but my family crest wasn't very important back then, so who knows who they would have found for me if he hadn't asked. I couldn't be choosy." She sighs. "Too many things have changed since then and they keep on changing. Doing the right thing is hard."

As we pull up to the Wallace's, Naani waits for me to get out and help her. "All I can say is that boy of yours is doing things backwards." She shakes her head. "And no good will come of it." She takes my arm and lets me lead her down the slippery path to the porch where the sound of a television blaring and lots of noisy conversation filters through. "Don't bother waiting for me, honey," she says with a wave of her hand. "Someone will take me back later."

Wolf Clan

♐♒♐♒♐♒

The next morning I'm up early, before first light. In the darkness I can feel the presence of the wolf nearby. This time I'm more curious than afraid. I'd expected to sense him more often as all totems become a part of life here, but after a while I began to think he wasn't one of mine. Perhaps he had simply accompanied me here from the Mainland and had gone home once I'd found my way.

His musky scent fills the room, and within the measure of his soft breathing somewhere out of my line of sight, I remember all the dogs I had growing up, how I would feel their small presence curled in a tight ball on the bed near my feet, how we comforted and warmed one another through the long winter nights. And yet they were all temporary; either ran off, got old, sick, pregnant, or died. We never seemed to be able to keep an animal in our house for very long. I want to invite the wolf closer, to touch its fur, the soft, deep thickness of it where one could bury one's head and fall asleep pillowed there. But he keeps his distance.

I hear a soft noise outside. The creak of the screen door, but no knock. Footsteps recede into the darkness. Jonah! I leap out of bed, stumbling through the dark to the door. It opens with a cold blast, but there is no one. Instead, propped by the door is a large manila envelope with my name on it. The writing I recognize: Naani's.

There is no time to light a fire. I huddle under the covers with the bedside lamp on, the wolf still sitting quietly in the corner, waiting. Inside the envelope is a collection of letters, all on very old stationery with blotched fountain-pen addresses, and penny stamps bearing the King's likeness in sepia.

I gingerly open the first one. It's a letter on school notepaper from a teacher, Miss Seaton, at a long-closed residential school in the B.C. Interior. In spindly, delicate script, she writes to a Reverend McIntosh in Masset about one of her students, Rose Graham, who had been caught drinking alcohol and was about to be expelled. For reasons she explained in the letter, she had come to feel pity for the young girl. "She has exceedingly bad nightmares," the letter explained, "and when I asked Rose what was troubling her, she refused to say." What puzzled the teacher was that although most of the Indian students in the school would have given anything to return to their villages, Rose seemed terrified at the prospect.

"What could I do but give her my sympathy, as the school is determined to send her home?" Miss Seaton wrote. "I tried to reason with the school authorities but wasn't successful."

There were several accompanying letters wrapped in a ribbon, as if they had been saved for someone. The script was childish, marred by many blotted mistakes and scratched-out words.

Dear Alice:

The teacher here says we must learnt to write letters home as practice for our English studies so this one is to you. How are you? I am not fine. This is not a good place. They punish us for every small thing we do. I hate being here but not more than I hate Masset (except for you). How is Reverend McIntosh? He taught me many things in the months before they came to take us away. Most importantly he taught us that we are children of God. I want to believe this and yet the more I think about it the angrier I get. I can only think of my sister, Skliee, and I miss her very much. She is dead. I grieve for her, but never to speak of her or to honor her in the way we have been taught. She has no grave, she has no marker. It is as if she never was. I have to go now.

Your friend, Rose.

Each successive letter from Rose was longer, densely scribbled to fit onto a single sheet of paper.

I think about Skliee's spirit and wonder, how can it be at peace? There was no peace for her the day we left K'yuust'aa. She was crying and screaming, "Sister! Sister, don't leave me!" My uncle was shouting at her to stay on the beach. He said he would come back for her. That's what he said when we left. I still hear her screaming, Guulaas!!! Guulaas!!! over and over. I still hear it even though my uncle told me to shut my ears. I've kept them shut ever since. Remembering makes me think of the night my parents died in the tent and Skliee and I were so scared and didn't know what to do. I don't like it when these pictures come back into my mind. The reverend says the pox was not God's way of punishing us, but I hear others say differently.

Maybe Skliee did not go to the kingdom of Heaven because she never knew Jesus. I asked my auntie and she said that it didn't matter, because

Skliee was nothing, and stop she told me, stop making trouble in the family by talking about it so much. She got scared and scolded me to keep quiet or something would start with my uncle. But I loved her and how could I if she was not the same? You taught us this is true. I wish I could talk to Jesus and ask if Skliee is at peace.

The sun is now up, ready to blaze past the cold, flat rays of morning. I put on my boots and coat and take the letters down to Naani's.

The big cast-iron oven is hot and full of baking. First out is a loaf of blueberry bread, fluted top crusted with sugar and butter. The old woman has already put out cups. Her good ones with purple flowers and real gold trim. "I had my neighbor's boy take those over to you this morning," she says, pointing to the envelope. "He's a nice boy. I woke him up real early."

"How did you come by these letters?" I ask, pulling one out.

She recoils. "Oh, honey, put them away. Every time I think of those things I feel real bad."

"Why?"

"Because I took them from the reverend's desk, just after he died. I was cleaning up in his study when the flu took him in '49 and I just couldn't help myself. They were in a fancy box and I thought they might be important. Then I saw that lady's name, Miss Seaton, and I remembered she'd visited the reverend many times over the years." Naani began vigorously banging on the blueberry pan to shake the loaf loose. "Until I read those letters I never understood why. Fact is, those papers were trouble and I knew they should be thrown away with the talk of *xaaldaang* and all, but when I saw some of them were written by Rose Graham I just couldn't destroy them. She was a good friend of my mother's."

"Alice," I guess, and she nods.

She looks off as if to find a memory picture stored away of her old life. "The girl in those letters died not long after she came back to the Reserve. She got drunk and drowned in the Yakoun River during a spring flood. They said she was a little off in the head when she got back from the Mainland and no one here wanted anything to do with her. Too many fights in the bar." Naani sighed. "But Rose was my mother's best friend and they loved each other just the same. I was told she'd suffered too much to live in this world, but her heart was kind and that's why I'd been named after her."

The plates clatter as Naani puts them on the table. "I have a Haida name, but my mother called me Rose after the Church told us our family names were too hard to pronounce. The ministers came here and started preaching the Gospel, so most of our traditions were forgotten and my other name just faded away." A troubled look crosses her lined face and she cannot help but glance toward the letters. "I kept those letters because they were about my mother's good friend, but this writing down of things, it's not our way. I never liked having them here, talking the way they did about one of our families." She shook her head and with a deliberate motion plunked down the silverware for our tea. "The way we remember our past is through our stories or by saving it in carvings and drawings. To my way of thinking this is much better than words on paper." She stops, her dentures clicking, head shaking back and forth. "These letters are a burden. They dig up terrible things about the girl Skliee and how she was left behind. I don't want to stir up any trouble."

"Who was Skliee?"

Naani puts her large, old hands flat on her apron, one hand on each thigh and sighs. "You might as well know. She was a house companion. A *xaaldaang,* bought to serve Rose. My mother told me they were best friends from the time they were babies because their Clan owned her mother too. There were a lot of different stories about how she got left behind during the smallpox, but that's the way it was back then. Everybody was dying and, oh, well, you can read about it in there someplace." She drinks deeply from her cup, face drawn and tired. "It was during the time when our families were getting rid of all their *xaaldaang* anyway."

"The shacks down the way, they belonged to these families?"

"We couldn't have them in our village, but they were scared to go. Living with us was all they knew, but we were too ashamed. They moved to that little clearing you found, and built a few shacks out of scrap wood. It was a terrible place, all buggy and hot. Not long afterward a fire started and burned the whole thing down before anyone could stop it. That was when they moved off the Islands for good."

"What made your families set them free?"

The old woman grimaces. "Oh, the government told us we had to do it and they made a lot of fuss. Said the United States down south had fought a whole war over the injustice of owning people. Made us feel dirty. Then the Church people came in said we should let it go because we'd all go to Hell. They were pulling down our totems and making us ashamed of everything. Skliee, she was one of the last of them we had around here, and I think Rose's mother and father were going to adopt her. But then they got the Fever."

With a poke towards the package on the table, she looks up at me sadly. "I don't want those letters anymore. And to tell you the truth, I don't know why I'm giving them to you. All I know is, I'm tired of keeping them." She gestures around the room. "I'm getting too old to remember where everything is now."

Though wearied, she makes a show of standing up and taking me to the door. "My feelings are all mixed up right now but we can't afford to lose any more of our kids—they're forgetting too much and remembering the wrong things. But if you have to leave us, maybe that's why I'm passing this story on to you. It's a strong *kokol* that will keep you close and bind you to us forever."

I step out into the cold morning and we hug. "Your child isn't going to be disgraced like Skliee was," she whispers, "just because she didn't have a proper family name."

From the highway I turn back to wave. She is still standing behind the glass screen door, watching out for me as she did for Jonah when he was little.

Alice, you remember Auntie was married to a very bad man, and after he died she had no one to take care of her. She went up to Haidaburg to stay with family. I was made a ward of the Social Services peoples and the Church gave me a little room in the Rectory to sleep. I miss Auntie. It's hard to think about Skliee. When Uncle came to rescue us we was wandering on the beach by K'yuust'aa. Our family was going to Masset but mother and father got sick and stopped moving. We were alone for many days, four or five I think. We had no food and the tent smelled bad. We slept outside in the cold.

Then one day I saw the canoe with Uncle and the other men in it and I was so happy. We ran into the water but the canoe stayed out deep. I told him, "Mother and father are still sleeping!" and still they did not come closer. Skliee and I were holding hands. Then Uncle got out, but then he stopped. "Come to me, Guulaas!" Skliee and I started coming but he shouted, "Let go of that girl!" But I didn't want to let go. She was my sister. I told him, "No!" But then Uncle got real quiet. The water was pushing him back and forth, he was wet like an otter. "Guulaas, I cannot carry you both to the canoe. We will drown. You must let go of her." At first I wouldn't, but he reached for me so I let go. I let go of my sister and I want to tell this because Reverend McDonald has promised me that Jesus will forgive all of our sins.

Uncle took me into the canoe. They wrapped me in a blanket. Why did they not take my sister?

"Don't dishonor your family name by calling that xaaldaang your sister!" Uncle shouted and he got even angrier at my wailing. I wailed for days, remembering her in the water, crying out for me. I should have made Uncle go back. I keep thinking about that. Skliee was my only true friend. She would have never left without me, so I must be to blame that she is dead.

I cannot sleep good anymore. If I ever get a canoe or a boat I want to find the place next to Dogfish River where Skliee died and take her bones back to Masset. Then the reverend can give her a proper Church burial.

June 10, 1905

Dear Alice:

My auntie is up north and she is well.

I have been trying my best to remember Skliee's family name. Her mother lived in Masset and may have gone to the slave-town set up by the Government. But I never saw her after my Uncle took me in. I am forbidden to cross the salt marsh between towns and they never came back to the village.

Skliee was xaaldaang and not of our class but she told me her mother secretly gave her stories that had once belonged to the Old Ones. She said their family was Salish from far down country but who can say since they were the property of our Clan for seven generations. Her father was given to the same family as a gift from one of the Chief's, who got him in trade from the Chinook upcountry but he did not know from where his people came and had no crest to protect him.

People called Skliee "low class" and a "flathead" but she didn't pay any attention to that. She said her ancestors were great warriors and it was only by the great fierceness of the Hayda that they came into this disgrace. Because they were xaaldaang, Skliee's mother and father were not allowed to marry. When she was born my parents made her a present for me. Her father died soon after because the smoke house burnt down and they said someone was bringing bad luck on the village. Skliee told me he was given to the sea so their luck would change.

Skliee said she was protected under the Salish Wolf crest, and the nights we were together after my parents got sick, she promised me the wolf would come from far away to watch over us. She told me stories her mother had given her and kept me from being afraid. I forgot those stories and I am ashamed. If I find her bones I could take her back to her ancestral home and then she will be at peace. Now I know that many are buried without ceremony on our lands or lost to the sea. I cannot sleep nights thinking about where they have gone. They do not have family names or stories for their children to hear. They have no houses or totems or honor. They will be soon forgotten.

There was one last letter from Miss Seaton.

January 20, 1910
Dear Reverend McDonald:

These letters from Rose were never sent. The Matron here thought them too provocative. But I managed to hold on to them for safe keeping. Rose didn't want them but I thought someone should. She has often spoken of you so I can safely assume they will remain with you until such time as Rose asks for them.

I have failed to help Rose at the school and it is distressing. She will be returned to Masset within the week. Please let me know how she does.
Until then I remain respectfully yours,
Gertrude Seaton

According to Naani, Rose lasted only a few months before her death at fifteen years of age. Whose fault this was I couldn't say. I'd seen too many others like her in Daddy Cools. The burdens are great and are not spoken aloud.

♐♒♐♒♐♒

True to his promise, Dobie arrives the next day as soon as he is off work. It's late afternoon and the sun is as sharp as a fishbone, slanting through the living-room windows.

"Can you come with me to Port Clements?" I ask him before he has his jacket off.

He has his knapsack with him, and some presents wrapped in newspaper. He studies my drawn features with concern. "Are you not feeling well today?"

"No, it's just that I've been up late, working on something."

Without further words he turns around and together we head down the highway.

"Why are we taking this trip?" Dobie asks quietly. He sits next to me on the front seat, legs apart, back straight. He is so small, his shoulders barely crest the windshield.

"I need to meet with my editor, Judy." I focus on the road, not daring to look at the envelope in the back seat. "And Charlotte City's too far a drive today." He nods and we lapse into silence for a few miles.

"Those King George men," he says suddenly, "they made the world too big. Things got complicated, didn't they?" His posture is strong, hands sitting regally on his lap. This is his canoe, and behind us the Eagle rises up in fierce regalia, warriors with their cedar paddles digging into the ocean. There is nothing faster, nothing greater.

"Dobie, that speech you gave back in the fall." I can feel him stiffen next to me. "You said our people had destroyed the earth." My whole body is trembling. Dobie's is trembling too. He says nothing.

"You spoke as a Chief, a learned man." And my friend. "Despite how much the words hurt, I had to believe the differences between us couldn't be so great. And I have to believe that things can change."

In the darkness I can feel him thinking, trying to find the way to me. "Now that the big lot of you live next to me I'll have to separate out the good from the bad," he grunts, "and find another word to describe the Old Ones. The Colonials may be dead and buried but their spirit lives on in the inheritors. These are the ones I have to call out." He takes my hand in his. "I guess we have to be careful when we choose our battles."

Jude's car pulls into a deserted parking lot behind the Port lumberyard. It is after dark and everything in this tiny town is closed. Dobie doesn't move as I retrieve the envelope and walk over to where my editor is parked. With a wary eye to the old Haida sitting like a statue in my car, she greets me with a grumpy hello and opens the door. I slide in next to her.

"Is that your article on the Congress?" she asks.

"Listen, Jude…"

She slumps down and sighs. "Oh, Lord, no."

"I'm leaving the Island."

"I've heard this before." Her eyes are glittering in the dark. "I thought you had more in you than the others."

"Sorry, I don't really have a choice." She rolls down the window, takes out a cigarette, but at my expression, puts it back in the package.

"Why the hurry?" she asks gloomily.

For answer, I slide the package toward her. "I do have a piece for you. If you decide to run it I can promise it will make your life on the Mainland very interesting and a bit sticky here on the Island."

She regards me with some interest. "So you did get inside the Congress?"

"It's not what you think."

"Something you dug up there?"

"There is no dirt. Only a lot of misunderstanding and political bullshit that's as old as time itself."

"That might do," she says with a quick laugh.

"Look, Jude. I can't give you what you want. Either way I'm finished."

She looks at the package. "What's this, then?"

"It's a story."

She gives me a jaded look. "What use do I have for stories?"

"The ones that have been kept secret for far too long in a history kept alive by stories. This one deserves a storyteller who is willing to own it."

"So that's you, I presume?" she asks.

"I'm afraid not. The rightful owners will come forward eventually." And the tale of the girl who came from the Wolf Clan will someday stand alongside those of the Raven and the Eagle. Her name will join thousands of others' who have a right to be part of the land here because their bones make the soil rich and the Islands worth fighting for.

Jude's profile is in shadow but I can make out her crusty features and the lines that draw down from her eyes. Sad eyes like mine. On this moonless night we both stare out into the darkness outside, broken only by a distant dot of light from Dobie's cigarette.

I turn to open the car door. "Thanks for doing this."

The envelope remains on the seat.

"I didn't say I'd absolutely do whatever it is you're asking, but," she reaches out and pulls it toward her, "I'll see what I see."

I reach over and grasp her arm. "So long, boss."

She waits in the parking lot as Dobie and I take off into the night.

♐♒♐♒♐♒

For the next week Dobie comes by promptly at the end of the workday to spend the evening with us. Some days he shows up with food, others with small gifts. Things he's carved or a pretty stone he has been keeping on his dresser. Lots of things for the baby: small totems made of cedar and argillite, a T-shirt emblazoned with the sun crest. If I need to run an errand he comes with me in the car, sitting resolutely in the front seat, staring down passersby as they watch me come and go. Because of the old man we have no dark nights in the house. He keeps fresh wood in the bin, the house warm and tea on the stove for the occasional visitor.

I haven't told him of my desire to publish the story about Rose and Skliee. I can't find the right time and place. But too many days are going by and I know Jonah's wedding is coming up soon. The opportunity finally comes one evening when he brings over a salmon his nephew has caught over by Langara Island. It has been cleaned, the bones and guts returned to the sea so that the salmon may return again the following year.

We bake it in the oven, silent for a time as the aroma fills the house.

"Dobie?"

He puts his hand on mine. "You know, I had a dream last night about you." He lifts his head in memory, looking off into the pitch of night outside the window. "I dreamed you were dancing." He pulls himself up, then, seeing the vision before him, watching it unfold carefully.

"I knew then that you were an Eagle." He turns to the blanket. "Like me. You were doing an Eagle dance."

He sees my expression.

"You thought you were something else, eh? Maybe a Raven? One of those clever tricksters always getting into people's business, full of songs? That's not your place. You're an Eagle and I know it because I saw you dancing the steps."

We look at each other silently for a long while. Then he stands up and comes over to where I am sitting, stiff with fear.

"You can dance, you know." His eyes are kind. "I've seen you."

"Dobie, I'm not allowed."

"It's okay," he murmurs kindly, pulling me upwards, taking my arms and showing me where they go, then leading me forward with a slow, measured gait. "*Yaay noo ngaa, yee,*" he sings, his old voice rough and dry. "Like this." His hands are curved down past his waist, arms out like wings. Dipping this way and that, I follow him tentatively in a circle around the room. His singing gets louder and we dance the steps over and over. I know he wants me to always remember them. Remember this one true time I can at last let my arms curve into wings, hands on hips, matching his stride. Proud and purposeful, my feet find the beat and they sing with silent joy with every step. We dance together and celebrate what has become undeniably ours, like no other.

He hums the Eagle song, his voice like a strong drum, resonating and bending with every step. Then he stops and turns toward me, his hands at his sides. Puts up his hand to stay my voice. "I know you're going from here. That's your way, up there in the sky, all alone and thinking about things."

I start to protest but he puts up his hand.

"The earth here has claimed you."

Rose's story is weighing heavily on my mind.

"I know what you've done." He puts his hands together, fingers twined inside. *This is the church, this is the steeple, open your hands and see all the people.* "Life is sacred. The darkness is sacred. Without it the Raven would never have noticed the sun." Then he takes something out of his pocket and hands it over. "This is yours, now."

An eagle.

The wings of my new clan are beautifully and sparely carved in argillite. From within the depths they are opening, curved for flight. And in the Haida way, hidden within the curve of the wings is the Wolf Totem. Skliee was now protected forever by the great Eagle Clan. She had been right: her people were great warriors after all, living far beyond the centuries of bondage to rise again.

He closes my hand around the carving.

"Don't ever be ashamed of being an Eagle. It's who you are. The Raven and the Eagle have been fighting it out since the world began."

He looks straight at me in that way he does.

"You came here because you needed to. And your path was created so the Wolf could follow. Who knows how many of our people are out there in spirit, free to roam from this Island when the world opened up all those years ago. Free to come and go because that's the way it is." Then he finds a place to sit down. The dancing has taken it out of him and his knees are acting up. As we face each other he reaches out and grasps my arms. "We were once so powerful we could have taken all the land and ruled the seas. It was everything we knew. Everything we respected. We had everything we wanted." Then he smiles. "I don't like to see the things we have in common, it makes life around here complicated." Sitting down he shakes his head. "This isn't the life I would have chosen."

We consider the arrow of time in companionable silence. "It's not good to live in fear for too long," he says thoughtfully. "It crowds everything else out until all that's left is shame."

We sit together like old friends. He takes my hand and I don't object.

After one more cigarette he folds the red eagle blanket up with great care and accepts a ride home. In his knapsack I have hidden a gift for him, knowing one day he'd pack up for good and that would be it.

♐♒♐♒♐♒

The Monday after the old Chief's departure from our house I have a small party and distribute most of my valuables to friends who have gathered to say goodbye. To Quinnie, I present the antique inkwell she had always admired; in Harry's lap are cradled two crewel pillowcases packed away so long ago in the California house I abandoned. Colleen gets the blue glass bottle that will sit upon her windowsill and catch the morning light. After some protest, Matty accepts a first edition of *Gulliver's Travels,* bought at auction the year I got my first job.

"If I tear out the illustrations and paste them on the walls, they'll go very well with the décor, don't you think?" she asks wickedly.

Naani Rose gives a good speech. In Haida she says that the rains have come early this year because the skies are crying. "They are crying because you are leaving," she translates into English, and then sits down. For Rose, I've chosen a nearly new cashmere sweater bought at Macy's before my trip.

"I'm going to sew a little heart on it right away," she promises, patting my hand.

We eat the last of the salmon I had canned back in the fall, then everyone leaves early to give me time to finish packing up. Naani is the last to leave.

"We have made a decision about Jonah," she says after we are alone.

"Yes?"

"The aunties said no when Jonah asked us to the wedding." She sighs and shakes her head firmly. "A blessing from the Village is important to him but we can't give it." She clucks and shakes her head. "Did you know they made this girl into an Eagle for his Raven just so everything would be like the old days? He got all the important things wrong." I know her memories are clear from the days when the villages had totem poles, and vast long houses so magnificent it seemed impossible that anything could surpass their beauty and power. A city of creativity and pride so huge it touched the sky. Each family crest was like no other, carved in rich detail to honor the history and accomplishments of a world memorialized from the very beginning of time. Back then, everyone knew with powerful certainty that all of humankind had begun on the rocky shores of Haida Gwaii, discovered beneath a clamshell by the inquisitive Raven.

In the deepening silence she reaches out and takes my hand, holding it gently as if in blessing. "In the old days a child of our village would not be leaving before he came to know his people." She smiles kindly. "Don't cry, *scundula.* I know what you're doing is for the best, but I'm very old and just a little selfish sometimes."

Without further word, she gets up.

"Can I take you home?" Matty has materialized out of her room and she is holding Naani's heavy wool coat.

"Thank you, dear." Then she turns and lets me hold her before stroking my hair and whispering, *"Guusd-uu di ging st'i tlajuu-gang, dii gudangee-aa?* Goodbye, my dear."

I pack alone for the rest of the evening. The door opens just as I get the last bit of tape on a box.

"Can I come in?" Jonah stands in the frame, rain dripping from his hair and collar. Out of habit, I examine his face for something familiar. He looks tired and beaten. I imagine the Naanis have been on him all week. I step back.

"I wish you wouldn't go like this. I have to explain." He slumps down on the sofa in his wet coat and his soaking hair and a little yellow tissue-covered package that he is twisting around and around his hands. They are blue with cold.

"What's left to say, Jonah?"

I remain by my boxes, ready for flight. He can't look at me so he just bends down his head to the cradle of his blue hands, a little crush of yellow against his cheek. In the gray of this room he is collapsing into something smaller and less significant, face mottled, defenseless, dissolving into the mess he's made for himself. His pain is genuine, and for a moment I forget mine, coming closer to crouch down at his knee. He puts his hand over mine and I realize he can't help me anymore, no matter how much I deserve it. I am beginning to understand the power of the inexplicable. I have worshiped the inexplicable and now it has come to own me.

"If you could only understand," he says, taking a deep breath to steady his nerves.

"Try."

"My uncle. He's not going to last much longer. Day after day I sat with him and watched the life flow from his body." Jonah is drained of emotion, body stiff. "He was always so full of energy, he was my link to my past and I took it for granted. You have to understand, all he could talk about was how proud he was of what I'd done to bring honor back to our clan. He said just having me near gave him peace. It was at the hospital he told me of a woman from his cousin's clan who was living in Vancouver. My uncle and his cousin dreamed of their families uniting one day. But there were no children. Only this woman. She needed to come home, wanted to come home, but she was stubborn."

At this confession, Jonah can't disguise a small, pleasurable glimmer of memory made visible on his face, and with it comes the unbidden image of the newly minted couple making a pact together, whispering, laughing, as excited as children with an unwrapped package. He senses the danger and continues on in a rush. "It was his deathbed wish that I do the right thing. I thought it was too much to ask."

He glances up, still hopeful that I might understand, take on part of his burden. To draw on all that has grown between us is like an old habit. From his expression, I wonder if I am giving him the sympathy he is asking for, and look away.

"Elle, I spent two nights out in the bush going over and over things, and my grandfather's voice kept coming back to me, begging me never to marry outside our people. My father, he hurt my mother so much and my grandfather never forgave him. I don't know what to do … he made me promise."

I can feel his close and warm thigh, there where it meets the softness of his wool sweater, and I know the secret places beneath the wet cloaking where I once burrowed, and realize then that he could never be a stranger to me no matter how much separates us.

"It has nothing to do with my coming to the Congress?"

He is taken aback.

"Or asking too many questions?"

"No! I told you. It's about the promise I made." I take his hand and put it on my belly. "And what about *this*?"

"I suppose you're better off taking him away. They're not very nice to the mixed ones in the Village." He rubs my hand as if in a trance. "There won't be any other children for me. The woman … she's divorced and much older. And when she comes back to Masset it will be my responsibility to support her." *My sacrifice for yours.* "In our tradition, someone has to be named to protect the family crest." *You're a trickster to the very end.*

"You are to be her *levirate?*"

"Please understand!"

"I do. You finally found someone who, like you, is confusing honor with being a manipulating shithead. You'll probably eat each other alive."

He backs away.

"So you see, I do understand perfectly well. And now I want you to get out of my house."

"Elle." He is as pale as a white man. "I want to know my child."

"Out."

The bedroom door opens and Matty appears. "You heard her."

He turns away heavily. It is only as he is letting himself out the door that he offers up the sodden yellow package. He tries to speak, but I push him firmly forward. The rain is pounding down and the sound of it mixes with the last thud of his boots on the porch steps.

Inside his last package, layers of tissue paper envelope a finely embroidered hankie. It is Victorian in design, with jonquils cresting the border, twining into the center where they create a bouquet. It is very old and smells of lavender. There is no note.

South

♐♒♐♒♐♒

Matty shakes me awake. I roll over and take the proffered cup of milky tea.

"You'll want to get an early start."

I still have *The Sentinel*'s car and I've arranged to drop it off with Judy at the ferry dock. She had taken the news of my departure with glum fatalism. "I haven't made up my mind about publishing your story." In the moment of silence that follows I can hear the waves outside an open window. "But I read the letters, and I'm starting to lose my own argument." She puts her hand over the phone. "Hold off on the print run till I get back there, Wilma!"

"Did I ever tell you, Elle, that you've become a pain in my keister?"

"Finally, I'm a real reporter!" We both laugh.

"What do you want me to do with the letters?" she asks, in her brisk tone.

"Send them to Jonah at the Band Council office." I look over at Matty and she nods. "He's the politician now."

We make arrangements for my last check, and she rings off gruffly. "I don't like all these comings and goings."

The day is lightening well with the promise of dry weather and Matty quietly thanks her personal totem for such a blessing. While she starts the stove fire, I put on my hat and coat and walk down to the docks, where the boats left fallow for the winter lie quietly in their berths. No foghorns call out this morning, as the air is dry and clear. A good day for traveling.

I follow the water line along until I am down by Harry's house, down where he first gave me the North Shore scallops he'd collected himself, so sweet and fresh. Then further along is the charred circle where we had bonfires to roast chocolate and howl at the moon. A promise is nothing if it lives for itself.

Remember. That was the last thing Matty had said to me the night before, catching my hand in hers and looking steadily into my eyes. And we understood each other. I had what Matty wanted most: time. And another chance. I would keep my promise to her and not waste it.

Along the shore, there are waves of small stones brought in by the last storm, a plain necklace of sparrow brown relieved by bits of colored glass worn soft and smooth into raw jewels of aqua, green and pink. I retrieve a tiny scallop shell and put it in my pocket, where it falls into a crevice to be discovered years afterward. The tide is out so I venture deep out onto the wet tide plain, far enough out to see the curve of the bay and the open sea beyond.

Chi, chi*!*

It is the familiar sound of the raven, up deep in the trees. For a moment a dark shadow sweeps against the marine sky and then it is gone.

The air smells of sea and otter, raven, crow, eagle, feathers, fire, wind. Forgiveness. I know now that in the end nothing much else matters. I know that before coming here I had only skimmed the surface of this world. I had always been a skimmer and now was the time to forgive myself for not knowing who to be angry at and giving up the way I did. If I do then I can forgive Jonah for not knowing anything different too, and for not being up to the rigors of the life he had been given, in all its glory and justice. In all its bitterness. There is still time, after all. These things have been occupying my mind for far too long now, these secrets of others, and it's time to let them go.

Long ago, when life seemed the size of a grouse grass yard filled with the cries of cicadas instead of the voices of others, I listened intently. I spoke too late.

And in the infinite space between, entire lifetimes came before God without an answer. In the knowing of this I can make my peace.

Acknowledgements

I am indebted to Ucross Foundation's Artist Residency Program in Wyoming for giving me the time and encouragement to complete the first draft, and to the late, great Fred Rochlin (*Old Man in a Baseball Cap*), who was my inspiration and mentor. Many individuals helped me along the way, but this story wouldn't have reached its potential without the insightful input of editor Mollie Gregory. Thanks, Mollie! Red Square Press, small but mighty, has two great assets: Vladimir Lange and Carol Reed, who provided critical input when I needed it. And kudos to Claire Valgardson, whose excellent polish on the manuscript is proof I should have paid better attention in English grammar class. I must mention Andrew Blauner for his encouragement and support early on; presenting this book to him will be a true joy. I also have to thank those who encouraged the creative process so essential to a writer: Sally Williams, friend and artistic collaborator; Michael Garnett and Mari Miller, my first readers; my parents, Yvonne and Bill, who shepherded a young artist in their midst; and my daughter, Mimi, whose *joie de vivre* is a daily reminder to count my blessings. To Bob, I reserve my deepest gratitude. Husband, father, and true patron of the arts – your partnership has been the greatest gift in my life.

The research necessary to explore the themes in this story would not have been possible without the months spent in Haida Gwaii as an observer and participant in a unique place that has been shaped by so many unforgettable individuals. A culture with a rich heritage to draw on has found its footing and begun to flourish again, ending a long cycle of diminished national pride.

As for the more sensitive issues: Very little information is available on the subject of slavery along the Northwest Coast, but it did exist for many generations (likely hundreds of years) until the end of the nineteenth century, making it arguably the last generational sub-culture of human property in North America. My research on these specifics came primarily from academic sources; the UBC Libraries and Vancouver Public Library have the most extensive periodical resources for British Columbia dating back to the early 1800s, including *The Official Report of the Exploration of the Queen Charlotte Islands for the Government of British Columbia, by Newton H. Chittenden (1840-1925).* However, I am most grateful to my Masset friend, Maureen McNamara, and the gracious and generous Naanis who provided me with the human side of this and other stories. Their courage and wisdom gave me the motivation to tackle a difficult (and sensitive) subject by putting a face to a part of history that has mostly been forgotten. From small snippets given to me as inspiration, I created characters and situations with details that came entirely from my imagination. It is up to those who may still have the real stories in their oral histories to bring the true facts to light.

photo: Bob Caseres

Valen Watson is a writer/producer who has worked in a variety of media, including film, television, advertising, and as a syndicated columnist. Originally from Toronto, Canada, she currently lives with her husband and their daughter in Southern California.